Henry Inman

The Delahoydes

Boy Life on the Old Santa Fé Trail

Henry Inman

The Delahoydes
Boy Life on the Old Santa Fé Trail

ISBN/EAN: 9783744681148

Printed in Europe, USA, Canada, Australia, Japan

Cover: Foto ©Andreas Hilbeck / pixelio.de

More available books at **www.hansebooks.com**

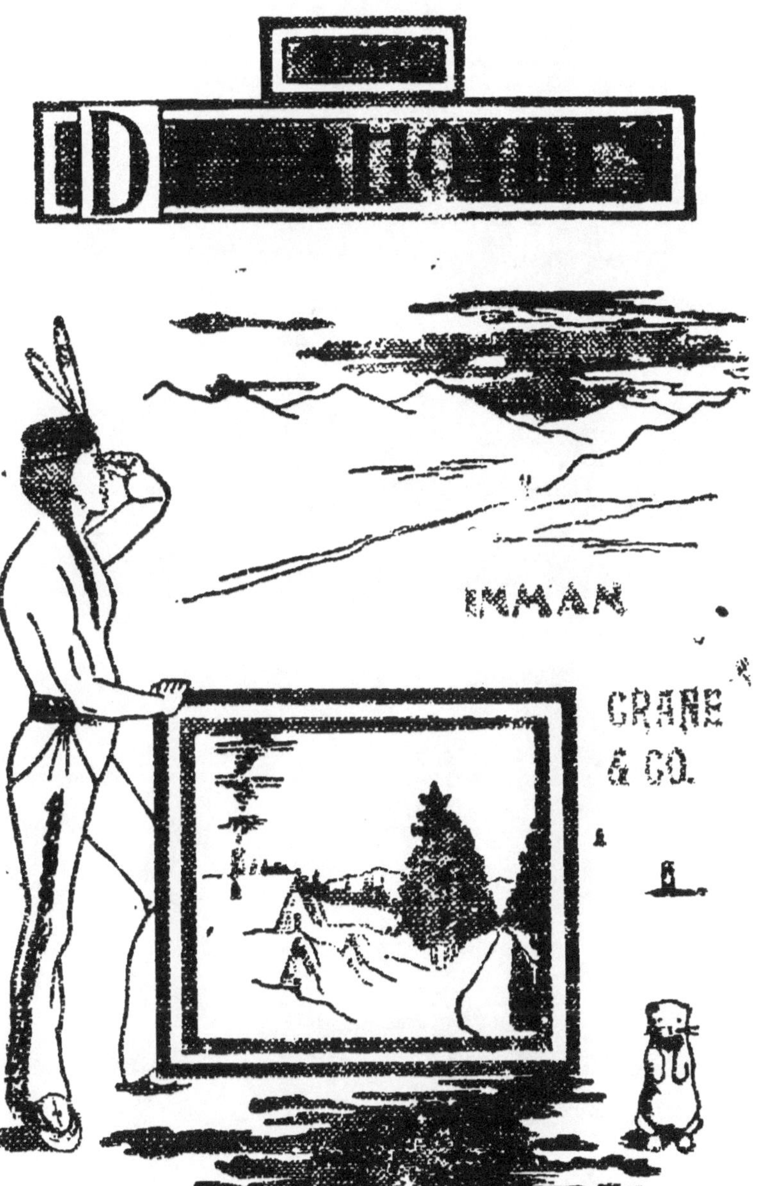
INMAN
CRANE
& CO.

HOME OF THE DELAHOYDE BOYS, ON THE ARKANSAS RIVER.

THE DELAHOYDES

BOY LIFE

ON THE

OLD SANTA FÉ TRAIL

BY

COLONEL HENRY INMAN

AUTHOR OF "THE OLD SANTA FÉ TRAIL," "A PIONEER FROM KENTUCKY," "TALES OF THE TRAIL," ETC., ETC.

CRANE & COMPANY, PUBLISHERS
TOPEKA, KANSAS
1899

PREFACE.

THE story of the Delahoyde Boys is not pure fiction, as is the general juvenile tale of the frontier. The characters are all drawn from life: in some instances the names only are fictitious. The localities are true in their geographical description, and the incidents of the plot are real experiences.

In its natural history, the author, who has always been a close observer, has supplemented his own knowledge of the habits and characteristics of the animals, birds and fishes referred to, by a careful study of eminent authorities on the subject, and it is believed that the descriptions in this book are correct.

The incidents in the lives of the famous men who figure in the story are true to history, and are not creations of the author's brain. In these instances real names are given, and events are recorded which are based upon actual occurrences.

While the scenes are sometimes a little sensational, and perhaps may have a tendency to shock the sensibilities of a refined nature, unfamiliar with the thrilling events which make up the history of the border, now vanished forever, they confirm the adage that "Truth is stranger than fiction." H. I.

CONTENTS.

CHAPTER V.

CHAPTER VI.

CHAPTER VII.

CHAPTER VIII.

CHAPTER IX.

CHAPTER XIII.

THE DELAHOYDES.

CHAPTER I.

ANCESTRY OF THE BOYS.—THEIR HOME ON THE ARKAN-
SAS RIVER.—ANIMALS AND BIRDS OF THE REGION.—
EARLY EDUCATION OF CARLOS AND PIERRE.—THEIR
AMUSEMENTS.—INTERIOR OF THEIR DWELLING.

PIERRE DELAHOYDE was an old-time French-Canadian trapper,[1] who had been an employé of the American Fur Company as early as 1820. He died at the ripe age of ninety-three, at his home on the North Platte, Wyoming, in 1865. As was the custom of men of his vocation, he married a squaw, a Cheyenne,[2] and had one son, also named Pierre.

The younger Pierre[3] Delahoyde was sent, when about fifteen years old, to school at St. Louis, as his father did not want to subject his only boy to all the demoralizing influences incident to the life of a trapper, and he remained away from his home until he was twenty-three, after having been graduated with honors by the University of Missouri.

[1] Trappers were men who in the days before the settlement of the Great Plains and Rocky Mountains were employed by the fur companies, to live out in those wild regions and catch the beaver, mink, and other animals valuable for their skins.

[2] The Cheyenne tribe of Indians take their name from the French word *chien*, meaning dog.

[3] Pierre, from *petrus*, Latin, meaning a piece of stone; and is French for Peter.

Pierre, however, having an instinctively unconquerable love for the wild life of the mountains and plains, inherited from his father, and the natural savage tastes of his Indian mother, chose to be a trapper, too, in which vocation he continued until 1866, when the advent of the railroads into the interior of the continent, and its incident rush of immigration, virtually ended the traffic forever.

In 1850 he squatted on a piece of land bordering the Arkansas river, near the mouth of the Walnut, a short distance from where the historic Santa Fé trail crossed that stream.

He had married the daughter of Carlos Beaubien, another old-time trapper and boon companion of his father, and had two boys to whom were given the ancestral names of their grandfathers.

He lived in a primitive dugout near the bank of the stream, and there his children were born. It was merely an excavation in the bluff, walled up on the inside with stone; the roof formed of saplings placed close together, over which about three feet of grass was lain, the whole covered with dirt, a layer of sod and rocks. It had three doors but no windows, the light from the entrances being deemed as sufficient; while the floor was the natural earth, pounded to a hardness as compact as that of the toughest wood.

No rain ever filtered through the thick roof, and it was as dry as the best of shingles could have made it.

There were five rooms in the dugout, one of which

was called "the museum," and claimed solely by Pierre and Carlos, for their collection of objects in natural history,—of which farther on.

The furniture was of the rudest character. The beds were formed of the crotches of small saplings, driven in the ground, in which were placed short pieces the same width of the bed, over which poles were laid lengthways, and the mattresses composed of seven buffalo robes each, their coverings also buffalo robes, and the pillows flour-sacks stuffed with prairie-grass. There were three or four chairs, fashioned by the old trapper of the natural wood, and which in an Eastern home would be considered rather artistic, rustic affairs, such as are often to be seen on the lawns of country gentlemen's homes. The only table was also a crude thing, made of slabs from the tree, smoothed with an axe.

The fireplace was a huge one, built of stone, the chimney above leading out of the roof, formed of sticks laid crosswise after the manner that children build their corncob houses in the country, and the interstices chinked with mud. There was an abundance of timber in the region at that early day on the Walnut, and it would have required much less labor to construct a cabin; but a dugout is cooler in summer and warmer in winter, hence the character of their dwelling was purely a matter of choice.

So remote from the nearest settlements was this ranch on the Walnut, that it was impossible to procure any furniture less than hundreds of miles distant; so

the primitiveness of the appointments of their home
was not from lack of means on the part of the trapper,
or indisposition to have it, but due to the difficulty in
procuring it. Rude as everything was, their home was
kept scrupulously clean, for Mrs. Delahoyde had been
reared in a semi-cultured family in one of the large
towns in New Mexico.

As the era of trapping had closed about sixteen years
after Mr. Delahoyde took up his claim, he engaged in
the stock business, which was just then developing all
over the "Far West."

The site selected for his home was a perfect wilderness of beauty. The silent river which flowed rhyth-
mically a few yards from the crudely picturesque home,
and the gentle soughing of the breeze in the forest
which surrounded and overshadowed it, were a sooth-
ing lullaby, which only those can appreciate who have
tasted the solitude of Nature in all her charm of isola-
tion from the conventionalities of a busy civilization,
an absolute immunity from all the disturbing elements
which characterize the features of a great city.

The whole region was a veritable hunter's paradise.
The deep woods which fringed the river on both banks
for many miles, was the home of the Lynx, or wildcat
as it is commonly called,—though in fact there are no
wildcats on the American continent; all so-called wildcats are lynxes. The lynx has a short tail a little
longer than its head, while the wildcat's tail is as long
as his body. Another difference between the two ani-

mals is that the ears of the lynx are tufted, while those
of the wildcat are not; and the lynx also lacks the pre-
canine molar which is found in the teeth of the wildcat.   On the open prairie beyond the timber, vast herds
of buffalo and antelope roamed, and the wolves were
found in great numbers all along the stream for miles,
where their dens were made in the rocky, precipitous
bluffs bordering it.

The different varieties — the white, the gray, the
brindle, and their despicable congener the coyote, the
latter a thorough vagabond, outcast and Ishmaelite[1] of
the Plains — were almost as innumerable as the cottontails and the jack-rabbits.

It is not generally known, perhaps, that with the exception of an obliquity in the position of the eyes, and
a variation in the matter of ears, there is little anatom-
ical difference between the wolf family and the dog.
The ears of the wild animal are always pricked, the
lopped or drooping ear being essentially a mark of civilization.

In the era of which I write, through the geographical
region described, where there were no restraining influences, the mountain wolves and the gray wolves of the
prairie joined forces and hunted in packs, and were
then seen at their greatest and bravest, fairly exceeding all other animals in shrewdness.

---

[1] Ishmaelite, a term taken from the Bible: one resembling Ishmael, whose
hand was against every man and every man's hand against him; one at war
against society. Hence the coyote is called the Ishmaelite of the Plains, because
he is "against" every other animal, and they against him.

In the springtime great squadrons of cranes sailed high in the air, and the eagle, our national bird, built his nest far up on the limbs of the dead cottonwood and elm trees. The river and its branches abounded in fish, principally cat and buffalo, together with little sun-perch, and that most ancient of all fish, whose ancestry dates back to the Devonian period,[1] the garpike,[2] a non-edible species. The catfish sometimes weighed sixty or seventy pounds, and when one of these great fellows was hooked, it required all the strength of the boys to land it.

Pierre and Carlos, as soon as they were old enough to handle a rifle, were carefully taught by their father how to use it, so that when ten years of age they became experts and could hit anything within range, though it were only a bird as small as a wren. Well educated himself, as has been stated, the devoted father became the tutor of his sons, setting apart a portion of the morning and evening of each day to their education. They could both read and write well, had a fair knowledge of the history and geography of their country, as well as that of foreign nations, and were prob-

[1] The Devonian period is one of the great divisions, geologically speaking, of the earth's strata, next to the oldest of all. Rocks of the Devonian period occur widely in the United States, as well as in Europe. They abound in fossil plants and animals, including fishes of many varieties, one of the largest of which was probably fifteen feet long, and according to the opinion of geologists could have easily taken off a man's head at a bite. They were, in fact, armor-clad like the garpike, from which the latter common fish has descended. The latter has degenerated, being much smaller than its remote ancestor.

[2] The garpike is a fish belonging to the genus of pikes, with a very long snout, the under jaw much shorter than the upper. Its scales are hard and knobby.

ably better educated than the average American boy
born and reared on the extreme Western frontier.

As is generally the case, boys reared remote from the
confines of civilization necessarily hold closer communion with the visible forms of nature than do those of
the great cities. To this rule Carlos and Pierre formed
no exception; or rather, in them it was developed beyond the ordinary. Baseball, billiards, marbles, kite-
flying and other amusements incident to civilization
were as unknown a quantity to the little trappers, as is
the x in algebra. Having no neighbors nearer than a
hundred miles, excepting the rough crowd at the stage
stations, they were thrown upon their own resources
for amusements, and their talents were directed to the
study of the various animals and birds whose habitat
was in the region where their home was located. They
observed and studied all the animals, and not even the
reptiles failed to escape their attention. In a few
years they collected such a large number of pets that
they alone would have constituted a small menagerie.
Their father's knowledge of the fur-bearing animals
was very extensive, because of his life-long vocation in
that direction; and as he loved his boys, and was a
most indulgent father, he took great pains to train
their young minds to the study of animate nature, in
which he himself was so well versed.

CHAPTER II.

THE absolute work which Pierre and Carlos were
required to perform on their remote ranch was
very light; in fact, it was so little laborious
that it seemed like mere play. It consisted solely of
herding the relatively small number of cattle their
father possessed, which duty was always performed on
horseback, as each of the boys owned three of the hardy
little Indian ponies. They met with many adventures
while herding, and had such unusual opportunities for
observing the habits of the many wild animals and
great variety of birds with which they became acquainted during their life on the ranch, that nearly
all their hours of sunshine were filled with amusement,
rather than with what could strictly be called labor.
The only thing that approached it was the cultivation
of a small garden-strip along the margin of one of the
creeks near home, where the soil was exceedingly rich,

and which was irrigated[1] by a spring flowing out of the wall of rock forming the cañon through which the stream ran. There was no attempt made at farming on a large scale, as climatic conditions precluded its possibility, excepting under a complicated system of irrigation, which for that then remote region was something very far in the future.

With an abundance of leisure on their hands, and virtually having no neighbors, the boys were thrown upon their own resources for amusement, and their efforts in quest of it were directed to the study of natural history.

Pierre and Carlos had a variety of living pets,—as what boy on the frontier does not ? Among these were a coyote, an antelope, several prairie-dogs, a bear, an elk, some moles, and even a rattlesnake. They had made several attempts to tame young lynxes, but had to give it up as a failure; so they were compelled to kill the quarrelsome brutes, as all the kindness bestowed upon them was fruitless of beneficial results, and they were mounted and placed in the museum, with other animals and birds the boys had captured for that purpose.

Of course both Pierre and Carlos owned dogs, several of them,—for what would a young boy's life

---

[1] IRRIGATION.— In the early days of watering by artificial methods, simple little ditches were constructed, often with only a common hoe, through which the water flowed to the garden-patches. Irrigation on a large, complicated scale, requires the construction of expensive ditches, miles long, the water being directed into them from some river, like that of the Arkansas, in western Kansas, or the erection of pumping stations; these enterprises sometimes costing a million dollars, and being controlled by a company.

—2

be worth on a ranch without his most faithful friend and companion, even though the animal should be the meanest of mongrels? Most of those belonging to them, however, were hounds,—some of rare, large breed, great shaggy-haired fellows that hunted by scent alone, and were a match, singly, for the biggest and most ferocious of wolves. Many times they had been engaged in hard-fought battles with them, and when not outnumbered, had invariably been the victors. The boys also possessed four common greyhounds, noted for their swiftness, but which hunted by sight only.

The country was filled with hares, or jack-rabbits, as they are called, and the little cottontails,—the genuine rabbit. One of the distinguishing characteristics between the species is, that the hare makes his lair[1] on top of the ground, generally in some thick mat of grass, while the rabbit-warrens are burrows underneath the surface, or in holes in the ledges of rock.

The boys had rare sport at all seasons, mounted on their ponies and following the greyhounds after the swift little animals, and the dogs were so perfectly trained that when they caught sight of one it rarely escaped: stewed or broiled rabbit was quite a prominent factor in the family larder.

The hounds were broken to chase the hare or cottontail in the following manner:

The dog which first sighted one went directly after him, the others keeping in the rear of the leader, but

[1] *Laír*, an Anglo-Saxon word meaning, literally, a couch; hence, the resting-place of any wild beast.

spread out at intervals of ten or twenty feet, keeping their eyes on their quarry, watching closely when he bolted sideways or suddenly doubled on his tracks, and then the nearest hound, having plenty of room to turn himself, would take up the chase. Then the first hound, whose impetus had sent him far ahead in a straight line the way he was going, would drop behind, and take his place in the rear, watching for his chance to run ahead when the rabbit turned again. Sometimes the little animal succeeded in getting no farther away from where he was flushed than twenty or thirty yards, when the hound that was directly after him would get close enough to shove his long nose under him, toss him in the air, catch him in his strong jaws as he came down,—and instantly that rabbit was dead!

Often at night—as the lynx is a nocturnal prowler—Pierre and Carlos would sally out from the dugout accompanied by their large hounds, and have many an hour's rare sport watching them tussle with the plucky beasts. The lynx was easily tracked to where he was prowling, for it has a cry strangely similar to that of a child, which betrays its whereabouts. The animal is no coward, and will fight to a finish, especially when cornered, and then he makes the fur fly as he stands at bay, and the hounds "go for" him. The dogs rarely came out of the battle unscathed, as many a long and deep scratch on their bodies, which they carried all their lives, indicated.

Although the boys possessed a great number of pets,

they had not been obtained without many a spirited adventure, attended sometimes with real danger.

One afternoon while Carlos was returning home with the herd of cattle he had been tending, as he reached the edge of the timber he saw a young elk had strayed from the side of its mother; so he determined to attempt its capture, failing in which, he intended to kill it for meat, as he always had his rifle with him. He was an adept at throwing the lasso, however, which was always attached to the horn of his saddle, ready for any emergency; so, swinging his rope over his head as the fawn ran, he started for the beautiful little animal. Throwing it swiftly, it caught the creature around the neck and brought him to a sudden standstill. So abruptly was the frightened beast stopped, as Carlos's pony braced his fore feet when he felt the lasso drawn tight, as he was trained to do, the elk was thrown sprawling on its side. The moment Carlos loosened the lasso so as not to strangle the animal, the latter sprang quickly to his feet, and, bristling with fight, made a rush for the pony. The hair on his neck was all turned the wrong way, just as the dog's is when he is going to have a tussle with another of his species, and it was with great difficulty that Carlos could control the little fellow until he hobbled his fore feet and subdued his fiery nature.

Fortunately, the place where the new pet was captured happened to be but a quarter of a mile from the dugout; so, tying his prize to a tree, Carlos jumped on his pony again, and thumping its sides vigorously with both heels, he fairly flew down the trail toward home. Arriving there full of excitement, he told Pierre of his great fortune in lassoing an elk, upon which Pierre jumped on his pony, which was already saddled, and both boys hurried back to the spot where Carlos had left the animal. Reaching there in a few moments, they found the young elk safe and unhurt, although it was evident he had made desperate efforts to free himself, as the earth all around the tree to which he had been fastened was cut up by his sharp hoofs as if it had been dug with a spade.

Getting their valuable capture safely home, the boys were soon at work building a corral for the pet, from saplings, large enough for him to have sufficient exercise but high enough to prevent his jumping out, at which he made several abortive attempts, the moment he was placed in the inclosure. This was intended as a temporary structure only, as the boys, knowing well the nature of elk, were satisfied that as soon as he was tamed he would follow them around like a dog, and becoming accustomed to his surroundings would feel perfectly contented and not stray away.

Fortunately for the boys, the elk had been weaned, so all they had to do was to cut the tender grass and feed the little animal, which in less than ten days had become so attached to its young masters that, as they had predicted, it was apparently never perfectly contented when out of their sight.

The elk grew to be an immense fellow, and grazed around the dugout in company with the cows.

The boys named him "Tom," and his neck was fitted with a broad collar of red flannel, wrought with beads in the highest style of Indian art by their mother, and to the collar was attached a small bell.

The milk cows, numbering half a dozen, never roamed far from home; they took a strange fancy to Tom, and would follow him everywhere. The tinkle of that bell seemed to infatuate them as does the bell-mare of a train of pack-mules. Tom always led them to the best pasturage, or where the choicest browsing was to be found, as he instinctively seemed to know just at what time the different varieties of grasses on the prairie, and the shrubs in the great woods, were at their best. The boys were never at a loss to know where the cows were, or how far off, being ever guided by the "tintinnabulation" of that never-silent bell, as its sound was wafted through the pure atmosphere, —rarely any other noise disturbing it, excepting in the summer-time by the monotonous droning of innumerable insects, or in winter by the occasional howling of a wolf.

Tom's fate was a sad one. Going out together after the cows one evening about sundown, as was their custom, the boys noticed with surprise the absence of that familiar tinkle of the bell on the elk's neck, and soon coming up to the animals, which were in one of their favorite haunts at that time of year (it was early in the spring), they saw at once that Tom was not with them. The cows appeared uneasy, and commenced to low the moment Pierre and Carlos came in sight, as if they wished to indicate to them that their companion was gone.

Both Carlos and Pierre were dumbfounded. At first they were at a loss what to do, or which way to turn. They knew that there were no wild beasts in the region excepting the wolves, large enough to kill their pet, and as these animals generally go on their predatory excursions in the night, it was not at all probable that they had killed and devoured him; besides, some signs would have been visible if such had been the case. The hide, or at least pieces of it, would have been left, and it would have been impossible for the wolves to devour Tom's antlers, which were now large, as he was fully two years old.

The boys looked at each other in mute astonishment for a few moments, when Pierre suggested to Carlos that he drive the cows home, while he wandered around through the woods to find out what had become of Tom.

Pierre was a natural trailer, having studied the art so well that he could tell by the pressure upon a leaf or the grass what animal had trodden upon it, and in which direction it was going.

Pierre stood for a few minutes until Carlos with the cows was out of sight, then commenced to hunt around for tracks of the elk, as he wandered forward and backward over the ground where the animals had been feeding, and was rewarded at last by discovering the hoof-prints of his pet leading toward the river. He followed them very intently, now knowing well he could track the elk to where it was. After walking slowly for about a mile and a half, he saw ahead of him, partly hidden in a patch of timber, a steep precipice formed by the bluffs, at the foot of which the river flowed. He walked to its edge, looked over, and to his great grief and astonishment saw the body of poor Tom lying upon the cruel rocks below. It required only one look, as he recognized the red collar with its bell attached, to satisfy him that, alas! poor Tom was dead!

Almost overpowered by his feelings, Pierre scrambled down to the river bank; and it must be confessed the boy shed a few tears, as he laid his hands upon the cold body of Tom. Then, philosopher as he really was, he began to theorize as to the cause of the animal's death. It required but very little observation to determine the fact that the elk had incautiously approached too near the precipice, and probably in stepping upon the loose stones which were scattered around, had tumbled over, and the fall had broken his neck.

Pierre slowly retraced his steps to the cabin, and when he told the fate of poor Tom there was genuine grief in the little family, for the old folks as well as the boys were sincerely attached to the elk.

During the two years the boys had lived on the ranch they had made many attempts to catch a young antelope, but had signally failed. One morning in May, while Pierre was out on the prairie about five miles from the dugout herding the cattle, he saw in the distance a herd of about a hundred, with lots of the coveted little animals among them. They were quietly feeding, and as the family had been out of fresh meat for three or four days, Pierre thought that here was an opportunity to replenish their larder and capture one or two fawns. He called Cyrus, one of the most intelligent hounds, a dog that he claimed for his very own, which always went hunting with him, and which he had taught a series of tricks. Taking a piece of paper out of his pocket, he wrote a few words upon it, and tying it to the dog's neck, he ordered him to take it home. The intelligent animal promptly obeyed, and started on the run for the dugout; arriving there in less than a quarter of an hour, he immediately hunted up Carlos, who was working in the little garden-patch. Noticing the note fastened to the dog, Carlos took it off and read it. It said:

"Carl, there's a big herd of antelope about a half-mile from me, and lots of little ones with it. You better come out as quickly as possible with your rifle, and let's try and get some. I cannot leave the cattle unless Cyrus is here; he'll guide you to where I am. Come at once. PIERRE."

Carlos, boy-like, dropped his hoe just where he was at work, hurriedly got his pony, which was picketed near the cabin, saddled him, and slipping the bridle-reins over the animal's head, led him up to the door, gave them to Cyrus to hold, while he went in for his rifle, buckled a belt of cartridges around his waist, came out in another moment, mounted the pony, and started to where his brother was, following the hound, which led out on his own trail beautifully. He arrived where Pierre was waiting for him, in about twenty minutes,—for Cyrus was somewhat tired, and had occupied a little longer time than he had in going home. Carlos plainly saw the antelope which his brother pointed out to him, still grazing peacefully, unconscious of danger; but they had gradually worked nearer to where the cattle were, than when Pierre first observed them.

Both of the boys knew very well how instinctively curious the antelope is, and feeling satisfied that the herd of cattle had attracted their attention, both got off their ponies, and putting the loops of their bridle-reins into the dog's mouth, ordered him to remain where he was and watch. They then took their rifles and crawled into a big patch of bunch-grass about three hundred yards away, which concealed them completely. They knew very well that if they patiently waited, the ordinarily timid animals, attracted by the strange appearance of the cattle, would approach near enough for them to get a shot, and if they happened to kill a doe with a young one at her side, it would not leave its mother and they could easily capture it.

Pierre and Carlos, long before their patience was exhausted, saw five or six of the leaders of the herd of antelope, together with about the same number of does, accompanied by their little ones, stop feeding, look up and gaze intently at the cattle, which were still grazing quietly. Then two or three of the males began to jump stiff-legged, the white patch on their rumps spreading out, an indication that their curiosity was unusually excited. Presently they stopped their antics, and deliberately walked with their heads erect, followed by their mates and little ones, right up to where the boys were concealed.

Before they came within range, Pierre said to his brother:

"Now, Carl, let's both of us shoot a doe, if possible, and let the bucks go, even if we have to do without meat, for what we want now is little ones."

"All right," said Carl; "you see those two does coming up this way: you shoot the one on the left, and I'll take the one on the right. Of course, we can get but one shot apiece, and if we kill the mothers, we are sure of the fawns."

"Hist! Carl," said Pierre; "here they come. Take good aim, and when I say, 'Now!' let's fire together."

The boys had been so well trained in the art of hunting, that they were always cool under the most exciting circumstances; so when Pierre gave the word, both rifles were discharged simultaneously, and the two does they had aimed at fell dead. The rest of the herd scampered off at the height of their speed, and were soon lost to sight in the purple mist of the horizon.

Pierre and Carl jumped up and rushed to where their dead game lay. The fawns, in their innocence, standing over the dead bodies of their mothers, were easily captured. Pierre took a piece of twine out of his pocket, fastened the legs of the little ones together, hurried to where the ponies were, and returned with them. Leaving Cyrus to watch the cattle, he packed the dead carcasses of the does behind the cantle[1] of the saddles, and, carefully lifting their prizes in front of them, rode back to the herd and started it back to the ranch, as they did not dare to leave it. Having captured the fawns for which they had so long wished, they did not want to take any chances of losing them by remaining out on the prairie until evening.

The boys were more than an hour in reaching the dugout, as they could not run the cattle, but no harm had come to the fawns. They were taken into the house, and given some milk, of which there was always more than could be used at the ranch, and it only required about ten minutes for the little ones to take as naturally to the new method of eating, as if they were nursing their mother.

The fawns throve splendidly, and in less than a week were as gentle as kittens, following everyone in the house around; so outrageously tame did they become,

---

[1] *Cantle*, the projecting part in the rear of those saddles used in the army and by plainsmen.

that they were ever getting under one's feet. They soon became used to their new surroundings; grazed on the bluffs above the dugout, rarely straying more than a quarter of a mile away, and never failing to return promptly at sundown, to the little corral and shed that Pierre and Carlos had made for them.

They were the most attractive pets of the many that the boys possessed; so graceful in all their movements, and so affectionate. They never appeared to be afraid of the dogs, which at first were inclined to inspect them too closely; but a word or two from the boys soon made them understand that the antelope were as much a part of the family as themselves.

The boys' clothes were as picturesque and wild as their surroundings. The nearest trader was at the military post of Fort Larned, on the Arkansas, forty miles up the river. Journeys were made there but two or three times a year, for such articles as were indispensable for the family — coffee, sugar, flour, salt, and dry goods, which latter comprised only calico for the mother's dresses, muslin for underwear, and stockings. For everything else in the way of clothing, the family depended upon the well-tanned hides of the animals shot or trapped in the vicinity of their home.

Carlos, Pierre and their father wore coats and trousers made of the finest skins of the common red deer, so abundant in the region. Their feet were covered with moccasins of the same material, and their heads by a fanciful cap made of the breast-feathers of the male mallard duck (so beautiful in their iridescence) for the summer, and a lynx or coonskin cap for winter. All these articles were fashioned by the deft hands of their mother, who was an adept in the peculiar bead- and needle-work of the Indian women, with whom, during her early life, she had necessarily been closely associated.

Although their apparel would have excited surprise and wonder among people in a highly cultivated society, it was nevertheless as comfortable, and fitted as well, as if made by the most fashionable tailor.

Their saddles, bridles, and other paraphernalia used in connection with their almost constant life on horseback, were also highly ornamented, the boys' tastes in that direction having probably been inherited from their dusky ancestors, as among all savage tribes a love for gaudy appointments is characteristic.

CHAPTER III.

IN midsummer Pierre and Carlos often camped out
for weeks at a time, their indulgent father cheerfully granting permission, and as cheerfully remained at home, herded the cattle and did the other
chores that generally fell to the lot of the boys.

They usually selected some beautifully shaded bend
in the river, a few days before they started, where they
knew big game and fish were abundant, intending to
hunt and trap during their stay.

One lovely morning in June, 1867, just as the sun
was gilding the bluffs above their dugout, they saddled
their favorite ponies, and after confining all but two of
the hounds, started on their journey.

They carried a small supply of flour, salt, coffee,
sugar, and a few other necessaries,—a frying-pan, a
kettle, and knives and forks; intending to depend
upon their own prowess in providing for the larder
during the trip.

Their beds, of course, were simply buffalo-robes, which with their other equipage was packed on a loose pony they drove before them.

They arrived at the appointed place long before noon, as it was only about ten miles up the Walnut from their home.

It was a charming spot: the river made a sudden sweep to the south in a most symmetrical curve, while the beach was perfectly level, composed of clean sand, but colored brown with the stain of iron with which it was impregnated. A few feet above, on the bank of the stream proper, were great groups of gnarled old cottonwoods, that must have withstood the wintry blasts of a century, their huge limbs reaching out far over the water, affording a most grateful shade.

At the foot of one of the largest of the trees, Pierre and Carlos pitched their camp. They needed no other shelter than the closely involved foliage, as it rarely rains in that region, excepting in the early spring or late fall.

After taking off the saddles, bridles and the load from the pack-pony, they picketed out their animals, which in a few moments were feeding knee-deep in the nutritious bunch-grass[1] growing so luxuriantly all around them.

Their beds for the present were thrown carelessly on the ground, while preparations for dinner were imme-

---

[1] *Bunch-grass*, a peculiar variety of prairie-grass which grows in tufts, or bunches; hence the name. It is sometimes as tall as a horse's head.

CARLOS CAPTURES A YOUNG ELK.

diately begun, as the boys, like their animals, were ravenously hungry, after their ride.

While Carl busied himself in cutting two sticks with forks in the ends, in which a pole was to be laid to hold the kettle, and gathered a lot of the dead driftwood to make a fire, Pierre shouldered his rifle and wandered off in search of meat.

By the time that Carlos had all his preparations completed, the fire briskly burning and the water sputtering in the kettle for the coffee, Pierre returned, having succeeded in killing a couple of Blue-winged Teal which he discovered swimming in an eddy under the edge of the bank half a mile from camp. He had crawled upon them, and waited with finger on the trigger until the birds got into line, when he pulled, and took off both their heads. In another instant he was in the water and out again, hurrying toward camp with his game.

While they were pulling the feathers off the birds, they commenced to talk together about the habits of the beautifully colored creatures which were sacrificed to the demands of their stomachs.

"Do you know, Carl," said Pierre to his brother, as he plucked the rich plumage from the wings of the bird he was dressing, "that in all my experience in hunting, these little fellows with their handsome blue wings, fly awfully swift, and when they are under full headway it takes a mighty quick eye and a snap-shot to bring one down?"

—3

"Yes," replied Carlos, "I know that they are the hardest birds for me to get. I can hit them easily enough when they are swimming, but on the wing I often miss them. And you know, when they are going to light, how carefully they sail about to see whether there is anything around to scare them; but the moment they are down in the water or on the ground they seem to forget all about enemies, and crowd so closely together while feeding that you can get half a dozen at a single shot sometimes."

"Did you ever see their nests, Carl?" inquired Pierre.

"Oh, yes," answered his brother, "I have found many of them; they are built on the ground in the coarse grass, or the reeds and rushes which grow along the edge of the sloughs[1] out on the prairie. They line their nests inside with down, which I suppose they pluck from their own breasts, and they lay from eight to twelve eggs — at least I have found as many, often. Don't you remember that set in the museum? It has a dozen eggs in it, that I found up the river last summer."

"Yes," answered Pierre; "and another good thing about them is that they don't leave until late in the fall, and I think they are the best birds to eat that we have here, not even excepting the quail."

'Well," said Carl, "we shall soon know how these

[1] *Slough* (pronounced *slew*), a low, wet or muddy place; generally a ravine into which water has drained. Sometimes they are very deep, and are difficult to cross.

taste; the water is boiling, and I 've made the coffee. I 'm going to stew them; I brought along some onions from the garden, and it won't take more than twenty minutes to cook them, if I cut them up into small pieces. So if you 'll mix the slapjacks, then water the ponies, by the time you get back from the river dinner will be ready."

Pierre jumped up, went after the three ponies, saying as he started, "I 'll mix the slapjacks as soon as I come back—it won't take a minute."

While he was busy leading the animals down to the river, Carlos put the teal into the pot, salted them, threw in a few onions to flavor them, and in ten seconds more the birds were sizzling and sputtering, and sent out a most appetizing odor to his hungry stomach.

In twenty minutes Pierre returned with the ponies, and picketing them out on a fresh spot, came to the fire and got the slapjacks ready for frying in a jiffy.

They were cooked in a long-handled frying-pan; and when one side of a cake was done it was tossed into the air, turning upon the other side as it came down. It was quite an art to toss them properly, but both of the boys were adepts at camp-life, and Pierre did not drop one on the ground.

By the time he had cooked a tin plate heaping full, Carlos took off the stew, and in a few minutes it rapidly disappeared, together with a liberal allowance of the slapjacks and black coffee. The dogs were lying near by, wistfully eyeing each mouthful as their masters devoured their dinner, with which the boys soon made sad havoc.

There was nothing left for the half-famished dogs, excepting a handful of cleanly picked bones; so Pierre said: "Carl, we 've got to go and hunt something for the hounds to eat, for they are terribly hungry, I know. I guess we can soon find a jack or two or a cottontail for 'em out on the prairie."

"All right," said Carlos; "I 'll be ready in a moment, as soon as I put out the fire."

That accomplished, so as to leave no embers that might burn anything while absent, both the boys took their rifles and sauntered out on the open prairie beyond the woods, the dogs following them, well knowing that it was for their benefit their masters were going hunting.

They had not proceeded more than a mile from camp when Cyrus flushed[1] a big jack, and both dogs took after him, but Pierre said, "You needn't run, you tired fellows;" and as he spoke, he raised his rifle and killed the animal before it had gotten twenty yards from where the hound had started it.

The jack that Pierre shot was an immense fellow, enough for two meals to each of the honnds; and as the boys fed their dogs only twice a day, there was sufficient food to last Cyrus and Jupe until the next evening, and before that time arrived the young camp-

---

[1] *Flushed*, a sportsman's term, meaning any animal or bird suddenly started, or " flushed."

ers expected to kill an antelope, deer, or perhaps even a buffalo.

As soon as the meat was secured for the hounds, Pierre and Carl, closely followed by the hungry dogs, returned to their camp, and upon reaching the big tree under which they purposed to sleep, the hare was chopped into four pieces, two of which were given to Cyrus and Jupe, who did their own skinning, and soon got themselves outside of their share of the hare. The remaining portions, which were to serve for their breakfast next morning, were suspended to a limb of the big tree, so as to be out of reach of the dogs.

The boys then sat down on the river-bank and discussed the probabilities of what their supper would be.

"What do you say about going fishing, and getting a young cat for supper?" said Carlos to Pierre, as he thought of their absolutely empty larder, so far as any meat was concerned.

"Well, we have got to get something, Carl," replied Pierre to his brother's interrogatory; "but I don't see any use of both of us going fishing. If we catch more than we can eat for supper, they won't keep in this hot weather until morning; so suppose you take a line and try your luck, and I'll go out after some bigger game?"

"All right, Pierre," responded Carlos; "but leave one of the hounds with me in case any wolves come around while you are gone, and you take the other; you would better take Cyrus with you, and I'll keep

Jupe, as he is not so good as Cyrus at hunting, but can fight off a wolf just as well."

"Well, let's do it," said Pierre; "you can take a piece of the hare for bait; cat will bite at it, if they bite at anything,— but they are a miserably slow fish to bite at all; they aren't a bit game like a trout, or a' perch. They will sometimes look at the bait half an hour before attempting to touch it; and then again they will not notice it although it hangs right before their noses."

"I may catch some perch," said Carlos; "they're better than cat anyhow, only they are small, and you've got to get so many more to make a meal, while a decent-sized cat is enough for five or six men."

It was now about three o'clock, as the boys guessed, looking up at the sun, their only timepiece; but they could usually come within a quarter of an hour of the real time, so dependent had they become upon nature in their wild surroundings. They had sufficiently rested, and while Carlos was getting his tackle ready, Pierre took his rifle, whistled to Cyrus, and started for the open prairie, where he had shot the hare a couple of hours before.

It took Carlos about half an hour to get his line in readiness, his bait cut up, and take a look at the ponies to see if they were all right, before he started for the river, intending to fish in the eddy where Pierre had shot the teal.

Arriving there in a short time, he seated himself on

the edge of the bank, while Jupe stretched out in the shade of the overhanging limbs of the trees not far from his master.

Absolute silence reigned; not even the droning of a bee could be heard, and there was not a breath of wind to rustle the leaves in the treetops. The dog was sound asleep, and Carlos, with line in the sluggish water of the eddy, was patiently waiting for a nibble. At last it came, and he hauled up a medium-sized perch, strung it on a willow wand, cast in again, and was soon rewarded with another. Thus he continued until he had caught half a dozen,—but not a single cat: they would not bite, although, boy-like, he successively spat on his bait, according to the superstitions of youth while angling.

More than two hours were thus whiled away by the patient Carlos, and it was now fully five o'clock, he thought, as he looked up at the sun, which was half-way between the zenith and the western horizon. The slow progress of his fishing was growing rather monotonous, and he was just thinking he would return to camp and await the return of Pierre, whom he hoped had been luckier than he in getting something for supper and breakfast, when his ears were suddenly greeted by a low growl, and the rushing of Jupe toward him. He looked around, and to his dismay saw not twenty feet from him a black she-bear, with two half-grown cubs by her side. She had evidently come down to the water to drink, and had not observed either Carlos or the dog (the latter having remained quietly sleeping all the time while Carlos was angling) until she emerged from the underbrush that grew to the edge of the bank.

The creature was immediately seized with powerful maternal instinct for the safety of her little ones, and made a savage dash for Jupe. The moment he smelt her, his fur all bristling with battle, he incontinently made a rush for her, but she sent him sprawling over and over on the sandy beach by one stroke of her dreadful paw, and then with mouth wide open, and jaws frothing with rage, made a break for Carlos, who was now on his feet, realizing the danger which confronted him.

Carlos had very foolishly left his rifle in camp, and had nothing to defend himself with but his pocket-knife, which he had already opened, however, resolved to do his best in the conflict which he believed inevitable.

Jupe had by this time recovered from the shock of his sudden tumble, fortunately unhurt, and gallantly came dashing on to the rescue of his master; but before he reached the ferocious animal, it rolled over dead, as the report of a rifle resounded through the woods.

It was his brother Pierre's unerring aim, that had sent a ball into the brain of the ferocious beast just in the nick of time!

He explained to Carlos, after the momentary excitement was over, that having failed to see any game

while out, he had returned to camp, and not finding him there, concluded that he was still fishing at
the eddy, and immediately walked down, happily soon
enough to prevent what might have been a serious
matter.

Carlos showed Pierre the very small string of fish he
had caught, and both concluded that the prospects for
supper and breakfast, if it had to depend on these,
were poor indeed; so they turned to the dead bear,
but discovered she was so thin and bony that she was
not fit to eat.

They then looked for the cubs, only one of which
was visible, the other having made off in the brush
upon the report of the shot that had killed its mother.
The other cub stood within easy rifle-range, bewilder-
ingly gazing at the boys, when Pierre by a well-directed
ball killed it in its tracks.

It was very fat, luckily. Then both Pierre and Carl
laughed with each other over the whole affair in relation to the visit of the bear, now that it had turned
out without any harm to them or Jupe, and with the
more pleasant prospect of plenty of meat for some time.

The cub weighed about seventy-five pounds — too
great a load for the boys to carry; so Pierre said he
would go back to camp and get the pack-pony, and
that Carlos could remain and watch the dead cub, for
if both went away the wolves would be sure to scent
it, and by the time they returned to the river there
would be no bear-meat to pack.

Pierre started on a rapid walk back to camp, leaving his rifle with Carlos, and half a dozen cartridges, should an emergency arise for their use.

It was fortunate that Pierre had the forethought to leave the rifle with his brother, for he had not been gone ten minutes before Carlos noticed the head of a gray prairie-wolf, popping up over a little ridge a few feet from where he was standing. Jupe saw it at the same instant, and made a rush for the intruder, which, the moment he saw the dog, tucked his bushy tail between his legs and scooted off.

Carlos called Jupe back, for he knew the cowardly wolf would lead him a wild-goose chase for more than a mile, and the dog would only get tired out for his pains. Besides, Carlos felt sure that the wolf he saw was not the only one in the vicinity, and he might have all he could do with both his rifle and Jupe, before Pierre returned.

The boy was right in his conjecture, for by the time that Jupe came up to him at his call, the deep snarling and growling of at least half a dozen of the impudent creatures could be heard, not far off in the brush.

Carlos had no fear of them so long as it was daylight and he had his dog and rifle, for they are most cowardly brutes, but at night are more bold and incautious. They seem to possess the most acute smell, and are attracted by the odor of a dead animal at most astounding distances; as the boys' father once told them, he believed that a wolf thinks it no uncommon thing to travel a hundred miles for his breakfast.

Although the continuous snarling of the wolves excited Jupe's combativeness, and Carlos with great difficulty restrained him from rushing into the brush after them, not another ventured to make himself visible.

In an hour Pierre appeared, leading the pack-pony, and carrying Carlos's rifle. Pierre reported everything all safe at the camp, and in a few moments the cub was securely fastened on the back of the pack-pony, and all started for the temporary home under the big cotton-wood.

It was nearly dark when the camp was reached, and the first thing to be done was to water the ponies and change them to a new grazing-spot. That was accomplished in a few minutes; then the bear was skinned, its viscera taken out and given to thē dogs, which gorged themselves on the unexpected meal, after which they stretched out on the grass and were soon slumbering soundly.

The cub's carcass was then hung to the limb of a tree, and while Pierre was attending to the animal's glossy hide, which he intended to make into a mat for his parents' bedroom, Carlos built a fire, started the kettle to boiling, and then cut off slices of the choicest portions of the bear. While the coffee was settling, and the meat nicely frying in its own fat, he mixed another batch of slapjacks, and by the time that his brother had scraped the cub's hide, stretched it out between two saplings and salted it, Carlos announced supper, of which the boys partook with great relish by the light of the campfire, as it was now dark and there was no moon.

The moment their meal was disposed of, the brothers prepared for bed; for they had always been in the habit of retiring early, and rising at an early hour,— before sunrise, in fact, the most delightful portion of the day, especially in summer-time.

Their beds were easily made: three buffalo robes were spread upon the ground, their saddles utilized as pillows, with a robe thrown over them, and another robe placed at their feet, to be used as a covering should it grow cool toward morning.

The boys took off only their moccasins and coats, and placing their rifles alongside, were soon snugly at rest; the dogs, when not prowling around within a short radius, lying at their masters' feet, ready to defend them at the instant of danger.

Very shortly after the boys retired to rest, the usual nocturnal[1] sounds peculiar to that wild region commenced, but which were a lullaby to their ears, for they had been soothed to sleep by them in their room in the dugout ever since they had lived on the Walnut.

The first of these familiar voices of the night was the Screech-owl, which utters a plaintive note, and then changes into a peculiar rattling sound, like the

---

[1] *Nocturna*, night; hence, those animals or birds which make their appearance and hunt their prey at that time are nocturnal in their habits.

chattering of teeth. It keeps up its alternating whooping and moaning during the hours between sundown and the appearance of the initial rosy tints on the eastern horizon, betokening the coming morning. Particularly does it love the moonlight, when it will perch upon the top of some blasted tree. On moonless nights it is not so vociferous; but it is never entirely silent.

It inhabits alike the woods and the abodes of man in the thickly settled States. It lives on mice, small birds, and insects; it makes scarcely any noise while on the wing in search of its prey, upon which it pounces with the swiftness of an arrow. It makes its nest in holes in forest trees, and frequently in buildings in civilized communities. The nests are sparingly lined with grass, leaves, or feathers. The eggs are pure white, and usually from four to six are found in one nest. In the boys' museum in the dugout they had six in their collection, which Carlos found one day in the hollow of a dead cottonwood on the bank of the Walnut.

As soon as it was fairly dark, the bird, known as "Poor-will," in contradistinction to the Whip-poor-will, of the East, began its wailing song of " poor-will, poor-will." It repeats it almost continuously at night during the breeding season. They love rocky, bluffy places, where they lay their eggs, only two in number, on the bare ground, but generally at the roots of a bunch of grass, weeds, or the low plum-bushes on the prairie. They do not line their nests with any soft material. The eggs, like those of the screech-owl, are pure white. The birds arrive late in April, begin laying the last of May, and depart in September.

The lynxes were peculiarly noisy that night the boys first camped out on the trip; they kept up an almost continuous mewing, and were probably attracted by the carcass of the cub hung up in one of the trees, but were afraid to approach it because of the presence of Cyrus and Jupe, whose special antipathy was a lynx, and who, when that animal commenced to mew, after Carl and Pierre had gone to sleep, were extraordinarily vigilant, prowling nearly all night around the tree, from the limb of which the young bear was suspended.

The boys slept splendidly, feeling perfectly secure with such admirable sentinels as Cyrus and Jupe, and at the first streak of dawn were out of their buffalo-robes, and down to the warm sandy beach of the Walnut to indulge in a bath.

They splashed around in the water, ducking and dodging each other in their brotherly sport, for at least fifteen minutes, then drying themselves in the first beams of the morning sun as its rays glinted on the beach, they dressed. Their initial duty of the day was the care of the ponies, but it was not an arduous task; all required was to lead them down to the river to drink, and re-picket them on a fresh spot of grass. The ponies' demands disposed of, the remainder of the hare that Pierre had shot the afternoon before was divided between Cyrus and Jupe, and then Pierre, acting the rôle of cook, began to prepare the morning meal; while Carlos, taking his rifle, and his own dog Jupe, who had already devoured his portion of the hare, sauntered up the bank of the stream to try his luck in providing meat for the larder.

He was gone but a short time, as it did not require more than half an hour for Pierre to get the usual breakfast ready, which consisted of black coffee, slap-jacks, and broiled bear-steaks; but instead of cooking the steaks in the frying-pan, he stuck them on peeled willow-twigs, the ends of which he put in the ground before the glowing embers of the campfire, and in a few moments they were done to a turn that would have satisfied the taste of the most epicurean gourmand.[1]

Carlos had bagged a young, wild-turkey gobbler, which the boys proposed to roast in old trapper fashion for their supper, as it would not be done by dinner-time by the treatment to which it was to be subjected. So, breakfast (which both the boys enjoyed immensely) out of the way, preparations were commenced to roast the beautiful bird which Carl had shot on his trip up the river.

A hole was first dug into the ground about two feet in diameter, and a foot and a half deep. In this was kindled a fire, and kept up for more than an hour, until the sides and bottom of the excavation were baked almost as hard as earthenware. Then the coals were scraped out, the turkey put in, just as he was killed,

---

[1] *"Epicurean gourmand,"* a lover of good food: to such an extent that he is a glutton.

feathers and all, after he had first been coated all over with mud. Then over the hole were placed a few sticks, sufficiently strong to bear up a covering of earth, on top of which the live coals were heaped, and replenished from time to time with freshly added fuel. Thus the bird was in a hot, hermetically sealed oven; hot enough to roast it better than can possibly be done in the most improved stove. It had to remain there many hours, to guarantee it being done when taken out. So, as the boys could not leave camp that day, at least until their turkey was cooked, which would not be before four o'clock, they sat by their watch-fire and discussed their favorite theme, natural history.

Both Carlos and Pierre were especially great lovers of birds, and made a study of the many species whose habitat was in the region where the dugout was located, as well as those which were purely migratory,[1] passing only a portion of their time in the vicinity during each recurring season, where they made their nests and reared their little ones. In the early fall these departed southward, to return at a certain time the next spring, either in flocks, singly, or in pairs, as their instincts dictated.

Of course the boys had no knowledge of the scientific names of the birds with whose habits they were so perfectly familiar, specimens of which they sometimes themselves shot or trapped, and mounted, under the

---

[1] *Migratory*, a term applied to animals or birds, especially birds, which reside in their ordinary home during only a portion of the year, *migrating* to other parts at certain seasons, where the temperature of the air and the surroundings are suited to their habits.

&uidance of their father, who was an expert taxidermist, he having learned the art during his college course.

Pierre and Carlos knew only the common names of the feathered beauties which congregated in such an almost endless variety in the woods bordering the Walnut, on the open prairies contiguous thereto, or swam in the quiet waters of the main stream or its tributaries.

Notwithstanding their lack of purely technical knowledge in these particulars, it is doubtful whether the most accomplished ornithologist could have taught the boys anything of the habits of the birds with which they were so familiar; their method of nest-building; the color and number of eggs which were laid by the different species; and the notes to which they gave utterance.

Of the swimming birds which frequented the waters of the Arkansas, Canadian, and Walnut, there were many varieties. The Ring-billed Gull was the most common, generally arriving during April and May, and remaining until September. They are as perfectly at home on the wing as in the water. They seemed to come so far inland, to feed upon the grasshoppers or red-winged locusts which abounded in such innumerable clouds on the Central Plains twenty or thirty years ago. The boys arrived at this conclusion, from the fact that of the hundreds they had killed, the crops of all were filled with those insects. They did not breed

—4

in the region of the boys' home, but far away on the southern seacoast; so that although Carlos and Pierre had several finely mounted specimens, neither nest nor eggs were obtainable.

The White Pelican was a common visitor, coming with the early spring and departing early in the fall.

The boys were particularly fond of watching those large birds. They admired them for their sociability among themselves, and their peaceful nature,—hardly ever quarreling, as do nearly all the feathered tribe. It was a rare thing to find a pelican alone; they soared in large numbers at great heights; for hours Carlos and Pierre often studied them, as they performed their strange evolutions in mid-air.

The pelicans live principally upon fish, and have a regular method in their angling. They get together and drive the fish into shallow water up the stream, where they catch and devour them at their leisure.

Even while Carlos and Pierre were quietly seated on the ground, carefully attending to the fire, which they knew must not be permitted to slacken, or their turkey would not be ready when evening came on, a slight rushing of wings was heard, and both boys glancing at the smooth surface of the river, flowing only a short distance away, saw a flock of ducks settle on its bosom.

"Those are Pintails," said Pierre, as he threw a handful of dry twigs on the fire, "and they are always the very first of the ducks to come in the spring."

"Yes," said Carlos; "and they eat a greater variety of things than any other species, so far as I have studied them,—seeds, roots, worms, snails, and even acorns; for I have found all of them in their crops."

"See how funny they act, Carlos," said Pierre, as he saw the flock with their bodies tipped over, and working their feet in the air.

"Yes," replied Carlos, "they seem to stand on their heads; that's because they don't really dive, but keep their bills under the water, searching for food."

"Just look at them, Pierre! Now they have turned over and are swimming again. How gracefully they sail around! There they go; something scared them, —and how fast they can fly!"

"Their eggs are handsome, too," said Pierre, as he watched the flock rush off, their wings making a whirring noise, so rapidly did they beat them against the air.

"Yes," said Carlos, "but their eggs are not always of the same color. I have found them from pale green to yellow, or rather, the same shade as the egg of a Plymouth Rock hen."

"They don't seem very particular about their nests, either," continued Pierre; "you remember that when we spent a whole morning last summer, searching for them out in the grass near the creek, we found only a sort of little scratched-out place, with a few scraps of down in them."

"They lay seven to ten eggs," said Carlos. "Don't

you recollect we got a great basketful that day, and that both mother and dad liked 'em so much?"

At noon the boys cooked a light dinner, saving their appetites for the turkey which would be done for their supper. They fed Cyrus and Jupe on a part of one of the hind legs of the cub, took "turn about" in caring for the ponies, watched the many varieties of birds which flew around in the solitude where the camp was located, and idled away the day in that manner, yet really were learning something all the time, for nothing escaped their notice.

At about five o'clock the boys concluded their turkey must be done. Carlos made coffee, mixed up the indispensable slapjacks, and got all the preliminaries ready for their evening meal. Pierre hunted around for a piece of clean bark, to serve as a platter for their big bird, as a tin plate was entirely too small to hold it, and in a short time, having succeeded in finding just what he wanted, he came back to the camp. Then he raked off the coals from the improvised oven, scraped away the earth, took off the sticks which held it up, and lifted out the turkey, whose coating of mud was now baked hard, and with a slight tap of a piece of wood, struck the shell, and off it flew, all the feathers sticking to it,—and there was one of the most beautifully white birds that was ever cooked. He laid it on the bark plate, and everything else being ready, the boys seated themselves on the ground and commenced their attack upon the turkey.

It was so juicy and tender that it fell to pieces under the touch of their knives, all the rich juices preserved by the unique way in which it had been cooked.

Its viscera were dried up into a little bunch inside, which was easily removed, and there never was turkey which tasted more delicious than that which comprised the principal portion of the boys' supper in that remote camp on the Walnut.

Carlos and Pierre had limited themselves to such a light dinner at noon, that scarcely more than the skeleton of the turkey was left when they were through. The remains, together with an addition of cub-meat, were fed to Cyrus and Jupe; and after looking to the needs of their ponies, they were almost ready for bed again, as it was now dark. But having eaten so heartily, they were afraid to retire until some time had been allowed for digestion,—thinking they might be visited by that equine quadruped known as the "nightmare."

The boys sat up around a little campfire, or rather a "smudge" to keep the mosquitoes away, until more than an hour had passed beyond their usual bedtime, when they threw themselves on their robes and were soon sound asleep.

Carlos and Pierre were out of their buffalo-robes betimes in the morning, watered the ponies, ate breakfast, and fed the hounds. After putting out the fire, they shouldered their rifles, whistled to Cyrus and Jupe, and started off for the open prairie, intending to have a grand hunt for two or three hours,—when

Carlos suddenly stopped, and said, "Pierre, what noise is that?"

Pierre listened for a moment, and said: "It sounds like horses' hoofs; the ponies are not stampeded;[1] I can see them quietly standing at the end of their picket-ropes, but they appear to notice something strange."

The boys remained where they were, eagerly listening to the approaching sound of hoofs, which there was now no mistaking; and presently they saw their father, mounted on his favorite saddle-pony, coming in sight as he emerged from a dense box-elder copse, through which the trail along the river-bank ran.

As he rode up, and after a filial greeting, Carlos said to his father:

"Dad," (the boys had always called their father "Dad" from infancy,) "I hope nothing has gone wrong at home?"

"No, boys, everything is all right at the ranch; but Dick Curtis, the Indian trader, arrived last night from the Cheyenne village on the Washita river, away south of us, and has traveling with him two young gentlemen from Boston, who have never been out in the "Far West" before, and they want to learn something of the wild life out here. When I told them about you boys, last evening, nothing would do but I must have you home, as they are going to remain several days.

---

[1] *Stampede*, a Spanish word meaning a sudden fright scaring a herd of cattle or drove of horses on the plains, and causing them to run; a hurried rush of an army or any body of men or animals.

They are nice, well-educated young men, both sopho-
mores of Harvard University, and nothing of the dude
about them. I thought you would like to meet them
and entertain them while they stay. So I started before day this morning, hoping to reach here before you
went out of camp, and it's lucky I arrived just in
time.''

"All right, Dad," said Pierre; "we expected to remain here until day after to-morrow, but will go back
with you, of course."

"Have you had any breakfast, Dad?" queried Carlos; to which his father said "No."

"Then, Pierre, if you'll unsaddle Dad's pony and
picket him out, I'll get some coffee and bear-meat for
him in a jiffy," continued Carlos, as he gathered up
some pieces of dry wood to kindle a fire.

By the time Pierre had his father's pony picketed
out, Carlos had the coffee boiling,—for the pot was not
yet cold from breakfast,—some nice slices of the cub
were broiled before the glowing embers, and in a few minutes Mr. Delahoyde was enjoying the substantial meal
Carl had so cheerfully and willingly prepared for him.

The boys brought up their animals, packed up their
camp equipage, and it was placed on the pony; the
brothers saddled theirs; their father's horse had filled
himself with the rich grass, and after he was brought
up to where the others were standing, and saddled,
they all mounted. The boys whistled to their hounds,
and they started on the trail for home, where they arrived by ten o'clock.

CHAPTER IV.

AS Mr. Delahoyde and his boys rode up to the
dugout, they saw Dick Curtis, the Indian trader, and two young men sitting outside on a
log, smoking their pipes. They rose as the ponies
halted, and when Carlos, Pierre and their father had
dismounted, Curtis and his friends walked up, and after shaking hands with Mr. Delahoyde, Curtis introduced Carl and Pierre to Mr. Summerfield and Mr.
Burton, saying, as greetings were interchanged:

"Gentlemen, these are the two boys I have spoken
to you about, and I think during the four or five days
we propose to camp here they will turn out to be the
best guides and hunters you could find in the Territory."

"Well, boys," spoke up Mr. Summerfield, "we are
what you call out here, 'tenderfeet.' Have never been
West before, but want to learn something of its wild
life and adventures; and having spoken to your father
last evening about your giving up your time for about

a week to us, we hope you will look upon the proposition favorably,— as we learn from Mr. Curtis that you are better posted about hunting, and know more about animals and birds, than even he, although he has been on the Plains all his life."

"That's putting it rather strong," said Carlos; and both he and his brother blushed at the compliment. "To be sure, we have given a great deal of time to the study of the animals and birds of this region, and perhaps know a lot about them; and as Dad is willing that we show you around here, both of us will do our best to give you some sport. Turkeys are plenty now, and they are the largest bird we have."

"Yes," interrupted Pierre, "both buffalo and antelope can easily be found only a few miles from here, to say nothing of wolves, lynxes, and an occasional bear. We killed a she-bear and her cub on this trip."

While the boys were talking to the young men, their father had unpacked the meat and camp equipage, unsaddled the riding animals, and picketed them out. When he returned, the boys and their visitors were sitting on the log, the latter listening to a description of the beauties of the region, and asking all sorts of questions, which the strange scenes around them had provoked.

Then the young men invited Carlos and Pierre to go down to their camp and dine with them, where they could lay out their plans for the week they proposed to remain on the Walnut.

Pierre and Carlos, accompanied by the Indian trader and the young gentlemen, upon this invitation proceeded to their camp, which could be seen from the dugout, about half a mile up the river under a large box-elder tree. Arriving there, they were invited inside of the tent, which was a Sibley, patented by an army officer of that name, after the Sioux tepee. It was conical in shape, with capacity for a dozen men. It had a small stove, the pipe of which ran out of the top, and the pole that held up the canvas rested in an iron tripod in the center. Scattered around were the buffalo-robes and blankets, which were the beds of the party, three saddles, four rifles, fishing-tackle, and a couple of valises.

Outside were two wagons, such as are used by freighters on the Plains, with white canvas covers; four mules and three ponies picketed near; a brightly burning campfire, at which stood a Mexican, who was the cook employed by the young men for their trip, now busily engaged in preparing dinner for the party, as it was almost noon.

Dick Curtis, who had left Fort Dodge eight or ten days previously, his wagons loaded with goods suitable for trading with the Cheyennes, was an old trapper, Indian fighter, guide and scout.[1] He had been on the Plains and in the Rocky Mountains for more than

---

[1] Scout, a person who goes ahead of the soldiers and spies out what the enemy is doing, how many there are, and gets all the information for the commanding officer. Especially is this duty necessary in Indian warfare. Kit Carson was the greatest scout of his time; Colonel W. F. Cody ("Buffalo Bill"), since the former's death thirty years ago.

twenty years, and was known by everyone in the whole region, from the Yellowstone to the Rio Grande.

At Fort Harker he had met the two young men from the East, who had brought letters of introduction to the officers of the post. These officers, upon learning that the mission of the Boston gentlemen was to "rough it" for a week or two, hunt buffalo and wrestle with the excitement of life on the frontier, suggested that they make the trip with Curtis to the Cheyenne village on the Washita, and stop for a time at the Delahoyde ranch on the Walnut,—one of the best parts of the country for big game. They were also told of the accomplishments of Carlos and Pierre Delahoyde, in the direction of the amusement they were seeking; so, without a moment's hesitation, they had acted upon the advice of the gentlemen at Fort Dodge.

Dinner was announced shortly after the arrival of Carlos and Pierre at the trader's camp, and as Curtis himself was a famous shot, the larder was always well supplied with wild meat.

The table around which they all gathered was formed of the end-gates of the wagons, over which an extra piece of canvas was thrown, to serve as a cloth. The appointments in the way of cups, dishes, knives, forks, etc., were of the simplest character,—generally tin, and such as constitute a regular camping outfit.

Buffalo hump, grouse [1] and hare constituted the meats; in addition, biscuits baked in a Dutch oven,

---

[1] *Grouse*, a family of birds, of which there are many varieties, with different names; in this instance, the well-known "prairie-chicken" of the West.

coffee, with milk from the ranch, together with a variety of canned fruit purchased from the sutler at the fort.

All did ample justice to the meal, and at its conclusion young Summerfield, Burton, Carlos and Pierre adjourned to the shade of the tent to discuss the program of the hunting expedition, while Curtis busied himself with some duty required about his wagons.

After Summerfield and Burton had filled and lighted their pipes (neither Carlos nor Pierre indulged in tobacco), the conversation opened with a discussion of the wild turkey, its habits, and the best time to hunt it.

Pierre took up the subject upon some interrogatories by both Summerfield and Burton, telling them that the wild turkey could be found in almost every piece of timber in the whole country, outside of the thickly settled portions. Sometimes places where they have been plentiful will suddenly appear deserted, but you will find them all again somewhere, where the acorns and nuts of other trees are ripe; so they migrate from one portion of the country to another, coming back in good time to where you first saw them.

"Is there as much difference in size between the gobblers and the hens as there is with our tame ones?" inquired Burton.

"Yes," said Carlos, "the hens are much smaller, not half so brilliant in their plumage, have no bristles on their breasts, no spurs, and the fleshy lump above the bill is not nearly so large as in the gobbler."

"As I understand it," said Pierre, "the wild turkey and the domesticated are really the same bird—so Dad says, and he has read all about them."

"It's a mighty big thing to find the nest of a wild turkey (though I have found a good many)," said Carlos; "for the hen always covers up her eggs with leaves when she goes to feed, and you have to watch her very closely to tell where the nest is, as she does not go directly to it; she never goes to it twice by the same path, and unless you are very patient and wait, you will fail to discover it. She lays from ten to fifteen eggs, and they are exactly like those of the tame species."

"When is the best time to hunt them?" asked Summerfield.

"Oh, by moonlight, on the roost," replied Carlos and Pierre, simultaneously; "there's lots of fun then."

"Besides," said Pierre, "they're so stupid and bewildered, you can sometimes shoot as many as fifty without moving from the spot."

"Let's see," said Carlos; "it will be full moon next Wednesday, and this is Friday; we can go to one of the great roosts in a day: what do you say for next Wednesday night?"

Summerfield and Burton readily and enthusiastically agreed to the proposition. The conversation was then directed to "ways and means" for the trip.

"We will go on horseback," said Pierre; "we don't

want to be bothered with a wagon; we can pack all our bedding and cooking outfit on two ponies. You gentlemen can stand thirty miles on horseback?" he inquired, directing his interrogatory to Summerfield and Burton.

"Oh, yes," they both responded; and Summerfield continued: "I guess we rode a greater distance even than that, some days, on our trip to the Washita. Did n't we, Burton?"

"I know we did," replied Burton; "we have become quite hardened to the saddle now. Besides, our ponies are wonderfully easy in their lope."

"What shall we do between now and next Wednesday, boys?" inquired Summerfield, looking appealingly at Carlos and Pierre.

"Oh, there 's lots," said Pierre; "we can fish, hunt jackrabbits with the hounds, go up to the wolf-dens——"

"Or have a night hunt after lynxes with Cyrus and Jupe; they 're thick in the woods now," interrupted Carlos; "but this afternoon I want to show you our pets and museum."

At that moment the young men's attention was attracted by a sort of croaking high up in the sky, and they looked that way, then inquisitively at the boys. Pierre said:

"There 's a flock of Sandhill Cranes sailing around away above us;" and stretching his neck upward he said, "Look there!" as he pointed with his finger at-most directly to the zenith, where all presently saw a thin circle resembling a small cloud, and listening, they learned that the sonorous croak emanated from it.

"Will they light," asked Burton, "so we can get a good look at them?"

"Yes," replied Carlos, "they are circling lower now, and if we wait fifteen or twenty minutes they will come down. If they light near enough, you'll see the funniest sight you ever looked at!"

"How's that?" inquired Burton of Carlos.

"Oh, they just dance, and go through all sorts of ludicrous antics; you'll see, if they light."

"Tell us something about them, their habits, and how they make their nests," continued Burton, keeping up an animated dialogue with Carlos.

"Well, they're very common here. They generally arrive from the south about the middle of March or early in April, and stay with us until the first week of October; sometimes a few will linger as late as Christmas — not frequently; it depends upon the weather. We often have the most delightful fall until then; but when a storm comes on you see no more of the cranes until the next spring."

"How about their nests, and how many eggs do they lay?" queried Summerfield.

"Well," answered Carlos, "they make a sort of platform of rushes about three feet in diameter, lined with the leaves of the cat-tails, and in this nest lay only two eggs; a kind of pale olive buff, spotted with brown and purple. I 've got a couple in our museum I 'll show you when——"

"There! they 're going to light on that bare sand-knoll," exclaimed Pierre, pointing to the spot about an eighth of a mile away, beyond the timber, "and if we sneak up behind the trees perhaps we can get close enough without scaring them away, and you can see one of their funny cotillions."

At this the boys stole quietly off, keeping in the shadow of the timber, and were successful in reaching a good point of observation without disturbing the birds. As Carl and Pierre squatted on the ground, making a sign for Summerfield and Burton to do the same, Pierre put his fingers on his lips, a sign for absolute silence. The cranes then commenced to bow to each other, leap into the air, skip backward and forward and circle about, letting their great wings droop as they did so, uttering their croaking whoops, and working themselves into a frenzy of excitement more intense every second.

So ridiculous did their movements appear to the boys who were watching them, that all simultaneously burst into a loud laugh, and the cranes on the instant, with a sharp croak, took to their wings, and were soon circling more than a half-mile above where they had danced.

"Now that fun's over," said Carlos, "let's go up home and look at our museum in the dugout, and our pets that are scattered all around the place."

DANCE OF THE SANDHILL CRANES.

So they started on a brisk walk for the ranch, Summerfield and Burton evidently delighted at what they had seen, and on the anxious lookout for fresh experiences.

When they arrived at the dugout, Carlos and Pierre led the way to the room on the extreme right, and when the Boston young men entered, their eyes fairly bulged with astonishment.

Around the rude walls, on shelves equally as rude, made of hewn slabs, were the nests and eggs of the several varieties of birds indigenous to the region, but there were no duplicates, for both Carlos and Pierre collected only to study; their natural love for animate nature was too great to permit them to destroy for pure wantonness.

Summerfield and Burton were especially attracted by the elk, which was once the favorite of the boys, and they had to tell the story of his capture, his long sojourn with them, and his sad ending.

Among the animals, nicely mounted, were the little lynxes the boys once attempted to tame, a couple of beaver, an otter, a badger, and a 'coon; all the varieties of birds, too, whose nests were there, had a place in the collection. Summerfield and Burton, after spending a most agreeable and instructive hour with their newly found friends, declared that if the collection were in Boston it would readily sell for many hundreds of dollars.

As they left the museum, Pierre said:

" Now we 'll hunt up our pets, and the first we 'll show you is ' Ephraim,' our bear. Dad says that all old trap-

—5

pers and mountaineers call that animal 'Ephraim,' so we christened ours by that name."

"How old is he?" inquired Burton, as Ephraim came crawling out of his den in the ledge of rocks just in rear of the dugout, whence the boys had led their guests, and called their rough pet by name. He was fastened to a tree outside by a long chain.

"How old is he?" inquired Summerfield of Pierre, forgetting that Burton had just asked the same question.

"About four years this month," answered Pierre.

"Dad and we boys were out one morning, getting a load of dry wood for mother to cook with, and we were not more than a half-mile from the dugout when Carlos, who was off by himself a short distance, after an eagle's nest he had discovered in the uppermost dead forks of a tall cottonwood, suddenly yelled as if he were hurt. We supposed at first that he had tumbled from the tree and broken his leg or arm; so, dropping everything, Dad and I ran with our rifles to where we had heard him scream, and when we got there we saw him sitting on one of the lower limbs, laughing at his predicament. At the foot of the tree was a she-bear with one cub, and the old one was examining Carl's rifle, which necessarily he had to leave on the ground when he climbed up the tree to get the eagle's eggs. The bear was turning the rifle over with her nose, smelling it, and once in a while touching it with her paw. You know bears are full of curiosity, and when they come across anything they are not familiar with,

at once commence to investigate it closely. Dad shot the
bear, and Carl came down from his perch. As the cub
was only a few weeks old it was very small, and we had
no difficulty in running it down after a spirited chase.

" Carl told us that he yelled as if he were hurt, so as
to attract our attention quicker, as he was not very comfortable in the forks of the tree, and had the eagle's eggs
in his hat, which he did n't want to lose. He was n't a
bit scared; it takes a good deal to frighten him."

" Those were the very eggs I showed you in the museum," said Carlos, after his brother had told the story
of how they captured Ephraim.

" We got the cub home," continued Pierre, " and as
we had plenty of milk, had no trouble in getting him to
drink it right away. He was very fat when we caught
him, and I don't believe he ever lost an ounce of flesh, so
kindly did he take to his change of living."

" Ephraim soon became a great pet," said Carlos, " and
as he grew we taught him lots of tricks; I 'll show you
one," continued he as he caught hold of the bear around
the body and began to wrestle with him. Over and over
they tumbled, the bear evidently enjoying the fun as well
as Carlos, but the bear was the stronger of the two, and
he succeeded in throwing Carlos on his back during the
scuffle. Effecting that, the bear would let go his hold and
stand up on his hind legs, ready for another bout.

" One of his dislikes," said Pierre, as Carlos ended the
wrestle with Ephraim, " is dogs — I mean strange dogs;

of course he will not make any fuss when he sees our own, but they generally keep clear of him. Once when an Indian trader who had a dog with him camped here about three years ago, and the dog tried to be too familiar with Ephraim, he just split his head open with one stroke of his paw."

"Ephraim will follow us around just like a dog, when we let him," said Carlos. Once when I had him out in the woods with me, it got dark so I could n't see my hand before my face. I lost my way, and did n't know in which direction to go. Whenever I started in a certain direction, Ephraim would act uneasy, and run in front of me against my legs, as if to warn me that I was going wrong. As he did this several times when I changed my course, at last I thought I would just follow him as he walked right in front of me, when, without halting once, or hesitating at all, he led me straight home, knowing the direction, although it was dark as pitch, as well as if it had been daylight."

Having watched the bear's antics for some time, young Summerfield and Burton were preparing to return to their camp for the night, as it was now about six o'clock, when Mrs. Delahoyde came out of the dugout and invited them to remain and take supper with the boys.

"We have plenty of milk," said she; "I will have hot biscuit, fresh butter, and will give you some broiled bear-steak from the cub the boys brought home yesterday."

The young gentlemen did not need a second invitation,

so gladly accepted the first. Then Carlos said he would show them the spring, where they could wash, as his mother brought out a clean towel.

The spring was only a dozen yards in rear of the dugout—a stream of cool, clear water as big as a man's arm, rushing out of the rocky bluff, forming a natural basin below, where probably for ages it had fallen on the ledge, and had worn out a hollow eight or nine feet in diameter and four deep.

"This is our bath sometimes," said Carlos, "when the river gets on a tear, and is too muddy; the only objection to the water is, that it is too cold. If you want to try it after dark, mother will let you have all the towels you want."

"I'd like it first-rate," said Summerfield; "I have always been used to taking a cold bath every morning at home since I was seven years old,—kept it up all through college, and until I came out West have never missed. But Carl, if it will make no difference to you folks, I would prefer to take a bath early in the morning. I have plenty of towels down in my tent."

"That's all right," said Carlos; "no one will disturb you, and as the pool is completely hidden in the willows, you will be as private there as if you were in your own tent."

After they had completed their ablutions at the spring, all walked to the dugout, where Mrs. Delahoyde surprised them by announcing supper ready, which she had set outside of the dwelling on the short, velvety buffalo-grass, which formed a natural lawn to the curious building.

On the grass was spread an immaculately white cloth, around which, prone upon the sod, reclining after the method of the old Romans[1] when eating, the little party distributed themselves.

The service was very plain, of course, but the variety of the viands, and the absolute cleanliness which characterized the meal, charmed the young Bostonians, who did ample justice to it, and were profuse in their compliments to their hostess for offering them such an entertainment, so delightfully and really *al fresco,* (as the Italians say for out-of-doors.)

A great pail of milk, which had been cooled to almost icy refrigeration by immersion in the spring; biscuits that in lightness and whiteness rivaled the fleecy clouds floating above them in the heavens; and most deliciously broiled young bear-steaks, which were a new sensation to the young visitors,—these formed the component parts of that supper, with marmalade made of the wild plum, as the last course.

After all had partaken heartily, and Mrs. Delahoyde had removed the cloth, the party lingered where they sat, and as the rays of the declining sun were gilding the crests of the bluffs, a delightful breeze came from the south, making the whole scene in its wild picturesqueness a de-

---

[1] The Romans reclined on a couch or sort of bench while eating; they did not sit on chairs, as we do.

lightful revery, they indulged in conversation full of interest and instruction.

"Boys," said their father at last, "you have not shown these gentlemen what I regard as the most curious and interesting of your pets—the Moles."

"Why, have you tamed moles, too?" asked Summerfield, in surprise.

"Yes, indeed," answered Mr. Delahoyde, "and the boys can tell you more about them than you ever knew, perhaps, because they have made a study of them,—particularly Carlos."

"We 've seen lots of them at home," said Burton, "but they are so common that we never took much interest in them."

"Go bring them, Carl," said his mother, who having completed her domestic duties inside of the dugout, joined the group on the lawn.

Carlos promptly obeyed, and in a few moments returned, bringing with him a cracker-box, into which the young Bostonians looked, and saw nestled in dry leaves and grass, six of the beautiful little creatures they had been talking about, which immediately rose up on their hind legs, as they felt the fingers of some one touching their nest.

As Mr. Delahoyde had said, one of the most beautiful animals in the region in which the ranch was located was the mole. He is a timid, unobtrusive creature, yet, as is well known in strictly agricultural districts, he exercises considerable influence upon the welfare of the farmer. In the East he is always to be found around country homes, and what boy who ever lived in rural districts there, has failed, as he wandered through the fields of his father's farm, to attempt the capture of the handsome little fellow?

Scientists aver that if it were not for this industrious little animal, our land would be overrun with those worms that live beneath the ground and do great damage to the crops so necessary to our very existence.

Carlos and Pierre discovered, after one or two failures, that the moles were easily tamed, and made clean, affectionate little pets. The box in which they were kept was well ventilated, and filled with earth and prairie hay. They had to be fed regularly, as the boys had found by a sad experience that if they were at all neglected they would soon die.

Differing from other wild animals, as soon as a mole is caught and put in its house it will begin to eat immediately.

Carlos had studied the habits of the mole very industriously, and said, as he handled one, that of all the animals with which he was familiar, it was the most skillful digger.

That his observations were true, anyone who has watched a mole working his way through the soil in search of food will admit. It would be difficult to find an animal any better adapted to his work. Nature has fitted him most magnificently for the work he has to perform. His front paws are made like broad shovels; have five strong claws, which set in a groove at the end of a finger-joint, and work perfectly in putting away the earth which must be moved in search of his food. His front legs are short, fixed to a shoulder remarkable for its strength, while his breast-bone is strongly formed so as to throw his head, when he is digging, on a level with his hands. His nose, too, has a mighty part to play in his excavations; it is long and slender, with a small bone at the very top, which helps him to push his way forward. His hind feet stand flat and firmly upon the ground, and altogether he is very strongly made. With his nose he picks out the worms and other insects from their hiding-places as he moves along.

The mole is always very hungry, and the deprivation of food makes him crazy and he soon dies; the boys discovered this fact from the experience they had while attempting to tame the first ones they caught, in putting no food in the cage and leaving them until night. When they returned with the cows they found their would-be pets dead. They however profited by their lesson, and found that moles would eat fresh meat when confined. Once when, by circumstances they could not control, they neglected to place food in the cage where there were two of the little animals, they found the one living had killed and devoured his comrade.

Moles go about on top of the ground at certain times, and are themselves devoured by wolves and coyotes. They are almost blind, but are able to hear well, which fact in part compensates for the deficiency of the other sense.

The mole's eyes are very small, and are almost hidden in the beautiful soft and fine fur which covers him, and his ears are almost closed.

Pierre, also, made a long study of the habits of these little animals, and found that they build themselves little fortresses. He discovered that their little houses are not indicated, as one would naturally suppose, by the ridge of earth which marks their hunting expeditions, but is a small hill thrown up by themselves which is protected by a bank, the base of a tree, or a rock.

The industrious little fellows first work the earth very well to make it convenient for use in building, and construct galleries for the purpose of communication with each other. At the upper part of the hill a round gallery is constructed, and from it five passages lead to another gallery below, which is larger than the first one. In the lower gallery there is a room which might be called the citadel of the fortress, and there the little animal lives. It is made very dry, and constructed with great care. Another gallery goes from the lower one in a straight line as far as the animal hunts. At the bottom of the sleeping-place is another, sinking lower into the earth. Several little passages are made to provide the house with water, and along which the mole goes for the desired liquid. It seems that these animals require a great deal of water, and their little homes usually communicate with a ditch or pond.

Their little ones are born in another department, which is placed at some distance from the main dormitory. The mother gives birth to four or five at a time, which in little more than a month begin to run about and provide themselves with food, although they are only about half grown.

Sometimes eight or nine defiles run around the hill from which the mole gets his food. If the hill is very large it may shelter several moles, but they are very careful not to trespass upon one another's hunting-grounds. If two should meet in the defiles, they fight until the weakest one is overcome and retreats.

The mole never searches for food near the spot which he has chosen for his fortress. He labors for two hours in the morning when he is building his edifice; then does not begin again until evening, when he works two hours more. The principal defiles of the fortress are formed in a circle, so that if anything happens he escapes through some of the many run-ways.

After listening to Mr. Delahoyde and his boys expatiate upon the merits of the pretty little creatures, Burton said that he had no idea that the subject of moles could be so interesting; that he had been delighted and instructed as well.

It was now fairly night, and Summerfield suggested

the propriety of going to bed, as he wanted to get up early, take his bath, and pass another pleasant day.

So they all got up, Mr. Delahoyde and sons accompanying the visitors to their camp.

The gibbous moon poured out a flood of light as they walked through the timber, and Pierre said:

"That will be a glorious moon for our turkey-hunt next Wednesday night."

"Suppose it storms?" remarked Burton.

"No fear of that," said Carlos; "it never rains here at this time of the year."

"Carl is right," said Mr. Delahoyde; "you can depend upon a most brilliant full moon." Then, having reached the tent, they bade their guests good-night, and walked back to the dugout and immediately retired.

CHAPTER V.

AFTER breakfast was over at the ranch, Curtis came to the dugout and inquired of Mr. Delahoyde whether his boys had any wolf-skins to dispose of.

He replied that he thought they had about twenty-five or thirty, and calling Carlos and Pierre, he asked them how many wolves they had poisoned since the trader was there a few months ago and bought all they then had.

The boys said they had thirty, fine ones; and upon Mr. Curtis telling them he wanted to purchase all, they took him to a sort of storeroom built in rear of the dwelling, and showed them to him.

The skins were in excellent condition, for the boys understood perfectly the art of preserving furs,[1] and Curtis told them he would pay the usual price of one dollar apiece for them.

[1] The art of preserving furs is the knowledge of that process which will keep them from spoiling when first taken from the animal. The best method is a solution of equal parts of saltpeter and alum, with which rub the skin on both sides two or three times a day for a week. I advise all boys to use this preparation, which is perfectly harmless to human life, and never to use arsenic, which is poisonous. I have used it for thirty years, and never failed. They are the same ingredients employed by the Smithsonian Institution, and are recommended by it.

The trade in wolf-hides was quite a remunerative one for Carlos and Pierre, amounting sometimes to two or three hundred dollars a year. Their method of procuring them was adopted by all trappers, and had been taught by their father.

Young saplings, generally of the cottonwood, about four inches in diameter, are cut into lengths of two feet, one end sharpened, and at the other a cup is made two or three inches deep. These stakes are driven into the ground out on the prairie, and into the cup is poured melted grease mixed with strychnine. The wolves lick the cups at night as they prowl around, and in a few moments afterward are dead. Frequently as many as ten of the wolves are found in the morning when the location of the bait is visited. Of course they are sought for only during two or three of the winter months, when their hair is thick and desirable.

During the period of wolf-poisoning, the boys confine their hounds at night, for even the most intelligent dog does not possess brains enough to discriminate between what is healthful and what would kill him, if the odor is attractive.

When the Indian trader returned to the dugout with one of his wagons to transport to camp the wolf-robes he had purchased from the boys, Summerfield and Burton came with him to learn what program Pierre and Carlos had decided upon for that day's amusement.

After the usual greetings, Pierre asked Summerfield

whether he had indulged in his bath at the pool, as he had proposed the evening before.

"Yes, indeed," replied he to the inquiry; "I was up at the first streak of dawn, and enjoyed my plunge immensely. When I came up through the timber, your dogs advanced to meet me, looked askance, but after smelling me, probably satisfied that I was all right, went back to their places on top of the dugout and curled themselves up again to sleep. I found the water in the pool very cold, as Carl suggested it would be, but I felt all right in a moment after I had splashed myself thoroughly."

"Have you decided how you and Burton would like to put in the day?" asked Carlos of Summerfield, as he got through telling about his early bath.

"No," he replied, "but Burton has expressed a desire to try his luck at fishing; we both have excellent tackle."

"Well, let's go fishing then," suggested Pierre; "only if we want to have lots of fun, it's better to stretch a trot-line across the river, and then we are more likely to catch some big cats. Carl and I have a fine one all ready for business, but baiting."

"All right," said Burton; "but I must confess my ignorance of what you mean by a 'trot-line.'"

"I'll tell you, then," said Pierre. "It is a long fishing-line, long enough to reach from one bank of the river to the other. At certain distances apart are fastened short lines, to each of which is tied a hook. The hooks are about two feet apart, and well weighted with sinkers, so

that they will stay straight down in the water. Sometimes
when you haul up the line, after letting it remain for a
couple of hours or so, you 'll get a big fish on every hook."

"I know now what you mean, since you have described
it," said Burton; "it 's the same thing all regular cod-fish-
ermen on the New England coast call a trawl; only a trawl
is frequently two or three miles long. It is coiled up in
a tub in the boat, already baited with clams, and when the
fisherman reach the location they started for, the long line
is paid out,—both ends being fastened to an immense float,
usually a small barrel."

"What do you use for bait on your trot-line?" inquired
Burton.

"Any kind of meat that we chance to have at the time.
Some of the cub that we killed the other day must serve
our purpose on this excursion; it 's all we have now on
hand, but it is just as good as any."

"Let 's start at once," said Carlos; "it will take two
hours to get the line ready and bait it up."

"Yes, all of that," said Pierre, "if you count in the
time it will take to get to where we want to go to set it."

"I guess I 'll take my pole and tackle along," said Burton; "perhaps I can catch something myself. I do so love
to angle."

"All right," said Carlos; "you 'll have plenty of time
to try your luck before we fellows get the trot-line set."

Then they all started for the store-room back of the dugout where Carlos and Pierre kept their odds and ends for

hunting and fishing. When they arrived there, Pierre said: "Carl, you and Summerfield straighten out the trot-line, and while Burton goes down to camp for his tackle I 'll cut up the bait, and then we 'll all put it on the hooks."

Burton went for his pole, telling the boys that he would hurry back and help them. Carlos and Summerfield then got out the line and began to untangle it, while Pierre started for a cottonwood a short distance off, to a limb of which the carcass of the cub was hanging, and commenced to cut off liberal slices of the toughest and most worthless portions of the young bear.

In a little while the boys got the trot-line straightened out, stretched it on the grass, and Pierre having gotten the bait cut up into suitably sized pieces, the three commenced to put it on the hundred or more hooks.

Before they had completed the job, Burton returned from camp with his fishing-tackle, and helped the other boys finish baiting.

"Where do you think we 'd better go?" inquired Carlos of his brother.

"Why, I was thinking the best place would be at the bend of the North Walnut, just below where Spring creek empties into it. You know we 've always been lucky fishing there; caught some of the biggest cats that were ever taken out of the Arkansas."

"I guess you 're right," said Carlos; "besides, it 's only

—6

a few miles from here, and we can make it easily in an hour and twenty minutes."

So, the question of location being thus quickly decided, the little party trudged off, whistling, laughing and gossiping on the way.

They arrived there at the appointed time suggested by Carlos, and found it a really beautiful spot, and said that Pierre had made no mistake in selecting their objective point, so far as beauty of scenery was concerned. There the Walnut made a graceful bend to the southeast, and both banks of the stream were heavily fringed with great cottonwoods and box-elders, whose limbs hung far out over the water, making one of those deeply shaded places that the sluggish catfish love to hide in. The banks, too, instead of shelving gradually to the edge of the river, as elsewhere, were four or five feet high, and washed out underneath to a distance of three feet, where the dark water moved very slowly,—a perfect paradise of a retreat for the species of fish the boys were after, where they love to secrete themselves under just such a protection from the sunlight.

Both Summerfield and Burton were charmed with the delightfully sequestered place, with its primitive grandeur, and so expressed themselves most enthusiastically to Carlos and Pierre, who, though brought up amid such magnificent scenes, declared that it was one of their favorite resorts of the many in the wild region where they lived.

The boys had brought a luncheon with them, which

Mrs. Delahoyde insisted they must take along, as it would be many hours until supper-time, and they did not intend to return to dinner, as it was after ten o'clock before they could get away from the ranch.

A dozen cold biscuits, a jug of milk and a small pail of wild-plum jam, she thought would suffice, although the party were not heavily freighted and could easily have taken more. The trot-line was wound on a stick, and they only had that and their luncheon to carry. Of course the boys took their rifles; Carl and Pierre never went a quarter of a mile from home without them, and so used were they to their guns, they really appeared a necessary part of themselves. Summerfield and Burton had theirs with them, too, because Mr. Delahoyde had told them the evening before, that it was one of the unpardonable sins of the frontier for a man to go anywhere without some sort of weapon.

Pierre told Burton he might as well cast in his line, as the rest of them were enough to set the trot-line; so he jointed his rod, baited his hook, and seating himself on the grass under one of the big cottonwoods, threw his line as far up the stream as he could, into the darkest part of the eddy.

"You'll not get a bite at once," said Carlos to him, as he looked so anxiously toward his cork float; "you may have to wait an hour before you get even a nibble; these Western cats are terribly slow at taking the hook."

Just as he spoke, however, Burton felt a fearful tugging at his line; his float entirely disappeared, and as he pulled up on his pole, he saw a curious-looking fish wriggling on his hook. It was about two feet long, and seemed mostly nose, while its body was covered with knobs like armor.

"What in the world is it?" he exclaimed, as he successfully landed it alongside him, and got a good look at it.

"Why that's a Garpike," said both Carlos and Pierre, as they laughed at Burton's apparent perplexity in attempting to classify his strange-looking monster.

"Why, so it is!" said Summerfield, coming toward Burton. "I studied that class of fishes in college. They are the real aristocrats of the whole world, if ancient ancestry is considered. They have descended without a break from the Devonian period, tens of thousands of years ago!"

"That is just what Dad says about 'em, too," said Carlos; "and you know he is a college graduate. We always throw 'em back into the water. They're no good but to bother a fellow when he is fishing.

"If that's the case, here goes," said Burton, as he unhooked his prize and tossed it back into the river. "But I take off my hat," suiting the action to the word, "and salute the most bloated aristocrat, so far as a lengthy pedigree is concerned, I have ever seen or heard of."

All laughed at Burton's apostrophe to the worthless fish, and Carlos said: "There's one thing I forgot to tell you about the garpike: it's a sign that you'll have good luck in angling now, for good fish always come to you after you 've hooked one of these fellows; at least, that 's what the old mountaineers say, so Dad has told us boys."

" Well, then," said Burton as he re-baited his hook and cast his line in again, " I have always been a little superstitious myself; believe in some of the omens[1] and auguries[2] that have come down to us from the Dark Ages, so I shall expect to haul up a big cat next time I get a bite." He then subsided again into passive indifference to everything around him excepting his cork float, upon which he fastened his eyes as intently as a snake does when it is after a bird.

The excitement ended caused by the little episode of Burton's hooking the garpike, Carlos, Pierre and Summerfield went to work in real earnest to set their trot-line. Unwinding it carefully, one end was fastened to a stout bush that grew on the bank, and the other carried across the river by Summerfield and Pierre, while Carlos kept in their rear to properly adjust the hooks as they dropped one by one into the water.

The boys had to take off their clothes while fixing the line and wade through the stream, which so varied in depth that sometimes they were in only to their ankles, and then up to their necks, when they reached the dark eddy at the opposite bank.

In less than an hour after they had commenced to

[1] *Omens*, signs of good or evil to come.
[2] *Auguries*, prophecies of future events.

stretch their trot-line across, it was secured and ready for the reception of any fish that might be allured by its tempting bait. Then, having nothing to do but wait for results, Carlos, glancing at the sun, remarked: "Fellows, it's a little after noon; had n't we better attack that lunch ?"

Summerfield replied: "Good! I 'm famishing already; this outdoor life gives me the appetite of one of your moles, which I think you said would soon starve to death if not fed pretty often."

"How is it with you, Burton ?" sang out Pierre across the water to the "lone fisherman" still absorbed in watching that motionless float; "do you want something to eat ?"

Burton upon hearing his name called, suddenly returned to his normal state of mind, and straightening himself out, replied, "Yes, I 'm as hungry as a wolf!."

"All right," responded Pierre; "we 're coming over to your side of the river. Stick the end of your rod in the ground—it can't get away—and join us at the foot of the tree below where the trot-line is fastened."

In a few moments they were all sitting on the grass at the foot of one of the big cottonwoods. The jug of milk, which until then had been immersed in the cold water of the eddy under the bank, the biscuit and the plum jam, together with a tin cup, were before them.

Courtesy demanded that as only one cup had been brought from the ranch, their guests should drink first; so Pierre, pouring out some of the milk, passed it to Summerfield, the eldest of the party, who, understanding the politeness which dictated that he must take the initiative, bowed to Pierre, and without any fuss drained the cup. Then Burton came in for second, and so on, by turns; all the milk was soon consumed, and each one took his portion of the biscuit, spread on the jam with his pocket-knife, and in a few moments not even the wreck of what they had brought along to eat was left.

Summerfield and Burton had just lighted their pipes to indulge in their postprandial smoke, when a loud whirring noise greeted the ears of the group, and a flock of large birds flew swiftly by a few feet above them.

"What are those?" inquired Summerfield as he withdrew the pipe from his lips to ask the question.

"Prairie Grouse, commonly called Prairie Chickens," replied Pierre, as he cast his eyes toward them to assure himself before he answered the question. "They are the finest birds we have out here," continued he, "always excepting the wild turkey."

"Do they stay with you all the time, or do they migrate in the fall?" asked Burton.

"Yes," answered Pierre, "all the year round. They live on the open prairie during the summer, and in the winter they go into the timber, and when the snow is deep and the weather cold they hide and roost underneath the drifts."

"What do they live on?" inquired Burton.

"Mostly on grasshoppers, seeds, buds, blossoms of the

many varieties of wild flowers we have here, berries, and nearly anything that comes handy," answered Pierre.

" They 're splendid eating too," said Carlos; " and they build their nests in tufts of grass under some low bush, into which they work their body, line the hollow they thus make with a few blades of the grass, and lay from six to thirteen eggs; I once found fifteen in one nest. The color of their eggs is light clay to brown; very often perfectly plain, but generally speckled with fine dottings of dark brown, and in shape more pointed than oval."

" They have several different notes," continued Pierre; " one very much like a wild turkey, and I have often been fooled by it. It 's awful fun to watch a flock in the spring when they are breeding; then they are very tame and you can get quite close to them, and if you keep perfectly quiet, can observe for an hour or more at a time all their queer cuttings-up. They usually get together on some ridge of the prairie, or little hill, always about sunrise, when the cocks begin to dance around in a circle, facing each other with their heads lowered, their feathers all ruffled up, like a fighting rooster, and strut around as if challenging some of the number to battle; but they rarely quarrel. Their meetings and dances are almost as funny as those of the sandhill cranes, and are kept up every day until the hens are through laying and commence to sit."

" They are most wonderfully careful and attentive mothers, too," said Carlos, " and will pretend to be dreadfully lame when you come near one with her little ones hidden in the grass. She will flutter along the ground, as if it were impossible for her to fly, to draw you away from her chickens, almost let you catch her, until she believes they are safe out of your reach, when with a whirr! away she goes, and you are left alone!"

By the time this dissertation about the prairie grouse had ended, Summerfield and Burton having finished smoking their pipes, the latter asked the boys how long they had been in the habit of fishing with a trot-line.

Pierre spoke up, and replied: "Ever since we have been old enough to go fishing alone; about seven years ago; after we had lived on the ranch four. At first we had terribly hard luck on account of the otters, which used to steal the fish we caught. At that time we always set our lines in the evening, baiting the hooks with young frogs, and did not visit them until the next morning. We always found that lots of fish had been hooked, but nothing excepting portions of their heads were left,—the pesky little animals had devoured all the rest. They got so bad that we had to give up fishing with a trot-line, and go back to our rods. Then, at Dad's suggestion, we turned our attention to the otters, as he had more than twenty traps, although he had not made a business of trapping since we were born."

"We had lots of fun too, catching the handsome little beasts, and in one season we got about thirty, the skins of which, after Dad had cured them properly, we sold for a hundred dollars to Curtis when he came along."

"They 've never bothered us since," said Carlos; "the traps seemed to have driven them out of the country. Of course," continued he, "once in a great while we see some, but very rarely; besides, we have always since then set our trot-line in the daytime, and watched it as we are doing now."

"How about Otters?" said Burton. "I don't think I have ever seen the animal, although I am familiar with the fur; I had an overcoat trimmed with it last winter."

"Well," said Pierre, "they vary greatly in size, but will average three feet and four inches long, counting the tail, which is long, and is more than a third of their whole length. Their fur is very soft, of a brown color, rather lighter on the throat and breast. It is made up of long, coarse, shining hairs, underneath which is another fur of the finest quality."

"He does not eat anything but fish," said Carlos, "and you seldom meet him far from the water on that account. Dad says that he has heard his father tell how when he was a boy in Canada, the otters used to bother the regular fishermen by destroying their nets to get at the fish."

"Do you know anything about how they breed, Carl?" asked Summerfield.

"Yes," replied Carlos; "they generally build a sort of nest in a hole in the bank of a river, or in the roots of some tree that hangs over the water. They have from three to five little ones at a time, and they are usually born in March or early in April."

"I 'd like to see one," said Summerfield.

"I don't believe you ever will here again," said Pierre; "I have n't come across one for three years or more; I guess they 've all cleared out."

Just then, Burton, who had all the time kept an eye on that float, saw it slowly disappear under the water, and the upper end of his pole pulled down close to the surface of the river. He ran as fast as he could to where it was, and hauling the line in, saw to his dismay another curious-looking thing dangling at the hook.

"Well, I 'll be blessed," exclaimed he, if I don't have the funniest luck in catching nondescripts![1] Things I never saw before or ever heard of; but I guess this is a turtle, but not anything like those we have in the East."

"That 's a Soft-shell Turtle," said Pierre, as Burton held the reptile up so that the other boys could get a good look at it; "they 're good eating, too, but are another of those things that play hob with a fellow's fishing."

"What shall I do with him?" queried Burton.

"Take him back to your camp; I 'll bet that Mexican cook of yours knows how to serve it," said Carlos in answer to his inquiry.

"What do you say, Summerfield,—shall we eat it?" asked Burton of his companion.

"Of course," replied Summerfield; "I 'm going to eat everything the natives of the country do; I 've a cast-iron

[1] *Nondescript*, something which cannot be described or classified.

stomach which never went back on me yet. Take him to camp with us by all means."

The strangely shaped creature that Burton had caught was about a foot in diameter lengthwise, and nearly the same transversely. His nose was as sharp at the point as a mole's, and his shell readily yielded to the pressure of the fingers.

"Will he bite?" asked Burton, as he tied a piece of cord to the turtle's hind leg, before taking the hook out of its mouth.

"Not unless you plague it," said Carlos. "He's a sluggish fellow, and won't bother you if you don't make him angry."

After the turtle was unhooked, Burton fastened it to the limb of the tree under which he had been fishing, and the poor thing hung there, only moving its claws slowly occasionally, indicating that it was still alive.

"I guess we'd better haul up our trot-line now," said Carlos; "it's after four o'clock. Don't you think so, Pierre?" he asked his brother.

"Yes, indeed," replied Pierre; "by the time we get the fish off the hooks, if we've caught any, and wind the line up, it will be time to start back home."

"Well, then," said Burton, as he began to unjoint his rod and put up his tackle, "I don't think I'll fish any more; I want to help you fellows, as I did n't do anything in putting the trot-line out."

" All right," said Pierre; " you 'd better take off your trousers, as we 'll have to wade in taking the fish off."

" Let 's commence at the opposite end," said Carlos; " then one of us can wind it up as we go along; it won't get tangled then, and when we get back to this side we won't have anything to do but dress and start for the ranch."

The boys all stripped, leaving their clothes on the bank, Pierre having first cut a long willow limb with the end having a crotch in it, to string the fish on, and then started across the river.

When they reached the opposite bank, Carlos and Pierre stepped out, the latter untying the line and handing the end to Carlos, who fastened it to the piece of wood on which it was wound when the boys brought it from the ranch. As Pierre then lifted yard after yard of the line out of the water, Carlos began to wind up the slack.

On the first ten hooks were six good-sized cats, which would average four pounds each, and selecting two of the best, with Summerfield's and Burton's help, Pierre strung them on the willow wand.

" There 's no use in taking home more than we can eat in two meals," said Pierre, as he tossed the four back into the water again; " they won't keep long in this hot weather."

" Will they live after you put them in the river again ? " asked Burton.

" Yes, indeed," replied Pierre. " The cat is the hardest

fish to kill of all that I 'm acquainted with. They don't mind the wound of a hook; it will get well again in a day or two, and then they are as ready to bite as at first."

When the trot-line had been all taken out of the river, the boys discovered that they had caught forty fish, all cats excepting half a dozen of the aristocratic garpike, which is always on hand where there is bait put out.

Taking only eight of the best cats, the boys, after dressing, picked up their traps and then started for the ranch, where they arrived at six o'clock. Their progress had been much slower going back than in coming out in the morning, as they were freighted heavier, with the fish, and as Burton was considerably handicapped by his turtle, which gave him lots of trouble.

The fish were divided, the greater portion given to the Delahoydes, as there were more mouths to feed, (including the dogs, that were fond of fried cats,) and two were taken to their camp by the Bostonians and given to the cook with orders to serve one for supper and the other for breakfast.

When they showed the Mexican the turtle and asked him whether he knew how to cook it, he said: "Yes, you bet—make good soup!"

After supper that evening, Mr. Delahoyde, Carlos and Pierre went down to Curtis's camp to talk to the old trader, who was going back to Fort Harker the next day, and to whom they wanted to give some commissions for the sutler, as he intended to return in about ten days.

The moon shone brightly, and after the Mexican had lighted a smudge to drive away the mosquitoes which swarmed rather thickly in the river-bottom where the camp was located, all the party gathered in a small circle around it, and talked of the adventures of the day. Then plans were formulated for the remaining time that Summerfield and Burton intended to remain on the ranch, which would, of course, be until Curtis returned from the Smoky Hill.

"To-morrow will be Sunday," said Pierre; "and as mother likes us to observe the day, we do not ever go fishing or hunting, but stay around home and read, whenever we have anything to read. Curtis brought down quite a large bundle of newspapers from Fort Dodge for Dad, so we can skim over them; and in the afternoon, if you and Summerfield," addressing himself to Burton, who sat close to him, "would like to take a stroll out on the prairie, and through the timber, we'll go. Mother does n't object to that, and perhaps you may see many things that are interesting and new to you. This is the time of year when the greatest variety of birds are here, and I know there are a good many kinds that you have not yet come across."

"That will just suit me," said Burton, "and you too,— won't it, Summerfield?"

"Certainly," replied Summerfield; "I should enjoy such a walk immensely."

"By the way," continued he, "I 've got a lot of magazines and papers in my grip that Burton and I bought while traveling in the cars, and I shall be delighted to give them to you boys. You can look them over during the morning, while Burton and I write some letters, as Mr. Curtis does not start until about noon, I understand."

" You 're right," said the old trader, " I can't get away from here until then."

" Monday we 'll go on a wolf-hunt with the dogs," said Carlos, " and Tuesday we must start early for the turkey-roost, which as I told you is about thirty miles from here. We must get our camp fixed up, and hunt some meat to eat before we get at the turkeys; besides, we want to get a good rest as well, for it will be a tiresome ride this hot weather."

" All right," said Summerfield; " Burton and I are under you boys' orders, and are ready to obey as promptly as regular soldiers."

The conversation drifted from one subject to another,—the young Bostonians asking innumerable questions of Curtis, Mr. Delahoyde, and the boys.

In discussing the various animals of the region, Summerfield asked Mr. Delahoyde which he regarded as the most ferocious.

" Well," replied he, " the wolf, if hungry, is terribly bold; the she-bear with cubs, and the lynx: all, under certain conditions, are insanely ferocious; but you know that, normally, it is the habit of every wild beast to run at the sight of man. If you had asked me which I regard as the most dangerous, I should have unhesitatingly told you the little black-and-white Skunk. We have two varieties out here, one much larger than the other; the smaller is to be dreaded, the bite of which is certain death. The savages are aware of the fact, too. Two or three of my old friends among the trappers and hunters have been killed by the apparently insignificant little beast. They generally attack one at night while asleep, often selecting the nose of their victim, which they bite. The result is hydrophobia, and a most horrible death. I would never allow Carlos and Pierre to camp out, were it not that in Cyrus and Jupe they have such vigilant sentinels, which will never permit an animal to come within dangerous proximity of where they are sleeping.

"Ordinarily," continued he, "the large skunk is harm-less, excepting the dreadful odor he emits when he con-siders himself in danger. The soldiers at the fort, where there are always large numbers of the animal to be found, have nicknamed him 'The essence peddler.'

"I once had a rather laughable experience with a lot of the larger variety a few years ago. I was going on horseback across the country from the Arkansas to the Smoky Hill river, and after I had proceeded about twenty miles, one of those terrible blizzards characteristic of the Great Plains region in the fall, came down from the north in all its fury. It was night when I started from the Arkansas, and when the storm commenced it grew so in-tensely cold in a few minutes, and the snow was so blind-ing, that I could hardly urge my horse to move at all. I

—7

knew that I was not far from a rude stone shelter, which had been erected by buffalo hunters as a place of refuge in case of just such storms, and fortunately I reached it before I was frozen or my animal absolutely refused to go,— which he would have done in a little while. It was a square structure with a dirt roof, and had a large fireplace in the one room, as a creek well timbered ran but a short distance away, so fuel was comparatively handy.

" Well, when I had turned my horse loose at the south side of the building (I knew that he would not run off), I entered, and found ten hunters already there, who like myself had been caught in the blizzard, and they already had a roaring fire blazing on the hearth. I soon thawed out, and hoping to get a little sleep, laid down with the others on the dirt floor. Near the fireplace in the wall were two or three great holes, and presently through them marched five skunks, with tails erect ready for action, evidently attracted by the warmth and blaze. They walked deliberately all over us, smelling our heads, but offered no violence, and we did not dare move, fearing a hostile demonstration on their part; so eleven men were held at bay by five little animals they could easily have killed with their hands alone. It cleared off about two o'clock in the morning,—those blizzards hardly ever last long,—and as soon as it was daylight the skunks departed through the same holes by which they had entered, and we men left shortly after, laughing over our ridiculous adventure."

When Mr. Delahoyde had ended his story, the party broke up; the Bostonians went to their tent and Mr. Delahoyde and his sons to the dugout, as it was now after nine o'clock, a much later hour than they had kept for months.

CHAPTER VI.

SUMMERFIELD and Burton were out of their blankets at the first indication of dawn; both of them intending to take a bath in the pool at the willows under the bluff behind the dwelling of their newly found friends, the Delahoydes. After dressing lightly for the purpose, Burton woke up the cook and told him to have breakfast ready by the time they had returned, which would not be more than half an hour. Summerfield then opened his grip and took out a large bundle of magazines and papers which he had promised Pierre and Carlos he would bring with him.

Both of the young Bostonians were charmed with the wilderness and solitude of their surroundings, and as they walked slowly through the timber toward the dugout, began to philosophize.

Summerfield remarked to his companion, as the deliciousness of the coming morning influenced his feelings: "Although there cannot possibly be any difference between one day and another out here in the wilderness, where there is nothing to mark the passing of the week like the relative quiet of the Sabbath by the cessation of all secular industries, as in our crowded civilization back East, still I feel a change when Sunday comes around. How is it with you, Burton?"

"I seem to catch the inspiration too," replied Burton; "suppose it is because on each recurring Sunday our thoughts are attuned to the legendary holiness of the time by our orthodox New England education. We should probably feel the pressure of the same obligation to hold it sacred wherever we chanced to be."

"Maybe heredity has something to do with it," said Summerfield; "but every Sunday I have passed out West seems to have been endued with a holier atmosphere; even the birds appear to sing more sweetly; from the flowers are wafted on the breeze a sweeter fragrance, and all Nature is touched with an exquisite calmness that is spiritual in its influence."

"I think that our closer communion with Nature, such as we are having out here, and which never fell to my experience before, may be the cause of our better feelings predominating; the soul's best inspirations coming to the surface," said Burton.

"Perhaps that's it," answered Summerfield. "You know that the old Ascetics[1] declared that when they hid themselves from the crowd, subordinated the flesh to the spirit, and communed with Nature, they had visions, glo-

---

[1] *Ascetic*, a person retired from the world, engaged in religious devotion; who spends his time in meditation upon holy objects.

rious visions of the alleged beyond; and from those dreams have come down to us through the ages, all the great religions of the world."

"Well, it's too deep a problem for me," said Burton. "I only know that I experience the same feelings you do on the recurrence of each Sabbath out here, but I cannot fathom the depth of the arguments you have presented to account for them. I was, never considered much of a logician at Harvard, anyhow."

When they arrived at the dugout, both were rather surprised to find Pierre and Carlos were already up and attending to the wants of their ponies.

As Carlos saw his young friends approaching, he walked toward them, and to whom, after the conventional salutations, Summerfield handed his bundle of papers, for which Carlos thanked him, remarking, "I guess Pierre and I can put in a good morning now at reading."

Summerfield told him that he and Burton were going to take a bath, hurry back to camp for breakfast, then put in all the time they could in writing, as they had many friends with whom they corresponded, but who had been sadly neglected, and it would take every moment of the time to get through by the time Curtis should be ready to leave for the Fort.

Burton said to Carl: "I wish that when you are ready for our proposed stroll this afternoon, you and Pierre would kindly come down to camp, and all start from there."

"Most certainly," said Carlos. "We'll be there about two o'clock; that's early enough; it will give us good four hours, and that will be all we shall want, for we'll be tired out then. We're going out on the prairie from your side of the timber anyhow, so by coming down there we'll save time."

It was a perfect afternoon when at the appointed hour suggested by Carlos in the morning, the boys, armed with their rifles, assembled at the little camp in the timber on the river-bottom, and in a few moments started for the open prairie a mile beyond the edge of the woods.

There was just enough breeze blowing from the south to gently move the treetops, and the air was redolent with the perfume of a hundred varieties of wild flowers, conspicuous among which were the melon cactus with its crimson blossoms, and its companion the broad-leafed species, with its beautiful lemon-colored crown,—all now at the height of their unfolding; the blue and white anemones, the sensitive and thorny rose, and that most wonderful of all the flora of the remote Western Plains, the compass-plant,[1] one edge of whose leaves is invariably turned toward the North Pole. It grows on the highest points, never in the bottoms, and is a certain guide to the lost traveler, when the heavens are cloudy.

"How true that saying of Grey's is," remarked Summerfield, as he walked along and contemplated the beau-

[1] *Compass-plant*, a coarse herb growing plentifully throughout the West, and well known under the name of "rosin-weed." It exudes a resinous juice, which, when dry, is gathered from the stalks by children and used as chewing-gum.

tiful blossoms the party were constantly crushing under
their feet:

> "Full many a flower is born to blush unseen,
> And waste its sweetness on the desert air."

"That Elegy is Dad's favorite poem," said Carlos, as
Summerfield finished the quotation from it; "he often
repeats the whole of it when he and we boys are out on
a tramp or hunt together."

Soon they arrived at the base of a little divide, separating two ravines, on the crest of which Summerfield first
saw an animal, slowly pacing backward and forward, evidently watching the aproach of the party.

"What is that, Pierre,—a wolf?" he said, as he
pointed with his rifle to the object.

"Yes, indeed," responded Pierre, "and a great big
gray one too,—one of the wickedest of the whole wolf
species."

As they neared him, Burton wanted to try to shoot
him, but Pierre restrained him, saying: "I'll show you
more fun than that. He does n't see the dogs yet."

Cyrus and Jupe were behind the party, close to their
legs, which completely masked them.

"Pick up a stone and throw at him, Summerfield, and
let's see what he'll do?"

Summerfield picked up a good-sized stone and threw it
quite accurately toward the wolf,—in fact, it struck the
ground within five feet of the animal,—upon which he
turned sharply around, sat down on his haunches, facing

the boys, and raising his upper lip, showed two rows of great white fangs.

"So! So! That's your game, is it? You want to fight, do you? Well, you shall have all you want," said Pierre, as he clapped his hands together, and yelled at the top of his voice, "Sic 'em, Cyrus! Sic 'em, Jupe!"— and in an instant the dogs were after him.

The wolf started the moment he saw Cyrus and Jupe, but they were too close to him, and were upon his neck before he was aware of it, and there was a grand shock as they came together. In a moment the very air was filled with dust, hair, and the most awful growling and snarling imaginable. However, the battle was of short duration, and as the dust subsided, the wolf was discovered to be dead. But Cyrus and Jupe had not escaped unscathed; they had two or three long gashes in their bodies, made by the terrible fangs of their antagonist. Carlos and Pierre examined the wounds, and declared they were not at all dangerous; the dogs had come out of many a tussle worse than that.

"Are you going to take his hide off?" asked Burton of Carlos.

"No. It's not worth anything at this time of the year," replied Carlos; "besides, it's all torn in strips where Cyrus and Jupe got in their work. We'll let him stay where he is,—the Buzzards will soon eat him up."

"Yes," said Pierre, you can see 'em already, sailing up

in the air. It's odd how those birds can so quickly tell an animal is dead."

"They will be down on his carcass the moment we are out of sight," continued Pierre, "and in less than an hour there won't be anything left of him but his bones."

"Yes," said Burton, "I know that bird very well. It is properly a vulture, and in some of the cities down South where I have visited, they run in the streets and are the only scavengers there. They eat all kinds of filth and carrion. No one is allowed to shoot them, either. I suppose they breed out here?"

"I have often found their nests," said Carlos in answer to Burton's question. "They are on the ledges of the bluffs generally, but sometimes in hollow trees and stumps. There is no building about them; they lay their eggs, two of them, on the bare rocks. The eggs are a sort of grayish white, spotted with brown."

"The only note they have," said Pierre, "is a hiss; and they are the biggest cowards of all the birds I know,— they won't even fight when you catch one, only stamp their feet a little."

The boys continued their walk along the edge of the woods so as to get into the shade of the trees occasionally, for it had grown warm since they left camp, and the timber shut off the breeze in a measure.

Presently they reached the confines of an immense Prairie Dog village, covering hundreds of acres. The little animals were sitting at the edge of their holes, barking vociferously as the boys approached, but soon turned tail and disappeared, while the solemn diminutive owls stood their ground, winking and blinking in the sunlight, hardly moving from their places on the burrows.

"What cunning things those prairie dogs are!" said Summerfield. "We saw hundreds of their villages on our trip to the Wichita' Mountains, and tried to shoot one, but never succeeded. They always ran down their holes, even after I knew that I had hit 'em."

"They're awful hard things to kill," said Pierre. "The only way to get them is to lay in the grass where they can't see you, and when they are running from one burrow to another shoot them, so they will die before they can reach one. I've killed lots of them that way."

"They are good eating, too," said Carlos; "taste just like a squirrel, which I think they really are. We had several of them for pets; they became very tame, and would follow us around like a dog."

"What became of them?" asked Burton. "I did not see any of them when you showed us your pets."

"No, they all died from some cause we could not tell. We kept them for over two years; they made a burrow just in front of the dugout and would run in and out of it and right into the house, and cuddle at mother's feet until she gave them some milk, of which they were very fond."

"They can be caught," said Pierre, "in two ways. One is to drown them out of their holes, if you can get at the water handily. Another is to take a barrel with both heads out, put it over their hole, and keep filling sand in the barrel until the dogs come up. You see, as the loose sand fills the hole they have to push it behind them all the time, and the first thing they know they are on top and in the barrel, and you can then get them easily. But they bite like fury, though soon get used to you. That's the way Carl and I caught ours."

"It's funny that you most always see one of those little Owls on the top of a burrow," said Summerfield; "they must live happily together."

"Yes," said Pierre; "but the owl lives in other holes besides those of the prairie dog. I have seen them in badger-holes, fox-holes, and even in the dens of wolves."

"Sometimes they make burrows of their own," said Carlos; "and they don't seem, like other owls, to mind the sun. You see," he continued, as he pointed to some sitting at the edge of the dog-holes, "they look right at you without blinking. All the other varieties of owls come out at night only, while these little fellows are seen at all times of the day. They have the dirtiest nests you ever saw: full of rotten bits of animals they have killed for food for their little ones, and swarming with lice. They lay several eggs, and after the young ones are ready to leave the nest you sometimes see six or seven of them sitting with their mother at the holes."

"They say that the rattlesnake also lives with the owl

and prairie-dog in the same hole: is that so, Carl?" inquired Summerfield.

" No. The snakes do live in the dog-holes frequently, but it is after they have killed the little dogs," said Carlos.

When they had stopped at the prairie-dog village for more than an hour, they concluded to go back to the river, as it was very hot and they were all tired of walking. The Delahoyde boys were not much used to traveling on foot, as they usually rode their ponies even for the shortest distances; so they were more fatigued than Summerfield or Burton, who had made a practice of taking long strolls through the country at home, and out on the Arkansas had kept it up, in a measure, at least.

Pierre and Carlos rested at the camp of the Bostonians a little while, and then went to their own home, after exacting a promise from them that they would visit at the dugout in the evening.

After supper, just at dusk, Summerfield and Burton walked over to the Delahoydes, and found the family sitting on the natural lawn before their dwelling. They seated themselves, too, and Summerfield asked Mr. Delahoyde to tell something of the " Old Santa Fé Trail," as he had been watching the stage-coach go by and long lines of wagons on the broad road which ran near their camp.

" Well," said Mr. Delahoyde, " it has been a ' line of way ' for many hundred years. The Spanish explorers were the first Europeans to travel it, but it had been used

by the Indians of the Plains and the far North for cen-
turies before that, probably, because history records the
fact of those tribes going over it to New Mexico and
farther south, to exchange their furs for the shells, feathers, and other things only to be found in those tropical
regions.

" Cabeça de Vaca, one of the noblemen who came to
this country with Cortez, was, it is believed by historians,
the first white man who traveled it. He was followed by
Francisco Vasquez de Coronado, another of Cortez' ad-
herents, in their search of cities which were said to be
filled with gold and precious stones. Coronado traveled
it about six years after Cabeça, in the year 1535.[1]

" Several expeditions by the intrepid Spaniards were
sent over the old trail, all of which had for their object
the search of precious metals, concerning which ridiculous
stories had been poured into the ears of the too-credulous
explorers, who were ready to believe anything the natives
of Mexico told them.

" It did not become a much-used road until the trade
opened up with far-off Santa Fé, in New Mexico, about
the year 1812. To be sure, numbers of old trappers
traveled it for many decades previously, hunting for the
animals whose skins were valuable; but the date I have
mentioned was the time that a regular traffic commenced,
since which it has grown into importance; aggregating for
years many hundreds of thousands of dollars.

[1] For a history of this great " highway," see my " Old Santa Fe Trail."

"The long lines of wagons, of which you spoke," addressing himself to Summerfield, "are called caravans, but at first only pack-mules were employed. Occasionally you may see them yet, as the Mexicans are loth to abandon the customs which they have been used to for so long.

"In 1849, after the conclusion of the war with Mexico, and we obtained possession of that country by treaty, stage-coaches were employed to carry the mail and passengers from the Missouri river to Santa Fé. They continue to run daily; you have seen some of them. But we shall soon have a railroad, as the survey has already been commenced, and the days of caravans and coaches will have passed away forever.

"The old trail is one of the most historic places on the continent, and I advise you to read as much about it as you can. It is full of thrilling stories of battles with the savages, and of hairbreadth escapes. It would take a month to relate even a portion of them."

Thanking Mr. Delahoyde for his interesting facts about the old trail, Summerfield asked him to relate some of his early experiences on the frontier.

"Dad, tell them that story about your tussle with a California Lion," said Pierre.

"Well, that was a good many years ago," said Mr. Delahoyde,—long before you boys were born; but if these young men think it will amuse them I shall be happy to tell it."

"Do please," said Summerfield and Burton simultaneously; the latter adding, "There is nothing so entertaining to me as stories of adventures of the pioneers in this wild country."

"It was after I had returned from school in St. Louis," began Mr. Delahoyde, "and I was about twenty-three years old. I had been on many a trapping expedition with my father (whom you have been told was one of the earliest employés of the American Fur Companies) before I went to get my education, and was as well posted in regard to the various fur-bearing animals, the manner of trapping and curing their skins, as any young man of my age.

"I thought I would continue in the same business as my father, because I liked the wild life, and besides, it paid well in those days.

"One winter I was trapping on Frenchman's creek, with a partner named Foote. He was a Scotchman, but much older than I, and had been on the frontier then for more than twenty years. He was a fine shot, and as good a trapper.

"We took turns at cooking and attending the traps, which were scattered all along the stream for more than six miles, and it was no easy job for a man to look after so many traps.

"I had finished my work, and was strolling along carelessly through a bunch of thick underbrush, when the first thing I knew I heard a 'spit' and a low growl, and looking to where the sound had come from I saw not five feet from me a California lion with three little cats about six weeks old.

"Now you must know that the animal is not a lion at all, but really the American Cougar. He does not resemble in any manner his African namesake, excepting in color. Once they were common all over the East, from Canada westward. I have often heard my father say that he had killed them when a young man as far toward the seacoast as in the woods of Quebec. There they were called 'painters,' a corruption of panther. Their principal prey is deer, and they seldom leave the timber, but prefer the woods, where, crouching on the lower limb of a tree, they watch until a deer comes along, then pounce upon him.

"The animal was just getting ready to spring upon me when I discovered her, and before I could get my rifle fairly to my shoulder she made a leap for me; so, without taking any aim, I pulled the trigger. The ball hit her on the side of the head, but glanced off, doing her no injury excepting to make her madder than ever.

"I could see her eyes gleam like a flash of lightning on a dark night, and she showed her great white teeth like a mountain-wolf when he is out of range of your rifle.

"She immediately recovered from the slight stunning my first bullet had given her, and crouched again for another spring, and I knew that unless I was quicker on the trigger next time she jumped for me, it would be all day with me.

—8

" You may be sure I lost no time in drawing up my rifle and letting fly at her again. But instead of seeing the ferocious beast roll over dead, she gave another spiteful growl and a vicious ' spit '; so I knew that I had not killed her.

" I had aimed directly at her left eye, knowing that the ball would easily enter her brain, and when I saw her only shake her head, I felt certain that in another moment she would come for me again, for she was frothing at the mouth, and her long claws were unsheathed,[1] ready for business; so something had to be done and that mighty quickly, for I was pretty well used up by the excitement.

" As she approached me, rather more cautiously this time, I watched my chance (as I had no time to reload my rifle) to try and blind her, by aiming a blow at her with my knife that I had drawn; but unfortunately I only cut her slightly on the nose, upon which the enraged beast gave a howl of pain, but paid no further attention to the wound than to give another shake of her head, a spit, and third jump for me.

" She pressed me closely, and I tried to dodge her, but my foot caught in a grapevine and I fell sprawling on the ground. In an instant she was on top of me, trying to bite, and to claw me with her hind feet. Luckily, I had on a new suit of buckskin, and that was all that saved me.

" With her front paws she had caught me by the left

[1] When in repose and not excited, all animals which possess claws fold them back in their sheaths; but when angry, stretch them out as offensive and defensive weapons.

shoulder as I fell, and the hinder portion of her body was toward my face. I caught hold of her long tail, while she caught me by the thigh, which seemed to afford her considerable amusement, as she tried to tear the flesh; but my good buckskins resisted all her efforts.

"I had hold of her tail with my left hand, and immediately began to tickle her ribs with my hunting-knife; but still the brute would not let go her hold.

"I knew it would only take her a few moments to work her teeth into my flesh, unless she was speedily shaken off me; so I tried to tumble her down the bank into the river, —for our scuffle had brought both of us to the edge of the bluff. So I stuck my knife into her side, and summoned all my strength to throw her over. She resisted her best, as if she divined my intentions, and was terribly desperate in her attempts to tear my flesh.

"At last I succeeded in getting her so far down that she lost her balance, and rolled over and over until she landed on the edge of the water; but in her tumble she dragged me with her. Fortunately I fell uppermost, and as we reached the bottom her neck presented a fair mark for my knife; so I lost no time in delivering a desperate blow. The point of the long blade entered her gullet, and by forcing the knife up to the handle it reached her heart. She struggled for an instant, and then died, much to my satisfaction.

"I got to camp a little later than usual that night, and

my partner was just on the point of going to hunt me, when I entered our cabin.

"I was only a little stiff and sore for a few days, and I thanked my stars that I got off so luckily."

"Well, that *was* an adventure," said Summerfield. I would n't have liked to be in your boots."

"What are we going to do tomorrow?" asked Burton, as the party broke up preparatory to retiring.

"Don 't exactly know," replied Pierre; "but you fellows come up early in the morning, and we 'll fix upon something."

By sunrise Monday morning, Summerfield and Burton, mounted on their ponies, and carrying their rifles, rode up to the dugout, just as Carlos and Pierre were coming out.

"Romeo says that we are entirely out of meat," said Sumerfield. We 've got lots of everything else, but have to go and hunt something."

"Well, get down," said Pierre; and the young men dismounted, and were about tying their animals to a tree, when Pierre, calling Cyrus, said, "Here, let the dog hold them. Give him your bridle-reins, and he 'll take as good care of them as he does of mine. You 've often seen him hold mine. I never tie my pony when Cyrus is with me."

The dog promptly took the two reins in his mouth, and upon invitation Summerfield and his companion went into the dugout.

Mr. Delahoyde and his wife, who were just finishing

their breakfast, invited the visitors to partake; but they declined with profuse thanks, stating that they had had theirs very early that morning, and had come up to get Carl and Pierre to go out hunting with them, as their larder was as bare as Old Mother Hubbard's,—not even a bone left in the shape of meat.

"Well, then," said Mr. Delahoyde, "you and the boys had best go after Antelope. I saw a large herd about ten miles down the river yesterday afternoon while you and my sons were out for a walk. I had occasion to go that distance, to look up better pasturage for the cattle, and I came across a herd that must have contained several hundred. I did not see any buffalo. I daresay you will find the same animals there yet; or maybe they have worked up this way some."

"Well, then, we 'll go antelope-hunting," said Pierre; "and let 's get off as quickly as possible."

"Won't we need a pack-animal to bring in our meat?" asked Burton.

"No," replied Mr. Delahoyde. "You can pack all that you need on the backs of your ponies; the meat won't keep in this hot weather."

The Delahoyde boys soon got their ponies and were ready to start, and after asking their father to keep the dogs back, all started down the river by the trail on the edge of the timber.

"We did n't bring any lunch," said Pierre to Summerfield and Burton, "because we are certain of shooting something, and we can cook it by a fire in the timber, as we shan't at any time be far from the river."

"That's right," said Summerfield; "I like to depend entirely on what we may happen to kill for grub. That's the real hunter style; and if we fail, why, we have to go without eating,—that's all."

"No danger of that," said Carl; "I never saw the time yet in this country when we did not find game of some kind. You can always kill a rabbit, if nothing else."

They hugged the timber, watching for signs of big game as they walked their animals on the trail under the trees, and were not rewarded by the sight of anything until they had proceeded about ten miles, when in the distance, far out on the prairie, Carl discovered a line of moving objects, which he declared were antelope.

"I guess they are," said Pierre, as he stopped his pony and gazed long and earnestly at the spot where there was evidently something moving.

"They are more than two miles off," said Carl, "and we had best make for that big patch of bunch-grass on this side of them. They won't be startled until we get within half a mile of them. There has been very little hunting done in this region, and the animals are not wild at all."

The party proceeded slowly toward the grassy area to which Carl had referred, where there were also two or three small trees. Upon arriving there they tied their ponies to them, and then crept carefully to a point through the excellent cover about seven or eight hundred yards from where the herd of graceful creatures were grazing.

"Now," said Pierre, "we 've got to attract them toward us by something. You know that they are very curious, and a bit of bright color will set them crazy to find out what it means. There, Burton, that red silk handkerchief you 've got around your throat, to keep the sun from blistering your neck, is just the thing."

"Take it, then, by all means," said Burton, as he untied it and handed it to Pierre.

Pierre then fastened it to the wiping-stick of his rifle, leaving the larger portion of it to flutter in the wind, and then stuck it in the ground twenty yards from where they were all concealed in the tall grass.

"Now watch 'em," said Pierre, as the bright flag began to wave in the breeze that was blowing gently from the south.

Presently some of the foremost of the herd, on looking up, noticed the strange object, and after gazing upon it for a few moments, slowly, with heads erect, moved towards the handkerchief. The rest of the animals soon followed suit, and the boys saw with great satisfaction that the antelope were unusually excited, and would get within range of their rifles shortly.

"There are four coming up together," said Pierre; "wait until they get close enough, then we 'll all fire together at them. We can only get one shot apiece, and if we all kill, there will be meat enough to go round, as long as it will keep.

"Here they are!" whispered Pierre; "now take them in regular order, just as we lie; I'll plug the one on the right, Burton the next, Summerfield the third, and Carl the fourth."

"Fire!" said Pïerre, as the animals came within thirty yards of the boys,—and all four of the creatures fell, quivering in their death-throes; while the rest of the herd, scared at the report of the rifles, rushed away as fast as their swift legs could carry them.

"Let's bleed them now," said Pierre, as they rose from their positions. "Each one take his own animal."

The boys were quickly at the heads of their game, with knives out, and just as Burton laid his hand on his antelope, up it jumped and was off before you could say "Jack Robinson."

Burton was perfectly bewildered, as he saw the other boys' animals still lying where they had been killed, but the one that he thought he had surely shot, flying down the prairie to join its mates far away in the distance.

"You only creased [1] yours," said Carlos as he looked at Burton's puzzled countenance.

"I thought I had killed it," said he. "It was all sprawled out and trembling just the same as yours, when I went toward it."

[1] *Creased:* Literally, to merely make a mark; to just graze. See chapter 10, where it is fully described.

"Well, never mind," said Pierre; "we've got all the meat we can possibly take care of. These antelope are awfully fat. Let's hurry up and get them on the ponies, and into the shade of the timber where we can take out their entrails; then they will keep better, and won't be such a heavy load, either."

The animals were packed on the backs of three of the ponies just behind the saddles, and in a few minutes were lying on the ground again, in the shade of the trees on the margin of the river, where Carlos and Pierre eviscerated them, then hung them to limbs, to remain while the ponies were picketed out to graze and the boys were getting their dinner.

"Boys, gather some light-wood, and we'll soon have something to eat," said Pierre as he proceeded to cut large slices off the choicest part of one of the antelopes with his hunting-knife.

The wood was soon gathered, for all to be done was to pick it up from the ground where there were cords of it lying,—dry limbs blown from the trees by the last winter's storms.

Carl then took out his flint and steel from a pocket, and selecting a few pieces of perfectly dry rotten wood, struck the flint, and in a few moments, after stimulating the sparks with his breath, he had a fire well started.

Each one fixed for himself a smooth wand of the willow which grew so thickly on the bank of the river, and presently was busily engaged in broiling the slices of antelope which Pierre had cut from one of the carcasses hanging to the limb of a tree. They had not forgotten to bring a little salt with them, and their frugal meal was most delightfully satisfactory to their hungry stomachs.

After they had eaten all they possibly could, Summerfield and Burton brought out their pipes, and while waiting for the ponies to fill themselves, sat on a log and talked of various things they saw and heard in the deep woods all around them.

Near them, in the middle of the river, was a marshy bit of island, covered with rushes and willows, and from which there came a curious sound of "Pump-a-lunk! Pump-a-lunk!"—a loud booming note, which caused Summerfield to exclaim, "What in the world is that, Pierre?"

"Oh, that's what we call out here 'a Thunder Pump.' It's the bittern, or shitepoke as some people term them, a wild, solitary bird, which like the owl, does not come out of his marshy haunts until dark, or at least twilight. They skulk and hide all day, and you can't get one up unless you get right on top of him. Then he comes out in a very slow, awkward way, dangling his long legs behind him, and uttering a deep note that sounds like 'Kawk! Kawk!'"

"They're the easiest bird killed I ever saw," said Carlos; "if a small shot strikes one he will fall. But he isn't worth anything even if you do kill him."

"What do they live on?" asked Burton.

" Minnows, mice, frogs, crawfish, insects, or anything that comes handy, like tadpoles and other small things," said Carlos. " Their nests," he continued, " are built upon hummocks in the low marshy water-grasses, and are made of sticks, weeds and rushes woven together. They lay some three or four eggs, of a brownish drab."

It was about three o'clock when the boys were ready to start back to the ranch, where they arrived in two hours. After dividing the meat, Summerfield and Burton went to their camp, stating that they would not be up again until early in the morning, as they wanted to get to bed soon, so they would not oversleep themselves and be late in going on the proposed turkey-hunt.

CHAPTER VII.

TUESDAY morning arrived at last, to which the boys, particularly Summerfield and Burton, had so anxiously looked forward. The day broke with its usual cloudless sky, and a delicious breeze from the south, the prevailing direction of the wind in the region at this time of year. It is caused by the great "Southwest trade winds," which bear down toward the Andes and are deflected by that lofty range of mountains directly north again, striking the interior of the continent at about latitude thirty-seven, where they join the constant current which crosses the whole United States from the southwest. Hence the country watered by the Arkansas, or at least that portion where the Delahoydes lived, was always fanned in summer by a breeze varying in intensity and velocity, according to the fluctuations of the atmospheric pressure.[1]

---

[1] *Atmospheric pressure*, weight of the volume of air on the earth's surface

The boys congregated at the dugout by sunrise, where all partook of breakfast prepared for them by Mrs. Delahoyde thus early, so they could get a good start. As soon as the meal was hurriedly disposed of they were ready to begin their journey to the turkey-roost, thirty miles north of the Canadian river, near the head of Eagle Chief creek.[1]

The Mexican cook who was to accompany them, and who was also an experienced packer, as nearly all of his race are, had already brought up to the dugout the Bostonians' horses and his own, on which latter he had skillfully packed the bedding and camp equipage of his employers, excepting the Sibley tent, which was left standing just where it had originally been pitched. He was provided with one of the Delahoyde animals to ride, the young hunters all, of course, using their individual ponies.

Carlos's and Pierre's outfit comprised the same articles they had taken with them on their last hunting expedition, when they shot the cub, and it was packed on the same pony which had carried it before.

When everything was ready, about half-past six o'clock, they "rolled out," in prairie parlance, the Mexican in the rear in charge of the pack-animals, which readily followed those the boys were riding.

Cyrus and Jupe, the never-failing companions on all excursions in which Carlos and Pierre participated, trotted

---

[1] *Eagle Chief creek.* So called after a celebrated Cheyenne Indian, who was named "The Eagle."

alongside their masters' horses, occasionally looking up into the countenances of the former with a sort of expression which seemed to indicate that they knew the boys were under their charge, at night at least, and that they would not be recreant to their trust.

They rode out of the timber slowly, and reaching the open prairie walked their animals at even a more mincing pace, as they did not want to "wind" them, for they knew that on the treeless plains it was all the time growing rapidly warmer, and they did not expect to arrive at their camp under six hours, which would be about noon.

On their route, both on the ground and sailing in the air, countless numbers of birds were seen. Those which particularly attracted the attention of Summerfield and Burton, Pierre told them were the Mountain Plover.

"Those birds," said he, "are fine eating, and arrive here in great numbers about the first of April, begin to lay early in May, and leave us again late in the fall. They love the high, desert-like prairies, and seldom go near low or marshy ground. They live on grasshoppers mostly."

"Their nest," said Carlos, taking up the subject, and to whom his brother conceded a better knowledge of eggs and nests than himself, "is only a little hollow in the ground, which is but sparingly lined with blades of grass, and they lay from three to four eggs, of a deep brownish drab, speckled with blackish-brown spots. I have found lots of them."

"There's another flock of birds over yonder," said

Burton, pointing to them, " that look very much like them. I watched them light, and the moment they touched the ground they raised their wings away up, and then slowly folded them."

" Yes, they 're Sandpipers,—splendid eating, too," said Pierre. " You can always tell them by the way you saw them fold their wings, and the sweet, long whistle they give utterance to as they fly. We must have some of those birds for our dinner. Let 's stop, and as there are so many of us, we 'll just pot-hunt them. Let me have your shotgun, Burton, and I 'll creep up; they are not shy, and I can get a dozen at one pop if I wait until they get into line."

So the boys stopped, while Pierre dismounted and threw the bridle reins to Cyrus, which the noble dog immediately took into his mouth; and while the others remained in their saddles, Pierre crawled cautiously along the ground until he came within range, where, waiting for a few moments, he fired and killed eight.

" That 's not quite enough," said he as he picked up the birds and handed them to the Mexican, who fastened them to the cantle of his saddle; but seeing that the flock had again lighted not very far off, he followed it, and presently got another shot, bringing down half a dozen more.

" Now we 've got enough for dinner," said Pierre, as he gave the birds to the Mexican to fasten with the others to the back of his saddle, and handing Burton his shotgun, mounted his pony again, and they all rode on.

They had made about fifteen miles from the Arkansas, when in the distance an immense herd of buffalo was discovered grazing on the broad bottom of a little stream to the right of the trail they were traveling.

"How I should like to get a shot at one!" said Summerfield. "Let's see if we can't hit one," continued he, looking appealingly at Pierre.

"We can't stop now," said Pierre; "we've a long way to go yet; besides, none of our animals here have been trained, and unless your pony understands his business, you can't come within rifle-range of the herd. We have four or five ponies at the ranch that are as good buffalo-hunters as there are in the Territory. Besides, you and Burton will have plenty of chances to go for them in a few days, after we return from this trip. Curtis can't possibly get back to the Arkansas for you from the Wichita Mountains in less than fifteen or twenty days. It will take him five to reach Fort Dodge, ten to get to the Cheyenne village, and five or six more to arrive at our place; so you will have plenty of time to shoot all you want."

"That's so," answered Summerfield. "I did n't think, when I first spoke, that we have to wait for Curtis to take us to Fort Harker. I did n't get a shot at one when we were with him on our trip to the Cheyenne village, though we saw thousands, but could not get near enough; perhaps it was because our ponies are not trained, as you say. But I do so want to kill one and take his head back to Boston with me."

" I 'll guarantee that, and will prepare it for you so that it will be sure to keep," said Pierre encouragingly.

" Thank you," replied Summerfield, who, now seeming satisfied, rode along in much better spirits.

In two hours more, without any adventure to relieve the monotony of their journey, there loomed up in the southeast a belt of timber, to which Carlos pointed, and told Summerfield and Burton that it was the head of Eagle Chief creek.

" You see that heaviest bunch of trees at the extreme end?" said Pierre. " Well, that 's the roost. Our trail runs close to the edge of it, but our camp will be made a mile below, where there is a fine spring. The banks of the stream are very steep, and it is difficult to get down to the water, yet the grass is so good for the horses out on the open prairie, and the timber is only about a hundred yards wide on the margin of the creek, that we always choose that spot. Besides, there is always plenty of driftwood for our fires without going to the trouble of cutting any."

" We ought to make it in another hour," said Carlos.

" I shall be mighty glad," said Burton, " for I am tired, and as hungry as a bear."

" Well," said Summerfield, " there won't be anything for us to do but rest, after we get our camp made and the ponies cared for,— will there, Pierre?"

—9

"No, indeed," said Pierre, "you can go to sleep, or anything else you want to."

"Can a fellow get a bath?" inquired Summerfield.

"Yes, the water is delightfully clear and cool; but, as I told you, it is difficult to get at,—though we can overcome that in some way," replied Pierre.

The party soon arrived at the first bunch of timber; both Summerfield and Burton were astonished at the size of the trees, and they saw with a feeling of delight the evident signs of a roost where large numbers of birds must have been for a great while.

At last they reached the beautiful spring which Pierre had told about, and the young strangers to the country were charmed with their resting-place.

The spring rushed out of a wall of rock, just like that at the ranch of the Delahoydes, excepting that the water in falling had formed two basins or pools, as it leaped from one ledge to another; the lower a few feet beneath the upper. Out of the lower one the animals drank, and the upper one was used for culinary purposes.

The ground on which the camp was situated, between two large trees, comprised about forty square feet, covered with grass as fine as any lawn. On it the robes and blankets for the beds were thrown, while a little distance away, on a slightly rising plateau, the Mexican distributed his pans and pots, for his kitchen.

The boys took the ponies out in the open to graze, after they had watered them; and as they started out to picket them, Summerfield said, "Romeo, you get us up something as quickly as you can."

"All right," answered the Mexican; "I get him quick!"

When Pierre, Summerfield, Carlos and Burton returned to the camp, Romeo had already gathered a lot of dry wood for his fire, which he kindled, and was now busy skinning the birds, (in camp, birds are not generally picked; it takes too long,) and his coffeepot was already beginning to sing.

While he was preparing other things, the boys unrolled their blankets and robes to air, and then sat down on the grass for a few minutes.

"I wonder whether we will have time to take a bath before dinner?" said Summerfield; "I'm dreadfully dusty."

"How long will it take to get dinner, Romeo?" asked Burton.

"Half-hour; can't get quicker; birds must be cooked well," answered Romeo.

"Then we can all take a swim," said Pierre; and they gathered a towel each, and started for the creek.

The banks of the little stream at the camp were twenty feet high, and very precipitous, as Pierre had said they were. So they walked down for a few hundred yards, where Carlos told them he knew of a trail which led by easy degrees to the water.

They found it in a moment, and hurrying to the stream, all plunged in, taking a hurried wash,—for they were awfully hungry, and did not want to be a minute late when Romeo should announce the meal ready.

"All ready," said Romeo, as he saw the boys approaching; "come set down; I give you fine grub now."

The invitation was obeyed with alacrity, and the boys gathered themselves around a big dish of beautifully broiled sandpipers, together with biscuit and coffee; both Burton and Summerfield declaring they had never tasted anything so delicious, even at Parker's, in Boston.

In a short time there was nothing left but a bunch of scraps, which were tossed to the dogs, but every one had had plenty. All now retired to their robes and blankets, to take a siesta before they attempted anything in the way of amusing themselves.

Pierre, noticing that the scraps left from the dinner were not half a meal for Cyrus and Jupe, got up and went for a piece of the cub, which he had purposely brought for them from the ranch, and then cutting it in two pieces he gave them to the dogs, who carried their portions a little way off and soon devoured every morsel.

It was nearly six o'clock before the young hunters awoke from their afternoon's sleep. Then Pierre said that the ponies must be changed and watered; so all went out to the prairie where they were picketed, and after leading them to the pool, re-picketed them, and returned to camp.

"We can't do much this evening but take it easy and loaf around camp," said Pierre. "The ponies are tired, we are tired, and even the dogs seem to be affected the same way. Besides, we will have to keep pretty close, as the turkey-roost is too near for us to be making much of a stir, or it might frighten them away, and then we 'd have all our journey for nothing."

" Well," said Summerfield, " after supper, and I have had my smoke, I 'm going to pile into bed and get as much sleep as I can, so as to be ready for tomorrow night."

" That 's a good idea," said Carlos; " I guess we had best all follow your example."

Supper was eaten and out of the way just about dark, and sticking to their resolution of the afternoon, they rolled up in their beds, and would soon have been sound asleep had the lynxes not kept up such a racket for awhile.

" They smell the cooking," said Pierre; " we 'll have some fun with them to-morrow night; would now, but it might interfere with our sport then."

The noisy beasts became quiet after awhile, and then the young hunters fell into a gentle slumber, the faithful Cyrus and Jupe keeping watch over the camp.

All were up betimes next morning, for this was to be one of the eventful days of the trip, to Summerfield and Burton. Breakfast out of the way, the animals watered and changed, the boys started down through the timber for the roost, intending to take their bearing for the work of the night.

They arrived there in less than half an hour, and found everything to their satisfaction, even to the very places where they intended to secrete themselves when darkness favored their coming down to have their sport. Having determined upon all their plans, they left the timber and wandered out on the prairie, to return to the camp by the open country, which they reached by noon, pretty well tired out, but without having met with any adventure worth recording.

They had another excellent meal provided by the versatile Romeo, and after they had finished, there was nothing to do but wait until night, when it would be time to go to the roost—for business, that time.

Carlos and Pierre cleaned their rifles, while Summerfield and Burton wrote in their journals the adventures of their trip thus far, as they had promised before they left home to keep an accurate record of all their doings.

They wished for supper-time to come, for time dragged heavily on their hands with nothing to do. At last it was announced, and they hurried to their places near the fire to eat.

When they had all gathered around their simple little supper-table which the cook had improvised for them out of a huge piece of black-walnut bark, enjoying the birds, and drinking their black coffee, Burton, his mind ever occupied with the thoughts of the coming sport, asked Pierre:

"Why is it that you select a moonlight night for turkey-hunting?"

"Because," replied Pierre, "the moonlight appears to

blind the birds' eyes, and they become bewildered, remain where they are, right in the same place, not seeming to know where to go or what to do."

"A fire has the same effect," interrupted Carlos. "Sometimes the hunters build great fires under their roosts, and they act in the same manner."

After their supper was over they became restless in their little camp, impatient for the seemingly tardy sun to set. At last, when more than two hours of the suspense had continued, the fading rays began to gild the summit of the divide which separates Eagle Chief creek from the Salt Fork of the Arkansas, many miles northeast. Then, still having to wait until the twilight curve met the western horizon, and the full moon appeared on the edge of the eastern sky, looking like a disk of molten gold, all excepting the Mexican cook and the dogs left the bivouac and sauntered slowly through the timber to the huge trees where the coveted birds were in the habit of congregating at night for many seasons. As the party walked on, not a word was uttered, against which both Carlos and Pierre had warned Summerfield and Burton.

Arriving at the edge of the roost, at the suggestion of the Delahoyde boys all took their positions on the ground, separating themselves from one another at distances of about twenty feet, each to watch from his individual vantage-point until the moment should come for the birds to seek their resting-place.

They did not have to wait very long. Before it had

fairly grown dark in the western sky, two or three flocks, numbering at least two hundred of the bronzed beauties, came walking stealthily down the sheltered ravines leading out into the broad bottom where the great trees stood in aggregated clumps, in the shadows of which the boys had secreted themselves.

Summerfield and Burton could hardly contain themselves, so excited were they at such (to them) an extraordinary scene; but a suppressed whisper from Pierre brought them back to their normal common-sense.

Presently the leader of one of the flocks arrived at the spot where his charge had been accustomed to roost. Then he suddenly stopped, glanced all around him cautiously for a few seconds, and, failing to observe anything suspicious, (so dark was it where his enemies lay prone upon the ground,) seemed satisfied everything was all right; and then he gave the signal—a sharp, quick, shrill note, at the instant of which, every bird with one accord, and a great fluttering of wings, rose and alighted in the loftiest branches of the tallest trees.

In a few moments, many more flocks arrived and went through exactly the same evolutions as the first two, when, having settled themselves for an undisturbed slumber, Summerfield and Burton whispered, " Can't we commence now ? "

" Not quite yet," replied Pierre; " wait a little longer until the moon gets higher, you may spoil all by a too hasty firing, and besides, are likely to miss them."

Soon the moon, having apparently intensified its brilliancy as it approached nearer the zenith, flooded with a golden sheen, as its light sifted through the interstices of the leaves, every limb, upon which could now be plainly seen each individual bird as it crouched in position on its roost.

“ Fire away ! ” said Pierre at last, and the boys began to shoot on their own account; and although Summerfield and Burton missed frequently in their excitement, the turkeys dropped from the trees like leaves in October. The birds not killed at the first fusillade did not seem to possess sense enough to get out of harm's way, but flew from tree to tree at every shot, persistently remaining in the immediate vicinity of the roost with all their characteristic stupidity on such occasions.

After indulging in the shooting for an hour, Pierre, determining to put an end to the wanton slaughter, said, “ Fellows, let 's stop now. We 've got more birds than we can possibly use, or take back to camp.” He had only allowed his conscientious scruples in this instance to be suppressed, because he wanted his guests to have their full measure of sport.

They then began to gather the dead birds, and found they had killed thirty; but not being able to pack that number, selected eight of the largest and fattest, and started,—compelled to leave the remainder just where they fell.

“ Shooting wild turkeys under such a brilliant full

moon, which nowhere that I have ever been shines so intensely," said Summerfield, "is the greatest sport I have ever had."

When the young hunters reached their camp it was long after midnight, and first suspending their turkeys to the limbs of the trees, all immediately retired, worn out with fatigue and excitement.

They had scarcely thrown themselves down on their beds, when there came on the still air, at apparently a great distance off, a snapping, snarling and barking as if it emanated from the throats of a hundred wolves.

Summerfield and Burton both sat up and asked what the terrible racket meant. They noticed that Cyrus and Jupe were uneasy too, having lifted their heads and were intently listening.

Pierre, without changing his position, answered the question: "They're Coyotes after the turkeys we shot and left down at the roost."

"Let's go and look at them," said Burton; "it must be a sight worth going for!"

"No use," said Carlos; "by the time we got there you would n't find a coyote on the ground. Probably there were more than a hundred of them, and you can guess how long twenty-two turkeys would last 'em; about five minutes, and away they'd go."

"There, hark!" said Pierre; "they're off already," as the sharp yelps grew suddenly fainter, and in a few seconds had ceased entirely. Upon the noise of the coyotes having ended, Cyrus and Jupe again curled themselves on the buffalo-robes at their masters' feet.

"It's a lucky thing for turkeys that a coyote or wolf can't climb a tree," said Carlos, "or there would n't be many of the birds left in this country."

"Of course they can't climb a tree," said Summerfield, keeping up the conversation, as the howling of the coyotes had awakened every one and all were inclined to talk for a few moments, "but I suppose they can get around pretty lively on steep places?"

"Not at all!" answered Pierre. "You know how clumsily a dog will scramble up a ledge of rocks? It must be quite an easy slope for him to make it anyhow. Well, a wolf is just like a dog in that particular: he can't make any headway on a steep elevation like a rocky bluff, unless it 's mighty easy footing."

The boys soon dropped off to sleep, and in a few moments not a sound disturbed the quiet of the little camp.

·By daylight, Carlos and Pierre, as usual, were out of their robes, but they did not disturb Summerfield or Burton, who were in a most profound slumber. They routed out the Mexican cook, however, who had slept all night, and inquired of him as they pointed to the turkeys hanging to the trees, whether he knew how to roast one in the old trapper style.

He answered affirmatively, saying that he had not only cooked birds that way, but buffalo-heads, deer, antelope, and mountain sheep. He then commenced operations, just as Carlos and Pierre had at the last camp; and, satisfied that he knew his business, the boys went off to attend to the seven ponies that were picketed out on the prairie.

When they had watered them and put them on fresh grass, they returned to camp, and found Summerfield and Burton just getting up, they having snuffed the breakfast the cook was preparing. They were profuse in their apologies for being so late, as they looked at the sun and noticed its rays were streaming over the tops of the trees.

"That's all right," said Pierre; "we thought we would let you sleep a while this morning, as we knew that the excitement of last night had worked your nerves up to a high pitch. How do you feel, anyhow?"

"I'm in a delightful state of both health and mind," said Summerfield; "slept like a top after those infernal coyotes had shut up. I guess I'll go and take a plunge in the creek, before breakfast. Come along, Burton!"

"In a minute," replied Burton, who, giving another yawn, and stretching himself again, remarked: "All night I had some of the most terribly exciting dreams that I ever had in my life. I couldn't get away from great flocks of turkeys which attacked me with their sharp bills like pick-axes; each bird being as large as an elephant, and all I had to defend myself with was a little stick."

The other boys laughed, as Burton rose, and throwing a blanket around him, accompanied Summerfield to the creek, remarking as he walked out of camp: "I guess a good plunge will cool my brain and quiet my nervous system."

"You come back soon," said the Mexican cook in his broken English; "breakfast be ready quick."

"All right, Romeo," said Summerfield; (his name was Romero, but they called him Romeo, because it was easier to remember;) "we'll be back in ten minutes."

In about ten minutes, as Summerfield had promised, he and Burton returned, shortly afterward all were eating their breakfast, which Romeo had told them should be an exceptionally good one. There were biscuits he had baked in his skillet; broiled slices of the breast of one of the turkeys; black coffee; canned fruit, brought along from the stores of the young Bostonians; besides plovers' eggs which Carlos had gathered from the nests he had found while Summerfield and Burton were taking their bath.

Gathered in a little circle near the cook's fire, all feeling in excellent spirits over their luck of the last night, and the really delicious things which Romeo had managed to serve, the conversation turned toward the subject of dreams, inspired by Burton's ridiculous experience.

"I rarely dream," said Summerfield, "but I am satisfied that there come to us in our slumbers, only visions of things and events that have happened. No matter how absurd, impossible and exaggerated the scenes that pass before us, they are based upon actual occurrences. Consider how ridiculous the turkeys appeared to Burton in his dream of last night, yet we can easily find the foundation for it in our hunt."

"I am certain that animals dream too, or at least some of them," said Carlos. "I have often watched Cyrus and Jupe when asleep in camp. They would suddenly tremble all over, their legs moving violently, and then they would utter a suppressed yell, just as they do when chasing a jack-rabbit or a lynx. When I woke them up, they would look as sheepish as possible, stare all around for a moment, then quiet down again, as if they realized they had been dreaming."

"I have noticed that in my own dogs at home, too," said Burton. "I don't see why animals should n't dream, as well as people."

"I am sure that Ephraim, our bear, dreams," said Pierre. "He will snort, tumble about, close his paws, and act just as he does when Carl or I wrestle with him, and I suppose he is dreaming of the fun he has with us that way."

"Well, Romeo," said Summerfield, as the boys rose from their places, "that was a splendid breakfast, as you promised; and here 's some tobacco, to make for yourself some cigarettes."

"You wait for turkey to-night," said the Mexican, grinning all over, "then you say *bueno!*" (good.)

"You and Burton ought to see how the old mountaineers and trappers cooked their large game," said Pierre to Summerfield, as the latter lighted his pipe with a coal from the cook's fire. "Romeo is going to fix one of our turkeys that way for supper. We can't have it for dinner, because it takes all day to cook it properly. Generally the meat, or whatever it may happen to be, is prepared in the evening, and allowed to roast all night, so as to be ready for breakfast. Carl and I had a turkey we served that way when we were camping out last week. It won't take long for Romeo to get his ready for the fire. By the time that Carl and I have shifted the ponies and are back here, you and Burton can learn the whole mystery; then we'll go out on a hunt."

"Very well," said Summerfield, "but I think that you should let Burton and I do our share of the camp-work this morning."

"Never mind that now," replied Pierre; "there will be plenty for you to do after a while."

Then he and his brother started for the animals.

Summerfield and Burton watched Romeo dig his pit, kindle a fire in it, and plaster the turkey all over with mud, ready for cooking in a style that they had never seen or heard of in Boston.

As soon as Carlos and Pierre returned to the camp, they all took their rifles, whistled to the dogs, and started on foot for a ramble along the creek-bank to pass the morning with some sort of amusement.

They had not proceeded very far when Burton, seeing a curious-looking bird at the edge of the water, said, "I know what that is: it's a kingfisher, is n't it, Carl? We have them down East; I 've often seen them along the rivers and brooks in Massachusetts."

"Yes, you 're right," replied Carlos. "That 's the Belted Kingfisher; he is here all summer, and sometimes stays with us during the winter, if the weather is mild, as our winters generally are. You see he has a band, the color of a chestnut, around his body, and that 's why they call him belted. They are always found at the edges of the streams, sitting on a limb of a tree which overhangs the water, ready to dive for the minnows which come to the surface. They seldom fail to catch one, either. The funniest thing about them is, that they always carry the fish they catch to some place where they can rest, and kill it by beating it before they swallow it, which they do head first!"

"They have a harsh, shrill note," said Burton; "it sounds like a policeman's rattle!"

"It 's exactly the same bird that you have East," said Pierre. "Hark! hear him?" as the bird struck up his unmusical screech.

After studying the kingfisher for a few moments, the boys walked on, and presently reached the open prairie, where they hoped to start up a rabbit for dinner, as the sandpipers were all gone and they had only turkey left, but did not care to eat any more of that kind of meat until evening, when the turkey which Romeo had put in the underground oven would be done.

They had not gone more than half a mile before Cyrus

flushed a big jack, and both the dogs went for him full tilt. They ran him a mile, though, before Cyrus caught him and brought him to Pierre.

"That will do for a beginning," said he to the dogs; "but we must have one more, at least, or you two hungry fellows will go without your dinner." And he started them on again.

In less than half an hour both Cyrus and Jupe had each caught another; and then, as there was meat enough for themselves and the dogs too, the boys concluded to return to camp, as it was growing fearfully hot.

"Well, we must get an early start for home in the morning," said Pierre, "and it is a pity that all our turkeys are spoiled by the hot weather; but we will have some sport with them and the lynxes to-night," he continued. "I thought that we never should be able to get any of them to the ranch; it's lucky that Romeo commenced this morning on that one in the oven, or we would be without anything to eat now."

"It's too warm to go anywhere until evening," said Carlos; "so we must content ourselves in camp until then. I'm going to take another bath. Don't you fellows want to go along?" he inquired of the others.

"Yes, indeed," said Summerfield; "you can't propose bathing too often for me. I'm a regular water-dog."

So all went down to the stream again, where they played in the water for an hour or more; then returned to camp, took care of the ponies, and threw themselves on the beds

—10

for a nap until time for supper, when the turkey would be ready.

About sundown, Romeo announced that the bird was cooked all right, and to it they fell with most ravenous appetites; for they had purposely refrained from eating much dinner, so as to get all the good they could out of the unique manner in which the cook had served the bird.

After they had finished, Pierre said, " As soon as it gets dark, we 'll take the turkeys and carry them out into the timber about half a mile from camp, so the lynxes will smell them, and then when the moon is up, which will be in a few minutes, we will go and hide under some tree near by them. Then when Mr. Lynx comes along we 'll have some fun."

They found a suitable spot, close to some big cotton-woods, where they could mask themselves behind their trunks, and placing the bodies of the spoiled turkeys within easy rifle-range of the trees they had chosen as a blind, all sat themselves on the ground to quietly await developments.

The moon had risen before they had tied their tempting bait to the bushes, and very shortly after they had taken their places the soft mewing of a lynx could be heard, then another and another, as they stealthily crept toward the bait.

When they reached it a tremendous snarling and spitting took place, just like tom-cats on a garden fence in a town; and the boys, waiting until they had fairly begun to feast on the birds, opened on them with their rifles. Carlos and Pierre both killed· one, Burton another, but Summerfield missed his completely; so they got three in all, which was pretty good work for the short time it took to effect it. And as there was no use in remaining there any longer, because the animals would not come back, the boys returned to camp and went to bed.

Bright and early the next morning they were all on their way to the ranch, where they arrived in time for supper. Very hungry they were, too, for their breakfast had been a light one, as all that they had depended upon, the turkeys, had been spoiled by the warm weather.

That evening Summerfield and Burton visited the dug-out, as was their wont,—the delightful moonlight forbidding thoughts of bed until they had passed an hour or two with their young friends of the ranch, and listened to some adventure by Mr. Delahoyde of his own boyhood days, of which he had a store.

When all were seated on the big log that laid in front of the dugout, Summerfield and Burton having lighted their pipes, the conversation drifted to what they had particularly noticed on their trip to the turkey-roost. Summerfield had been especially attracted by the deceiving pictures of the wonderful mirage,[1] and admitted that

<hr>

[1] *Mirage* is that peculiar phenomenon best observed on deserts, or on the arid mid-continent region of the United States. It is derived from the French word *mirer*, to look at, and from the Latin *mirus*, wonderful. Its cause was first explained by the scientist Monge, a Frenchman who accompanied Napoleon on his expedition to Egypt: "The layers of air in contact with the heated soil are rarefied and expanded more than those immediately above them; a ray of light from an elevated object has

he did almost believe that what he saw was real, and not the distorted images caused by the atmosphere.

Burton said that he would have sworn at one time on the journey, they were approaching a beautiful lake, and was only assured of his mistake when they reached the spot where he imagined it existed, to find that nothing was there but the dead prairie.

Mr. Delahoyde told them that emigrants in the early days, when crossing the Plains, often made long detours from the established route in trying to reach one of those deceptive lakes, which seemed about ten or twelve miles distant, and much suffering ensued.

Once, during an Indian war on the Plains some years ago, an officer of a cavalry regiment pursuing a band of savages that had been committing depredations on the border, when riding ahead of his troops, saw, as he believed, a party of the savages not more than a mile in advance, and who appeared to be coming toward him on a quick lope. Orders were immediately given for the troopers to move forward and meet the attack, as the distance between the supposed enemies was decreasing each moment. The command to charge was just about to be sounded, when what at first appeared to be a band of the Indians was found to be nothing but the desiccated car-

to traverse strata of air less and less refracting, and the angle of incidence continually increases in amount till refraction gives place to internal reflection." The objects distorted by the mirage are generally seen in the air inverted, and appear to be formed in water, so as to create the illusion that a lake or pond is near. Many a thirsty traveler on the Great Plains has been deceived, and followed for miles the phantom sheet of water he so terribly needed, only to find that it had no existence.

casses of some buffalo which the mirage had exaggerated by the effect of the peculiar atmospheric conditions; and that waving motion which always attends the phenomenon caused the buffalo to appear as if moving toward the command.

"You have to get used to a great many curious things out in this strange country," said Mr. Delahoyde. The mirage is one of them, and the other is the deception of distances; but the eye soon gets accustomed to it."

After more conversation relative to their hunt, all retired to their separate sleeping-places, anxious for the morning to come, which was to be full of new adventures.

CHAPTER VIII.

SUMMERFIELD and Burton did not get out of bed next morning until after seven o'clock, so stiff and sore were they from their long ride of sixty miles. They went immediately to the pool to take their accustomed bath, stopping a few moments at the dugout to talk with Pierre and Carlos; then returned to their camp to clean their rifles, and to fix their clothes that had been torn in the brush on Eagle Chief creek.

Carlos and his brother were just as fresh and lively as ever after their night's sleep, and went to work in their little garden-patch, which had been sadly neglected for the past week, while entertaining their young visitors, and did not go to their camp until after supper, to invite them up to the dugout and spend the evening.

Before dark, Summerfield and Burton were again seated on the lawn at the ranch, as had been the custom when not out on a trip with Carlos and Pierre. Mr. Delahoyde told them that just after they had left for their camp last evening, Tom Norman, a Government scout, on his way from Fort Sill to Harker, had stopped at the ranch a few moments, and reported the whole country south of the Canadian black with buffalo. "He struck the Arkansas about thirty miles west of here, then followed the Santa Fé trail right down to here. So if you boys want to go on a hunt before you leave for home, now is a good opportunity, for the buffalo will probably remain for a week or more in the vicinity of where Norman saw them."

"Let's go by all means," said Summerfield. "Why can't we start to-morrow?"

"I know of no reason why you can't," said Mr. Delahoyde; "but you do not have to leave here until afternoon, because you can't get to the ground before the second day, and will have to camp on Bluff creek the first night. So you can take it easy, and be ready the first thing next morning to go on to the Canadian, and arrive there by sundown."

"We won't want to take any camping-out things," said Pierre, because it is so warm now we can use our saddle-blankets to sleep on, and can cook our meat just as we did the antelope yesterday."

"Of course," said Carlos. "We don't have to take the dogs along, either,—they'll be in the way; and as there are so many of us—four—we can take turns keeping guard at night. Besides, we shall not be out more than four nights, anyhow."

"We'll have to take one extra pony along, come to

think of it," continued Pierre, "to pack a buffalo head that I promised to mount for Summerfield."

"Yes," said Summerfield, "don't forget that. I want to take a head with me back to Boston by all means."

"It's settled then," said Burton, "that we go to-morrow afternoon."

"As we have plenty of time for sleep to-night, can't you tell us some other adventure before we go back to the camp, Mr. Delahoyde?" appealingly asked Summerfield.

"Why, yes, if you care to hear one," replied Mr. Delahoyde. "I have a fund of them, but they do not always come to me when I want them. Let's see," continued he, musingly; "I once had two adventures on the same afternoon; one was very comical, the other quite serious.

"I was trapping on Powder river with my father, and as we were getting scarce of meat, he told me, just after our meager dinner one day, to go out and hunt for anything that was good to eat.

"I must have walked about five miles down the stream, —you know we never thought much of a five- or even tenmile tramp in those days,—and coming through a big patch of underbrush, I suddenly met, face to face, a monstrous grizzly bear. Luckily for me, it was a male, and not a female with cubs at her side, or it would have been the end of me.

"We were upon each other before we had any idea of it, the brush was so thick; and as he met me he looked at me askance, gave a snort, quickly raised one of his big fore paws, without stopping, and knocked my rifle clear out of my hand; it would have gone forty feet if it had not been for the chapparal. Fortunately, he kept right on in his tracks, without turning his head to take a second look. So did I as soon as I had picked up my rifle, which, as luck would have it, was not injured a bit.

"I don't know which was the worst scared, the bear or myself.

"Continuing down the river trail, in about half an hour I came upon a small herd of black-tail deer, and shot a fine fat doe, which fell right under a big mountain cotton-wood tree on the bank of the stream. While I was busy bleeding the doe, I heard a low growl immediately above, and upon looking up, saw a panther with the bristles on its back all standing, and glancing down at me, as if not perfectly understanding whether there was any danger to be apprehended or not.

"I knew that the brute was going to leap upon me in another instant, and raising my rifle, pulled the trigger, just as the dark figure left the tree. She was shot through the side, the bullet coming out and striking the trunk of the tree. I could hear it plainly. The brute spasmodically drew herself together, and laid for a moment absolutely motionless, excepting that her tail was gently oscillating, just as you have often seen a house-cat when watching a mouse-hole. This gave me time to load again, which I did immediately, and taking careful aim, hit her in the eye and stretched her out cold.

" All that saved me from a furious attack, and probable death, was her wavering for a moment to get into position for another spring, which gave me time to load my gun.

" I was scared when I saw that I had not killed her with my first bullet, and expected to have a hand-to-hand struggle with the ferocious beast, but fortune was on my side, and I did not get even a scratch.

" Now comes the funny part of the adventure. While the panther was entertaining me, half a dozen mountain wolves, attracted by the scent of the doe's blood, were soon drawn to the spot where she lay, and devoured every morsel of it, as I was unable to pay any attention to them, although I could hear them growl and snap, not a hundred yards away. We had to go without meat again that night, but had excellent luck next day.

" My father had an exciting experience to which I was a witness, for I was with him at the time. It was when I first returned from St. Louis and made my initial trapping-trip with him.

" It was on the upper Arkansas river where we established our trapping-camp, and had with us as partners two more old mountaineers, whose names I have forgotten.

" Father had heard somehow that the commanding officer of the regular troops stationed at Santa Fé, New Mexico, was desirous of obtaining a young panther, and that he would pay fifty dollars for it.

" We talked the subject over in camp, and father said

he was going to try and get a young cat and the fifty dollars.

"One afternoon, we heard the mewing of a young panther, not very far from our camp, and we all started for the direction from which the sound seemed to come, and presently arrived at the foot of a tree not a great distance off, where, sure enough, high up on one of the branches, we discovered the little animal. It was not more than six weeks old, and father at once began preparations for securing it. He sent me back to camp for a lariat. I returned very shortly with it, and father buckled his belt tighter, put his hunting-knife in it, and began to cautiously climb the tree, placing the rope around his shoulders. It was nearly twenty-five feet to the first limb, but he was a good climber, and soon reaching it, sat down on it to take breath and feel if his knife was all right. He then looked up, and saw that the young cat was still motionless, and clinging to the same branches as at first.

"Then, using the other limbs as natural steps, father ascended quickly and lightly toward the kitten, which, though it did not move in the least, still kept its fiery eyes on its approaching foe.

"But unknown to any of us, wilder eyes than those of the young one were watching my father's progress. The grim and dangerous enemy was none other than the mother of the kitten, which lay with tail gently waving on the limb of a dead tree standing alongside of the cottonwood on which father was, with its branches interlacing it.

" The old panther was apparently ready to spring, seemingly only waiting until the distance was lessened between father and her kitten, before she would make the leap and throw herself, teeth and claws, upon the audacious man who would dare to seize her offspring.

" Carelessly swinging from limb to limb, father was soon under the young one, which began to raise itself gently, after the fashion of the domestic cat with its back up, and stood on the branch looking down upon father, as if not perfectly comprehending the danger to be apprehended from him.

" Father, seeing now that he was in the position he desired, took the lariat from around his shoulder, and forming it into a noose with which to throw over the kitten's head, steadied himself between two limbs, and looking up for the proper moment to land his rope, saw for the first time, directly opposite him, and hardly ten yards from where he stood, the glowing eyes of the now enraged mother as she bent down for the fatal spring!

" The reason why none of us had seen the old one before was, that the leaves on the cottonwood were very thick, as it was the height of their unfolding, and we never thought of looking into the dead tree alongside it.

" Father had presence of mind enough to realize the situation he found himself in, and called to me, but I had fortunately at the same instant caught sight of the brute, and raising my rifle, fired just as the dark figure of the mother made her leap.

" The beast, pierced by the bullet, gathered herself, and sprang from branch to branch until she had reached the topmost limb, where, the thin foliage not being able to sustain her, she tumbled to the ground, dead.

" Father, now happily relieved from his perilous position, perfectly cool, as he always was, under the most trying circumstances, threw his rope so accurately that it caught the kitten just back of its shoulder-blades, when, bracing himself, he jerked it off the limb, and carefully holding on to the coil of the lariat, let the kitten down slowly, which I secured as soon as it touched the ground.

" Then father descended, and we tied the kitten firmly by all its legs. He then sent me to camp for a pony, while he waited and watched his prize. As soon as I returned, he tossed the kitten over the front of the saddle, and mounting, we rode back to camp, where we arrived about sundown, it having taken several hours to accomplish the capture of the young panther.

" The kitten, however, did not live to reach Santa Fé, having died of stubbornness,—refusing to drink the milk offered it at the several ranches on the trail; so father had all his trouble for nothing. But it was an exciting adventure, all the same."

The little party now broke up, Summerfield and Burton going to their camp, after having been told they need not hurry in the morning, for if they got away by ten or eleven o'clock they would be in time to make their camp on Bluff creek, only a day's ride from where Norman had seen the herd of buffalo.

The boys all retired in a happy state of mind over their prospective start for a buffalo-hunt on the morrow, but Summerfield and Burton did not get asleep until long after midnight, for talking about it.

CHAPTER IX.

THE next morning after breakfast, Pierre and Carlos went out to the herd and drove five ponies up
to the dugout. Four of these had been thoroughly
trained to hunt buffalo; the fifth was to be used as a pack-
animal to transport what meat they might want to bring
home, and the buffalo head for Summerfield to take to
Boston with him. Summerfield and Burton's own horses
had never been trained, so they rode two belonging to the
Delahoydes, that would know just what was expected of
them when they got close to a herd of the great shaggy

beasts; theirs were to be left in charge of the Mexican until the party returned.

About the middle of the forenoon, Summerfield came up to the dugout for the animals he and Burton were to ride, and leading them back to the camp, soon returned mounted, accompanied by his partner.

A coffeepot and four tin cups were fastened to the pack-animal's saddle, and that was about all he was to be burdened with, as the boys intended to use their hunting-knives instead of carrying others along, and in place of a frying-pan, to cook their meat before the campfire on small limbs of trees.

The Boston young men took dinner at the dugout, and in about half an hour after it was concluded, all were ready to start.

"Have you everything you will need?" asked their mother, as Pierre and Carlos swung themselves into their saddles.

"Yes, indeed," replied Pierre; "our wants will be few."

"You 're sure you 've got your flint and steel,[1] Pierre?" inquired his father anxiously; "that 's the most important of all."

---

[1] *Flint and steel* were used before the introduction of matches, and continued to be part of an old trapper's or hunter's outfit long after the latter were invented. The steel was simply a short piece of good steel, and the flint a piece of pure silica such as could be picked up anywhere near the margin of a stream, or even on the open prairie in the vicinity of rocks. Fire was made by striking the flint on the steel; the sparks generated by the friction communicated to a bit of soft rag, generally cotton, or dry splinters of wood, or grass, as the case might be. It was more reliable on the Plains and in the mountains than matches, for the latter were easily affected by the damp weather, and became useless.

WAR DANCE OF THE COMANCHES.

"It's right here," replied Pierre, as he struck his hand on the place where his pocket was in his buckskin jacket. "Good-bye," continued he, as he led out toward the river-bank.

"Good-bye," was reëchoed by Summerfield and Burton, as the little party rode away from the ranch, full of spirits, laughing and chatting,— not imagining they would not look upon it again until many weary months of excitement, hardship and adventure had passed.

"A good thirty-mile ride before to us to where we shall camp to-night," said Pierre; "for Norman must have struck the Arkansas at the main ford. A splendid place; plenty of dry wood, good grass for the animals, and a fine spring of water."

"I suppose he saw the big herd of buffalo not far south of the river?" said Carlos.

"I so understood him when he told Dad about them. And if they are there we can have a fine hunt and get back home by dark the fourth night."

"What do you expect to kill for supper?" asked Burton of Pierre. "I don't suppose it will be rabbits, as we have no dogs along to flush them."

"Birds," laconically answered Pierre. "Either ducks or sandpipers. No danger of our going to bed hungry."

"No, indeed," said Carlos; "our trail runs right along the river the whole distance to the ford, excepting a little cut-across, where it makes a bend below Spring creek; you remember where we set our trot-line the day we went fishing last week?"

"I'd rather kill some blue-winged teal," said Pierre, "because if we can get five or six,— and we may at one shot,— it will be enough for both breakfast and supper. So keep your eyes skinned for ducks upon the river, boys. We'll have buffalo for our dinner to-morrow, sure, I think."

They had passed the little cut-across, as Carlos had called the detour, and got back to the river again, when Burton, whose faculty for observation was very acute, suddenly stopped his pony, pulled up on his bridle-reins, and pointing to a spot under some overhanging trees, about five hundred yards up-stream, said, "Pierre, I think that there is our supper and breakfast, too."

"Yes, indeed," replied Pierre, "a flock of blue-winged teal, sure! Let's halt here, and I'll crawl up on them."

The boys all stopped, and Pierre dismounted, letting his pony stand,—it had been trained to stay just where it was left, when on a hunting expedition,— and cautiously walked along the trail. As he neared the ducks that were swimming along, totally unconscious of approaching danger, he crept into the thick willows that bordered the water, his comrades watching him intently until he disappeared.

In a few moments they heard the discharge of his gun, and then saw him emerge from the copse, holding in one hand a bunch of birds.

"How many?" sang out Summerfield, as he came within hailing distance.

"Seven, and all at one shot!" answered Pierre, who, when he reached his pony, tied the birds to the cantle of his saddle, and they all rode on.

They saw lots of all kinds of game on the way, but not caring to waste any ammunition, and having enough meat to last them until the morrow, they passed the time in chatting, and arrived at the Fort Sill ford about six o'clock.

They chose their camp close to the spring; and while Pierre and Carlos picketed out the ponies, Summerfield and Burton began preparations for supper, as all were fearfully hungry.

By the time that Carlos and his brother returned, the two Bostonians had the coffee boiling, the ducks skinned, cut up, and ready for each one to broil his own portion before the now brightly glowing embers.

While the birds were slowly cooking, Pierre said, " Fellows, we will have to tie our ponies in to-night, as we have no dogs to watch them, and the wolves might get after them if left away out on the prairie. So, after they 've filled themselves, we 'll bring them in and fasten them near where we sleep."

After supper was disposed of with great relish, Pierre told the boys that they must gather lots of wood. " We 'll have to keep up a fire all night, for if there are buffalo near us there 's bound to be lots of wolves hanging around the herd, and they're just as liable to pay us a visit as not."

Acting upon Pierre's suggestion, the boys all willingly pitched in, gathered great quantities of limbs of the trees which had been blown down by the wind, and portions of the dried trunks, until they had collected more than two cords.

"I guess that's enough, isn't it, Carl?" inquired Pierre, depending somewhat upon his brother's judgment.

"Yes, but don't let us make the fire too near where we are going to sleep; it's fearfully hot down here in the timber, anyhow," replied Carlos.

"Well, we'll put it a dozen yards off, then," said Pierre.

It was now just dusk, and noticing the ponies were standing at the ends of their picket-ropes lazily swinging their heads and switching their tails to keep away the gnats and mosquitoes, which were thick out on the prairie, Pierre said: "We had best bring in the ponies now; they're full, and we want to get them tied up before it grows too dark to see."

So all went out, brought the animals in, and after tying them to trees close to where they had spread out the saddle-blankets to sleep on, Summerfield and Burton lighted their pipes, Carlos and Pierre sitting on their robes, and they commenced to talk. The conversation opened immediately upon a subject that was uppermost in the minds of the young Bostonians—the proposed buffalo-hunt.

"How far east," asked Summerfield of Pierre, "can you find the buffalo now?"

"Well, Dad says he doubts if any have been seen east of a line drawn north and south, cutting the Arkansas at the Big Bend of that river, for a great many years. West of there, clear to the foothills of the Rocky Mountains, he says, as late as sixteen years ago, the whole country seemed fairly blocked with the shaggy animals; an immense moving mass, which made the very earth tremble with their clattering hoofs when from some cause they were stampeded. Now, there are not half as many as there used to be, even within my own recollection of thirteen or fourteen years; besides, they are getting scarcer every season."

"By the signs around here out on the prairie, that I noticed when Pierre and I went to picket the ponies, a big herd had been in the vicinity very recently," said Carlos.

"Yes, only as late as yesterday; for I could see the fresh trails leading down to the river where they went to drink. You need not be afraid that we shall not have all the sport with them we want, to-morrow."

Then Pierre said: "It's about time to turn in; now who's going to stand guard first to-night?"

"Let me!" promptly replied Summerfield. "I do so want to."

"All right, then," said Pierre; "as we shall start out

on our hunt at daylight, or as soon as we eat breakfast, it will be less than two hours apiece for us. What time is it now, Summerfield?"

Summerfield looked at his watch, and replied, "Just half-past eight."

"Well, then, your turn begins now," said Pierre, addressing himself to Summerfield; "and at half-past ten, call me; at half-past twelve, Carl goes on; at half-past two, Burton will take his turn,—but before his two hours are ended we shall all be up, as daylight comes then."

"That will give us plenty of sleep," said Carlos; "and the time will fly when you're on guard in camp,—it always seems so to me, anyhow."

The three boys then laid down on their saddle-blankets, while Summerfield, seating himself on a stump a short distance from the fire, his rifle resting between his knees, commenced to puff vigorously at his pipe, while he mused over the strange situation in which he found himself. He rather enjoyed the perfect stillness of his surroundings, as he watched the stars twinkle so brightly in the clear atmosphere, for he was inclined to love solitude, and was always contented when alone with his thoughts.

Occasionally he would get up and stroll around, his rifle on his shoulder, real army-sentry fashion; sometimes go to where his companions were wrapped in deep slumber on their single blanket, with heads resting on their saddles for a pillow, the ground their bed and the heavens their canopy.

After he had smoked two or three pipefuls, and wandered around the camp several times, he looked at his watch to learn how the time was progressing, when to his surprise he saw that it was already quarter-past ten. He thought that he had been on guard only about twenty minutes, so rapidly did the hours pass to him.

"Well," he said to himself, "I'll take just one more smoke, then call Pierre, and turn in for a little sleep."

He had scarcely seated himself on his favorite stump and pulled out his tobacco-pouch, before he heard, far away, a sound similar to that heard on the night of the turkey-hunt, when the coyotes were after the birds they killed and were fighting over them down at the roost.

Summerfield listened intently. The noise grew more distinct in volume, the yelping hoarser than that of coyotes, and he knew that, whatever it emanated from, it was coming nearer each moment; so he determined to apprise Pierre of the fact. He was just about to call him, when Pierre suddenly jumped up, and punching Carlos gently with his foot, exclaimed, "A pack of gray wolves! Don't you hear them?"

Carlos was on his feet in a second, rifle in hand, and in a minute all the boys had gathered around the fire, as the ferocious animals were evidently rapidly approaching camp.

"Look at the ponies!" said Pierre; "how they tremble and pull at their lariats, trying to stampede. Carl, go and speak to them,—they know as well as we what 's coming."

Carlos ran to where the ponies were fastened, and tried to soothe them by patting their necks and talking to them. It had the effect of quieting them in a moment, when he returned and took his place with the other boys.

Carlos had scarcely arrived at the fire, when ten of the ugly brutes came into plain view, growling, snapping and whining, as they were balked by the sight of the young hunters and the blaze of the campfire that shot high in the air,—Summerfield having thrown on a supply of fresh fuel at the instant of their emerging from the timber.

"Let 's kill them," said Burton, as he brought his rifle to his shoulder.

"No! no!" said Pierre; "we have n't any ammunition to waste that way. We can get rid of them without killing them. Throw a little loose powder out of your flask into the fire, Burton; the smell of burning powder is dreaded by nearly all wild animals."

Sure enough, as Burton poured a little powder into his hand and tossed it into the flames, which leaped into the air doubly brilliant, with a howl of evident rage and disappointment the wolves all "turned tail," and darted away into the shadow of the timber; nor did they return.

The boys as they stood at the fire could still hear their snarling as they rapidly retreated, the sound each moment, however, growing fainter, until it finally ceased altogether.

"Well, those confounded wolves have upset all our arrangements," said Pierre. "What time is it, Summerfield?"

Summerfield drew out his watch, held its face toward the fire, and replied, "Half-past one."

"Let me take your watch now," continued Pierre; "you and the others go try and get a little sleep; I'll stand guard until half-past three; then it will be almost daybreak. We'll get some breakfast while the ponies are grazing, and be off as soon as they are filled up, for daylight will be here by that time."

All excepting Pierre threw themselves on their blankets, and in a few moments were sound asleep. Pierre then walked to where the ponies were tied, spoke a few words to them, although they were perfectly quiet, returned to the fire, threw on some more fuel, and sat down on a stump with his rifle ready for any emergency.

Not a sound now disturbed the stillness of the little camp, excepting the occasional mewing of a lynx down in the heavy timber, or the hooting of an owl perched on the limb of some blasted tree near by, and the crackling of the fire when Pierre added fresh fuel.

Some boys would have felt very lonely under such circumstances, but not so with Pierre, who with his brother had been reared from infancy in the solitude of the remote Plains. There is an old saying that "The nearer we get to Mother Earth, the more we love her," and it was fully realized by both Pierre and Carlos, whose lives had been passed in the closest communion with Nature.

Pierre walked around and sat down by turns, musing upon the subject that occupied his thoughts,—to give his young guests as much sport as possible on their contemplated buffalo-hunt.

Throwing some wood on the fire, which had burned low while he was thinking, as it blazed up again he drew out Summerfield's watch, and looking at it, was rather surprised to find it was almost a quarter to four o'clock. Then casting his eyes toward the eastern horizon, he noticed the first faint, rosy streaks of light, announcing the approaching dawn.

He said to himself, as he put the watch back into his pocket: "I'll not wake up Burton; let them all rest; they're pretty well tired out, and I could n't sleep any more now if I tried. I'll picket out the ponies myself, then put the coffeepot on, and when it boils, call the boys."

He then took out two of the ponies at a time, picketed them on a spot of fresh grass, came back for two more, and at last led the pack-animal out. Returning, he went to the spring, washed himself, filled the coffeepot, put it on the fire, and sat down again on the stump.

In a few moments the pot began to sing, and as day was rapidly approaching, Pierre stirred up his companions, who stretched and yawned, but soon realizing where they were, they jumped up in a hurry, ran to the spring and washed, then returned to the fire, ready to help picket

out the ponies; but upon looking where they had been tied
the evening before, noticed they were gone, and saw them
grazing peacefully out on the open prairie.

"Why, Pierre," said Summerfield and Burton, "you
did n't call us to help you with the animals!"

"That 's all right. I did n't want to sleep, so I thought
I might just as well let you boys get all you could."

"Well, I 'm much obliged for your kindness," said
Burton; "for to tell the truth, I never was so tired out
and sleepy in all my life, that I can recollect of."

The ducks, which had been prepared the evening before
and placed in the spring to keep them sweet, were now
brought to the fire, where each one took his portion and
broiled it, and with the coffee made a good breakfast.

Pierre watched the ponies to see when they had filled
themselves, which would be as soon as they should have
stopped grazing and swung at the end of their lariats.

It was a whole hour after breakfast before the animals
ceased to feed, and almost six o'clock when they were
saddled ready to start on the hunt.

The boys took a straight line south from the Arkansas,
and after having ridden for about ten miles without seeing
the first evidence of the presence of a large herd, Pierre
said, "I 'm afraid that something has stampeded them,
and we may have to go clear to the Hackberry before we
find them."

"How far is it to the Hackberry?" asked Summerfield.

"About thirty miles, isn't it, Carl?" replied Pierre, referring to his brother.

"All of that," said Carlos, "and over a dry country, too. If we don't see them by the time we reach the creek, we can rest there, eat our dinner, graze the ponies, and then go ahead,—as I'm for keeping on until we come across the herd, if it takes a week."

"Well, that's just what we'll do; but if we don't come up with the herd by the time we arrive at Hackberry creek, we will have to shoot something to eat for our dinner," said Pierre.

"No danger of our not getting something, is there, Pierre?" inquired Burton, who was always blessed with a good appetite.

"No, I guess not; we'll find something if it's only a prairie-dog, and I know there are two or three big villages of the little fellows between here and the creek," replied Pierre.

Two more hours passed, and it was now after ten o'clock. The prairie was perfectly lifeless, so far as the presence of animals was concerned, although the signs were abundant that a vast concourse of buffaloes had recently passed over it.

The sun had reached the meridian; still the ponies plodded wearily through the alkali-dust[1] of the desert region between the Canadian and Hackberry creek, and not a sign of buffalo in sight.

---

[1] A chemical term. Employed on the deserts of the world to designate the white dust of arid regions.

It was fully three o'clock before the timber on Hackberry appeared, like a dark line on the distant horizon, over three miles away. The hunters arrived thêre in another hour, selected a suitable spot, pitched their camp, and turned out their jaded ponies to graze. While the others were attending to the animals, Pierre went on a hunt for meat.

The boys in camp soon heard the report of his rifle, and presently another discharge. In a few minutes he appeared with a wild turkey, and told them that he had missed the second shot at one; but they had enough with the bird he had killed, and more, too, than they could possibly eat.

"How did you come to see them?" asked Burton.

"I was walking along the edge of the timber," said Pierre, "when I started up a big flock. They did not fly, but did some tall marching. I tell you there is no bird that can outrun a wild turkey. They were on one side of a little knoll, and I ran around to head them off, but by the time I got there the turkeys were away ahead, nearly out of range. Luckily, I got one, but missed the other because he was too far off when I pulled trigger."

They broiled the turkey, after cutting it into small pieces so it would cook quicker, and, contrary to Pierre's statement that it was more than they could eat, every bit was devoured, so hungry were all, after their long and wearisome ride.

Summerfield and Burton indulged in their usual smoke;

Carlos laid down on his blanket to rest; but the nover-tired Pierre took a stroll on top of the bluff bordering the creek, to see if he could discover anything of the buffaloes which he believed must be somewhere in the vicinity.

He was not gone more than fifteen minutes, when he hurried back to camp and announced to the boys that the whole-prairie beyond the creek was literally black with buffaloes.

In a moment all were on their feet, full of excitement at the good news Pierre had brought them; and Summer-field and Burton, had they not been restrained by the better judgment of Pierre and Carlos, would have jumped on their worn-out ponies and gone after the herd, and the chase would have resulted only in failure and disap-pointment.

"We must wait," Pierre told the nervous young men, "until our ponies are in condition to run; that is impos-sible now. It will take a couple of hours at least for them to get rested sufficiently to do the work, and then it will be only a little after six o'clock. Plenty of daylight to kill all the buffaloes we want to, and get a bull's head for Summerfield."

"It will be much cooler then, too," said Carlos; "this has been an awfully hot day."

Six o'clock did not come a moment too soon for the young Bostonians, who all the afternoon had been chafing at the delay; but at last Pierre told them to help get the ponies in, saddle up, and then they would start out after the buffaloes.

They rode out of camp full of excitement, and when they arrived at the top of the bluff and saw the prairie beyond covered with the great ruminants, just as Pierre had told them, their enthusiasm knew no bounds, as they rode around to the leeward of the herd, which was about two miles distant.

Coming up to the herd, the ponies, well trained to the business, ran after the one which was selected by each of the hunters, and in a few minutes three of them were killed; but one was so old and tough that when Pierre and Carlos dismounted to skin him with the others, they abandoned him to the wolves, which could be seen trailing after the herd.

Pierre succeeded in killing an enormous young bull, with a magnificent head and horns, which he told Summerfield was the best specimen he had seen for a long time, and that when they got to camp he would fix it so it would keep until they returned to the ranch.

Summerfield was lucky enough to kill a very fat cow which ran in front of his pony. He bravely dashed after her, but at first only wounded her, the second shot laying her out cold.

Burton missed altogether, though he fired several times at the running animals, his pony acting superbly in its efforts to bring his rider up to them, and he was very much disgusted with himself when he found out that all the rest of the party had been successful in bringing down one or more of the huge beasts.

Summerfield had quite an adventure with a cow which he wounded; she turned on his pony and showed fight, but he bravely loped around her, and got in a death-shot.

Night was rapidly coming on when they had skinned their game and packed what they wanted of it on the pony, together with the large head of the bull which Pierre had shot purposely for Summerfield.

They intended to make camp on the Hackberry that night, take a fresh start in the morning for the Canadian, and the next evening reach home.

Unfortunately, as they rode away from the field of their slaughter a " norther "[1] began to make its appearance. Black, ominous-looking clouds rolled up on the western horizon, and it suddenly grew so dark that the boys could not see the ground.

They were at least ten miles south of Hackberry creek, the buffaloes having led them a chase that distance before they discontinued the slaughter, and Pierre said, as he noticed the coming storm, " I guess we won't camp on the Hackberry very soon to-night."

They traveled on in the dismal fog which soon began to overspread the earth, occasionally stopping to listen

[1] " *Norther* " is a name given to sudden storms of a very cold wind from the north, often accompanied by snow. They usually occur beyond the one-hundredth meridian, and are not of long duration. Farther east they are termed " blizzards," though a blizzard differs in many particulars from the Texas norther, principally in its continuing for a longer time.

for the roar of the creek, which Pierre knew must now be swollen; but nothing was conveyed to their ears but the whine of a distant wolf, and the rumbling of the thunder.

It is usually the case that when persons are lost on the prairie they unconsciously travel in a circle, and it was so with the party of young hunters,—and very soon the fact stared Pierre in the face that he was lost!

Neither he nor Carlos could agree as to the proper direction; one insisted upon this way, the other that, until they were both so confused they did not know which way to move.

Fortunately, they were caught on the edge of the norther only, and it was not so cold as to make the air uncomfortable, nor was the sky completely covered by clouds. There were great rifts in them, through which the stars twinkled at times, but both Carlos and his brother realized that the region in which they were now was strange to them. Not a landmark with which they were familiar could be recognized, and the darkness, which is always more bewildering on the open prairies than in the forest, soon had its effect on the brave boys,—for brave they were, —and they knew they were lost.

It grew darker every moment, and even the hundreds of old buffalo-trails leading to the streams, which those animals followed to drink once a day, became indiscernible; and as for catching a glimpse of the timber which fringed many little creeks tributary to the Canadian, it was impossible.

—12

At last Pierre pulled up on his pony, and said to Carlos: "Carl, we can't make Hackberry to-night; let's camp in one of these ravines, and wait for daylight."

"No!" insisted Carlos; "we must make the creek, or as near to it as we can. It won't do to build a fire, for we are not far from the Comanche country, and some of the Indians might see it, and if they should it would be all up with us."

Burton spoke up, and said, "We have to go directly north, don't we, Pierre?"

"Yes," replied Pierre; "Hackberry creek and the Canadian are both north of us. If we go in that direction, we are bound to strike them somewhere."

"Well, then," said Burton, "I know the North Star[1] when I see it, and we can guide ourselves by that if I can get a glimpse of the sky through the rifts of the clouds."

"All right," said Pierre; "pick out the North Star, and we'll follow on a straight line for it. All we have to do is to travel north, and as long as we reach the creek, whether we come out below the trail or above it, we can cross and keep right on to the Canadian,—for I know every inch of that river for forty miles either up- or down-stream."

Burton took a glance at the heavens, which at that moment happened to be quite clear of clouds in the direction he was looking, and said, "Come on, fellows,—follow me!"

---

[1] *North Star*, a star at the north, around which the heavens appear to revolve.

Unfortunately for the young Bostonian, although he perhaps had a very good knowledge of astronomy, he selected a bright star in the far south, and unconsciously led his companions in directly the opposite direction from that in which they should have gone.

On they plodded (their ponies giving evident signs of leg-weariness, frequently stumbling,—an unusual thing for them, as they were very sure-footed animals) for as much as ten miles more, vainly peering into the darkness for some signs of timber ahead of them.

Pierre now cast his eyes to the heavens, and saw to his dismay that the star which they had been endeavoring to follow had passed far down toward the western horizon, and he stopped and said to Burton:

"That cannot be the North Star you are guiding us by. You know it never gets so low down."

Burton very unwillingly had to admit that Pierre was right, and he felt much chagrined over the mistake he had made.

Then they halted to talk over the dilemma they found themselves in, when Carlos, who had particularly fine eyesight, said: "I see campfires ahead!"

All strained their eyes to the place Carlos pointed out to them, and sure enough, apparently far ahead of them, in the direction in which they had been traveling, they distinctly saw the dull embers of half a dozen fires.

"Some buffalo-hunters, probably," said Pierre. "We are all right now, for we can find from them where we are, stop with them all night, and get a fresh start early in the morning."

Then, thus encouraged, they moved forward again, hoping to reach the camp in a few minutes, when suddenly their ears were almost deafened by the yelling of a perfect canine cataract which came pouring around them as they naturally pulled up at the horrid din; and the next instant they were surrounded by a dozen dusky forms. They had struck an Indian village, instead of a hunter's camp as they had hoped!

Immediately a score of warriors closed upon them and yelled at the dogs, which instantly skulked off, and our young hunters found themselves captives. Pierre told Burton and Summerfield he supposed they were Comanches.

"Keep up your courage," said Carlos; "it always counts, Dad says, among the Indians."

"Besides," said Pierre, " the Comanches, Cheyennes, Kiowas and Arapahoes are friendly with the whites, and that fact may help us some; but you never can tell what a savage is going to do. They may kill us, and may not."

While they were conversing together, the warriors most unceremoniously jerked them off their ponies, took their guns away from them, and led them rather roughly to a large tepee[1] in the middle of the village; and having

[1] " *Tepee* " is the name given by the Sioux to their dwellings, and is now a general term for any Indian lodge. A tepee is built of from thirteen to seventeen poles, about three inches in diameter, the ends of which rest on the ground. They are slender in shape, tapering symmetrically, and are eighteen feet or more in length. The number of poles employed varies with the different tribes. They are tied together at

been told by signs to enter, they saw a rather dignified-looking Indian smoking a long pipe and blowing the smoke through his nostrils.

The old savage gazed at the boys, spoke a few words, which of course none of them understood, but in a few moments knew what they meant, for the same warriors who had ushered them in carried them to another lodge, where they were bound by the feet.

Summerfield and Burton thought that their time had come, surely. But the warriors laughed at them, and an old squaw made her appearance in the tepee, and, after jabbering a few unintelligible sentences to one of the Indians, returned with some dried buffalo-meat and a bucket of water. Then the warrior who had spoken to the squaw motioned to the boys to eat.

The alarm of the young hunters somewhat subsided at this demonstration of friendliness, because Pierre and Carlos, who were quite well acquainted with the Indian character, said they had been told by their grandmother that Indians rarely feed a person they intend to kill. The Bostonians, comforted by these encouraging words, fell to eating, as did Pierre and Carlos, for they were all terribly hungry, having had nothing since their turkey din-

the small ends with buffalo-hide strings, then raised until the frame resembles a cone, over which buffalo skins are placed, very nicely fitted ; and having been made soft by manipulation with the brains of the animals that wore them, the skins are sewed together with the sinews of the buffalo, taken from the strong and long muscle that holds up the great head of the beast. In summer the lower edges of the skins are rolled up, and the wind blowing through makes the tepee a cool retreat. In winter, of course, everything is closed tight, and the tepee is quite a comfortable place. Some tribes build their dwellings of rushes and other material, but the general name of "tepee" is given to the lodges of all tribes.

ner on Hackberry creek at four o'clock that afternoon,—
and it was now long past midnight by Summerfield's
watch, it having as yet escaped the eyes of the warriors.

After they had surfeited themselves—for there was no
stint to the old woman's rations—they were told by signs
to go to sleep, at the same time being shown a pile of
buffalo-robes in the end of the lodge. They immediately
took possession of these, for their worst fears were dissi-
pated, and they soon fell asleep, waiting for what events
the morning might develop.

At sunrise, which came too quickly for the tired young
hunters, they were roused up by one of the warriors who
had been sent to stand guard over them during the night,
to prevent any possible attempt to escape. The painted
and feather-bedecked savage had to shake them two or
three times rather roughly, so sound was their slumber
after their fatiguing journey to the Indian camp.

Breakfast was served to them by the same old squaw,
which consisted of the conventional dried buffalo-meat
and cold water. After finishing breakfast they were told
by signs to follow the warrior who had awakened them.

He took them to a magnificent tepee, which, by its appointments of rich furs, and the highly ornamented shield
that hung on a tripod before the lodge entrance, indicated
that it was the dwelling of the principal chief. He before
whom they were brought the evening previous was only a
subordinate.

The boys entered, as they were made to understand by

signs they must, and upon going in found themselves confronted by a very large Indian with a prominent nose, a broad, high forehead; his long hair falling down to his waist, braided, and ornamented with brass rings an inch wide, placed at intervals of three or four inches.

Summerfield and the rest of the young hunters found out afterward that these rings were peculiar insignia of the chief, no other of the principal warriors being permitted to wear anything like them. Also, that when he dressed in his best, he wore on his breast a polished copper plate as big as a dish-pan, which glistened in the sun as he strutted about the village.

This chief, whom they learned was "Red Bear," always remained in the village, only moving when the tribe migrated, for he was a very old man,—eighty years at least, the boys thought. He had a son who was regarded as a sort of chief too, and whose wife was a white woman, a raiding party of the Comanches having captured her in Texas some years previous to the advent of the young hunters in the village.

Pierre and the other boys made several attempts to talk with her, but at first were frustrated by the watchful savages, the chief having forbidden her to hold any conversation with them.

There was another white captive in the village, who was made an interpreter by the chief for the occasion, which was in reality a council to decide upon the fate of the boys. He was told to tell them that if they were not

Texans, would be good, and not try to run away, they would not be killed, but might stay with the tribe, and finally be adopted as members thereof. · While the interpreter was explaining what the old chief had to say, the latter pointed to a row of relatively fresh scalps which hung on a pole in his lodge, and said something, which the white captive immediately interpreted as follows: About three weeks before, four Mexicans were captured on a raid, brought to the village, treated kindly, and sent out to herd the ponies; but they attempted to escape. Some warriors were sent after them to bring them back, but the chief finally decided that as they had started, only their scalps must be returned to the village; and if the boys tried to run away, they would be served in like manner!

Red Bear was very impressive and decidedly in earnest, the young prisoners discovered, and made up their minds, after conversing together alone, that the best thing for them to do was to keep quiet, stay with the Indians without making any fuss, and bide their time, for it would only be madness to make any attempt to get away at present.

So the young hunters contented themselves as well as they could under the circumstances, gave a promise to the old chief that they would " be good " and obey all his orders just like the other young men of his tribe.

They were then told that they would not be tied any more; that a lodge would be assigned them, and a squaw

THE YOUNG CAPTIVES ARE CARRIED BEFORE THE CHIEF OF THE TRIBE, RED BEAR.

ordered to cook and work for them as the other braves were waited upon by the women, for men did not work. A warrior must only hunt and fight.

Having been assigned to a really nice skin lodge, not very far from that of the chief, they were sent out to herd the ponies, an immense number, with some Indian boys of about their own age.

Out on the prairie, like all boys the white captives and their dusky companions soon got on the most friendly terms, and before noon on the first day at herding, each side had picked up a few words of the other's language.

They were kept out all day, and did not get back to the village until it was quite dark. Going to the lodge, they found that the squaw who had been assigned to take care of them had provided an ample meal, of which they ate heartily, for all were exceedingly hungry after their romping and riding out on the hot prairie.

The next morning they were told that other of the young boys would be detailed to herd that day, and they must begin to learn how to become great warriors.

After breakfast they were escorted by some old warriors, together with about half a dozen young bucks, to a place out on the prairie, not far from the outskirts of the village, which might properly be called a training-school, and the exercises they were put through with their dusky companions were very amusing and exciting.

When they left their lodge for the race-course, as Summerfield afterward called it, they were mounted on very fast ponies, but as all the white captives, particularly Pierre and his brother, who had virtually lived on horseback since they were old enough to straddle an animal, were perfectly at home when in a saddle, they did not have the least fear when the frisky little Indian beasts were given to them.

Arriving at the appointed place, they found on each side of the track they were to race over, wolf-skins sewed together and fashioned in the shape of a man, which were stretched out on the prairie. They were given a bow and arrows, and showed by some of the young Indians just what they were expected to do.

Four of the young savages then went back for a distance of about three hundred yards from the supposed enemy, then turned and dashed down the track as fast as their ponies could be made to go. When they passed the skin images each shot an arrow right through it, by throwing himself on the side of the pony, holding on by his heel against the rear projection of the saddle. The left arm, with a shield on it, was thrown over the horse's neck, grasping the bow with the arrow in the right hand. The arrow must be delivered and hit the image while passing it, or it did not count. They also had to learn to shoot with the left hand as well as with the right.

Pierre, Summerfield, Carlos and Burton went at their allotted task with much trepidation,—not that they were at all afraid, but none of them had had any experience with such a primitive weapon as a bow, consequently they made some bad breaks in their attempts to shoot at the skin images.

The young savages and the white captives got many a tumble, at which all would laugh, for the average Indian boy is as full of fun and enjoys a joke as well as a white boy.

The riding of the young whites was infinitely better than their shooting, at the start, but after some weeks of constant practice they even excelled their dusky companions; for it is a fact, that the white man can do anything an Indian can, and always better, after he learns how.

Frequently bets were made on the daily drills, of skins, little trinkets, and sometimes even of ponies, for the savage is an inveterate gambler. The young trapper-boys often came out ahead in these friendly contests, and eventually accumulated quite a lot of savage gewgaws, the result of their superiority in such sports.

One day, about three months after the boys had been captured, and had become quite proficient in the Comanche language, a raiding party of warriors returned from northern Texas with several prisoners, among whom were three negroes. They had been slaves to a Cherokee chief; had run away from him, and while they were trying to reach Mexico the war-party of Comanche warriors caught them. They were on horseback, having animals they had stolen from their master; and why the Indians did not kill them might seem a mystery to those who are not acquainted with some of the peculiarities of the North-

American savage. They never scalp a negro soldier killed in battle; say they are "bad medicine," and call them "buffalo soldiers."

When the poor frightened negroes were brought before old Red Bear he was astonished, for he had never before seen a black man. He asked Pierre, to whom the old chief had taken quite a liking, why those men blacked their faces and curled their hair. He was even more astonished when Pierre told him that they were born so, but he would not believe it until he had rubbed his finger over their faces and examined very closely every portion of their anatomy. He pulled at their hair, and wonderingly inquired of Pierre how it got so kinky. In fact, the dark-skinned men were a great curiosity to the whole village,—men, women and children flocking to see and examine them.

The negroes were terribly frightened all the time, expecting they were to be killed; but Pierre and Summerfield, who had made a special study of the character of their captors, assured them that they would be turned loose in a few days, given food and ponies and treated kindly, for the Indians were rather inclined to regard them as "bad medicine," and were afraid to hurt them, as it might bring down upon the tribe some manifestation of their god, who would be angry if they were hurt.

In about a week, as Pierre and Summerfield had predicted, Red Bear sent for the negroes, and told them that as they had had a good rest now in his village, they might go where they pleased. He ordered a big supply of food, buffalo-robes to sleep on, good ponies to ride were given them, and he sent a party of eight of his warriors to escort them to the trail into Mexico.

The boys often went fishing with the young Indians, and learned how to catch trout with a bone hook. They were told one day while out on an excursion of this character, that very soon a party of warriors were going on a raid to the Pawnee country, to steal horses, and the boys were to go with them. The Comanches were the most accomplished horse-thieves of all the Plains tribes, and their wealth consisted principally in the number of ponies they owned, as a very large portion of their lives was spent on horseback.

As might have been expected, the boys' clothes soon became very ragged, particularly those of Summerfield's and Burton's, which were of cloth, while Pierre's and his brother's, made of the same material as those of the Indians, were not so badly worn; but the old woman who had charge of their lodge said they all needed new suits, and she was charged with making them.

Of course, they were to be similar in every respect to those worn by the warriors: a buckskin hunting-shirt, reaching to the waist, and trousers of the same material, but made so as to require a breech-cloth, as they do not cover the small of the back. Moccasins were the only foot-covering worn, but frequently they were elaborately beaded.

The women of the tribe wear a buckskin petticoat and dress, reaching to the knee, and trousers like the men. The dress of the squaws is generally fringed, and the most favored often wear a handsome red blanket in addition to the rest of their costume. The women, as usual in all savage tribes, perform all the labor. They are ever busy: they cook, wash, and with great skill make up all the garments worn. For needles, they use awls made of thorns or sharp bones. The thread is made of a species of wild flax, though they often use the sinews of the animals taken in the chase. All the skins are dressed and tanned by the women, and their taste in ornamentation, with both beads and small shells, is quite wonderful.

CHAPTER X.

AT THE time of the capture of the young buffalo-hunters, the Comanches were in all probability the most formidable and blood-thirsty savages of the Great Plains. They were the most perfect equestrians in the world. Forever on horseback, forever at war, they roamed restlessly from one point of the great prairies to another in search of the buffalo which supported them. They acknowledged no superior to that of their own tribe. They robbed indiscriminately all who ventured through their inhospitable hunting-grounds, murdering the defenseless who were so unfortunate as to fall under their hatred. They were a dangerous, implacable, cunning, brutal and treacherous enemy, half centaur,[1] half demon, living but to kill and eat.

[1] *Centaur:* In heathen mythology, a mythical creature, half horse, half man.

They were trained in warlike feats from their infancy. When perfected in the art of their splendid horseback-riding, they would dash along at full speed, then suddenly drop over the side of their animal, leaving no part of their person visible but the sole of one foot, which was fastened over the horse's back, as a purchase by which the rider could pull himself to an upright position. In that attitude they could ride any distance, and at the same time use their bow or fourteen-foot lance with deadly effect. One of their favorite methods of attack was to ride swiftly, at the top of their animal's speed, toward the enemy, and then, just before they came within range, drop on the opposite side of the horse, dash past, and pour into the surprised foe a shower of arrows delivered from under the animal's neck, or even under his belly. It was useless for the enemy to return the shots, as the whole body of the Comanche was hidden behind that of his horse. There was nothing to aim at but the sole of the savage's foot, just projecting over the horse's back.

Often the Comanches would try to steal upon their enemies by leaving their lances behind them, slinging themselves along the sides of their horses, and approaching carelessly, as though these horses were nothing but a troop of animals without riders. A quick eye was necessary to detect this ruse, which was generally betrayed by the fact that the horses always kept the same side toward the looker-on, which would seldom be the case were they wild and unrestrained in their movements.

"A GENERAL FREE-FOR-ALL SCRABBLE BETWEEN THE DOGS AND THEIR OWNERS."

Every Comanche warrior had one favorite horse, which he never mounted except for the war-path or for hunting the buffalo,—always using an inferior upon ordinary occasions. Swiftness was the chief quality for which the steed was selected, and for no price would the owner part with his favorite animal. Like all uncivilized peoples, the Comanche treated his horse with a strange mixture of cruelty and kindness. While engaged in a hunt, for example, he spurred and whipped the animal in the cruelest manner; but as soon as he returned, he carefully turned the valued beast over to his squaw, who stood ready to receive it as if it were a cherished member of the family.

The manner in which the Comanches replenished their stock of horses was remarkable. In many portions of the central regions of the continent, until within a few years ago (there may be some yet left in remote places), horses had become so perfectly acclimatized, had run wild for so many decades, that they had lost all traces of domestication, and were as truly wild as the buffalo or antelope, and assembled in immense herds led by the strongest and swiftest stallions.

It was from these immense droves that the Comanches supplied themselves with horses, which were so absolutely necessary to them. When a warrior wished a fresh animal he mounted his best that he had at home, provided himself with a lasso, and started out in search of the nearest herd of wild ones. When he arrived as closely as possible without being in danger of discovery, he dashed at them at

—13

full speed, and singling out one of the animals that suited him, (which, hampered by the multitude of its companions, ran on,) he soon threw his lasso over its neck. As the noose became firmly settled, the Indian jumped off his own animal. The pony was trained to stand where left, and allowed himself to be dragged by the frightened horse he had taken, and which shortly fell by the choking the leather cord effected. As soon as the horse had gone to the ground, the savage came up to it very cautiously, keeping the lasso tight enough to prevent it breathing perfectly, and yet loose enough to guard against complete strangulation, and at last was able to place one hand over its eyes and the other on its nostrils. The horse was now at the Indian's mercy. Then, in order to impress upon the animal the fact of its servitude, he hobbled together its fore feet for a time, and fastened a noose to its lower jaw; but within a wonderfully short period he was able to remove the hobbles, and to ride the conquered animal into camp. Of course, during the time occupied in taming the horse it jumped and struggled in the wildest manner; but after the one attempt for the mastery it gave up, and became the willing slave of its captor.

One of the most astonishing things in the whole process was the rapidity with which the operation of taming was accomplished. An experienced hunter would chase, capture and break a wild horse within an hour, and do it so effectually that almost before the herd was out of sight the wild animal was ridden as easily as if it had been born in servitude. The Comanche, cruel master as he generally was, always took special care not to break the spirit of his horse, and prided himself on the jumps and the bucking which the animal indulged in whenever it received its rider upon its back. ,

Of course, the very best animals were never captured from the herd. It was impossible to capture them, because they always placed themselves at the head of the troop, assuming the position of leaders, and dashed off at full speed as soon as they feared danger. Consequently they were often a half-mile or more in advance of their fellows, so that an Indian stood no chance of overtaking them on a horse impeded by the weight of the rider.

When the Indians began to receive firearms and had learned how to use them, they adopted a new method for capturing wild horses, called " creasing." Taking his rifle, the hunter crept as near the herd as he could get, and watched until he decided which horse he wanted. He waited until the horse stood with its side toward him, then aimed carefully at the top of its neck and fired. If the shot was correctly guided, the bullet just grazed the ridge of the neck and the horse fell as if dead, stunned for a moment by the shock. It recovered within a very short time, however; but before it had regained its feet, the Indian was able to go up to it, hobble and secure it. It was a very effectual method of wild-horse catching, but always broke the spirit of the animal, and deprived it of that fire and animation which the warrior prized so highly; therefore the Indians resorted to it only occasionally.

A Comanche funeral was a curious spectacle. They would carry for a hundred miles or more a dead warrior killed in battle, that his body might lie within the limits of his own nation. The departed warrior was wrapped in buffalo-robes, and laid on a scaffold made in a tree, as high as the body could be placed. His bows and arrows were laid beside him, buffalo-meat put under his head, and his horse killed at the foot of the tree. When all the ceremony was over, the assembled warriors dropped on their knees, and with hands uplifted and clasped, eyes raised to the sun,[1] in a deeply devout manner murmured their prayers to their deity; asking that the departed brother be taken into his bosom, and be happily revived in the heavenly hunting-grounds.

The Comanches believe that a dead warrior with his bow and arrows, sitting astride the horse at the foot of the tree in which his body rests, will ascend to the sun, bearing the provisions that have been placed under his head, which are thought to be sufficient to last him on his journey, where he is expected to find an abundance upon his arrival there. After the lapse of a century, he will return to his nation, with the same bow and arrows, riding the same horse! All men, women and children after death must return at the end of a hundred years of supreme hap-

---

[1] The sun is the god, or Great Spirit, of the Comanches.

piness in the sun, in order to keep up the population and power of the tribe.

The signals of savages by means of smoke are something wonderful; each particular kind having its special meaning. A sudden puff, rising into a graceful column, and almost as suddenly losing its identity, indicates the presence of a strange party in the vicinity; but if the columns are multiplied rapidly and repeatedly, they serve as a warning to show that the travelers are well armed and numerous. If a steady smoke is maintained for some time the object is to collect the warriors and the scattered bands of the savages at some designated point, prepared for hostilities. These signals are made in the same order at night, by means of fires, which, having been kindled, are either alternately exposed and shrouded from view, or suffered to burn steadily, as occasion may require.

The grass on the prairies, and especially along the banks of the streams, where it grows more rank, if pressed down during the dry season will retain its impress and grow daily more yellow, until the rains impart new life into it. The savages are so well versed in this style of signaling that they can tell by the appearance of the grass how many days have passed since it was trodden upon; whether the party were Indians or white men; about how many there were; and also of what particular tribe, if Indians, they were members.

To do this effectually they select some well-defined

footstep, for which they hunt with a marvelous avidity, and gently pressing down the grass so as not to disturb the surrounding herbage, they very carefully examine the imprint. The difference between the crushing heel of a white man's boot and the light imprint left by an Indian's moccasin is too striking to admit of a doubt; while the different styles of moccasins used by the various tribes are well known to all the others. The time which has elapsed since the party passed over the ground is determined by the discoloration, and by breaking off a few pieces of the grass. Numbers are arrived at by the multiplicity of tracks. Signaling by bent twigs, broken branches, and blazed trees, while traveling through the forest, is also common.

If a mounted party have been on the trail, their number, quality, and time of passing are determined with exactitude, as well as the precise sex and species of the animals ridden. The moment such a trail is discovered they follow it eagerly until some of the dung of the animals is found, which is immediately broken open, and from its condition of moisture and other properties the date of the passage of the party is arrived at with wonderful accuracy, as well as the region from which they came. This latter point is determined by the contents of the dung; whether of gramma-grass and other varieties which are grown only in certain parts of the country. When barley or corn is discovered, it is certain that whites have passed over the trail. Barley shows almost conclusively that they were Americans; if corn, they were Mexicans.

Signaling by stones is much more difficult to comprehend than any of the other methods, and few white men have ever reached a proficiency in this art. The celebrated Kit Carson was the most skillful, and, as is well known, no man had a keener insight into Indian methods than that famous frontiersman. The traveler is often surprised to find a lot of stones on the trail, apparently without observable arrangement. The only thing that attracts his attention is the utter absence of others anywhere in the immediate vicinity. He will know intuitively that they must have been placed there, and that is all. But they have a meaning according to whether they are laid in their original position, *i. e.,* with the same side toward the ground, or whether turned up, on edge, half turned over, etc.

In signaling they also make use of a piece of looking-glass, a kind of heliograph.[1]

The mirror also sometimes serves for another purpose: The warrior fastens a fragment of one to his shield, and is often able to dazzle the eyes of an enemy taking aim at him, thus causing his shot to miss.

The Indian would give a horse for a small mirror, but

---

[1] *Heliograph,* from the Greek *helios,* the sun, and *grapho,* I write. The modern heliograph, used by the United States Army for signaling on the plains and in the mountains, is a circular mirror, revolving on a horizontal axis, and is adjusted to the required angle of incidence with the sun by a telescopic rod, by which the rays can be directed to any point with accuracy. The dots and dashes of the Morse system of telegraphy are used in transmitting messages. Ever since the North-American Indian came in contact with the white man, and learned of reflecting surfaces, such as a looking-glass or bright metal, he has employed them in a crude sort of way as a means of signaling; but his usual method is by means of fire and smoke, his code being a marvel of savage ingenuity.

cares nothing for a valuable watch. This fact Summerfield soon discovered, for the chief took his watch and pocket-mirror, the latter with a grunt of evident satisfaction, but the watch Red Bear simply broke into pieces, which he gave to his favorite squaw to wear as ornaments.

"There goes my last Christmas present from my dear mother," said Summerfield, as Red Bear grabbed his watch; "but I suppose it would be of no use for me to protest," he continued, appealing to Pierre and the interpreter.

"Not a bit," replied the white captive. "He could raise your hair, if he wanted to; he could merely tell one of his braves to scalp you, and the red devil would do it with a grin of satisfaction. We had best take things as easy as we can, and trust to luck to get out of here one of these days."

By Christmas, after the boys had been with the tribe for nearly six months and had become quite proficient in the language, they were told that a party of warriors were going down into New Mexico to fight the Apaches, and that Red Bear wanted the white boys to go with them. He was to send five hundred of his best braves, who were to steal all the horses they could and bring back as many scalps as possible.

Pierre, Summerfield, Carlos and Burton talked the matter over at the first opportunity when they found themselves alone, and concluded that they dared not refuse to go with the party; that they rather liked the idea of such a trip,—it would be something to brag about when they got away from the savages: but they did not at all take to that part of the chief's program which included the murder of innocent people and wrenching off their hair.

In a few days, grand preparations were made for the raid. The best war-dresses of the warriors were brought out from their parfleche[1] boxes by the squaws, and cleaned up; the fastest ponies were selected from the immense herds of the tribe and brought closer in to the village; the shields and bows carefully inspected; many new arrows manufactured; and the squaws were kept busy until long into the night for several days, preparing the rations of dried buffalo-meat and other articles to eat. Every morning and afternoon, the warriors—particularly the younger ones, who were to make their first venture into battle, including the white boys—drilled constantly on the race-course.

At last everything was declared ready for the march, and early one morning, with the whole village out of the lodges to give them encouragement, the five hundred warriors in full war-paint and feathers, their long lances at poise, shields, bows and quivers of arrows in place, moved out, making the air hideous with their whoops and cries of defiance.

The party camped on some stream every night, and hunted buffalo on the way, in which the boys participated.

[1] *Parfleche* is the tanned hide of the buffalo.

Now that Summerfield and Burton had become experts in horseback riding, they killed just as many of the huge animals as either Pierre, Carlos, or any of the young " bucks."

It was a novel sight at night, just before the savages went to sleep, to see them get down on their knees facing toward where the sun had set, with their hands elevated and joined, and pray for the successful termination of the expedition,—lots of scalps of their enemies, and many horses. At sunrise the same ceremony was repeated, as is the daily custom of the Indians, both in their villages and in the field.

The party was absent from the village about two months, during which time it had many a skirmish with detached bands of Apaches, but always came out victorious. The warriors brought back with them six hundred ponies and fifty scalps, but lost seven of their own braves. Their dead bodies were transported on ponies for more than two hundred miles, until the boundaries of the Comanche nation were reached, and were there buried with all the ceremony described in a former paragraph.

The next morning after the arrival of the war party at the village, the warriors were ordered to assemble at the old chief's lodge, to make their report of the expedition to him, as required by the customs of the tribe.

Every warrior took his place in a circle in front of the entrance to the lodge of Red Bear, the old chief sitting in the doorway on a magnificently embroidered buffalo-robe,

—his son, the war-chief who had led the party on the raid, by his side. First, the medicine-pipe was lighted and passed from one to the other, and after a smoke,—which is always the preliminary to everything that a savage does,—in a very loud voice, so that all of his braves who had accompanied him could hear him, the events of the expedition to the minutest detail were narrated by the war-chief.

While he was talking, the most profound silence prevailed; and when he had concluded his narrative, he asked his warriors one by one if he had not told the story of their expedition correctly. These reports are usually very accurate, but if a mistake is made by the narrator, some of the warriors correct it. The war-chief was very profuse in his praises of the conduct of the white captives, particularly Burton, who had killed an Apache.

Many of the warriors were severely wounded during their battles. The majority of them, however, recovered very soon, by the careful nursing of the squaws; but three had been so terribly injured that between them the amputation of two legs and one arm was necessary. The wounded were returned to the village on buffalo-robes suspended between two ponies, forming a kind of litter, in common use among the tribes for transporting the sick and wounded in battle.

The amputation of the wounded limbs as witnessed by the white boys they described as barbarous in the extreme. The only instruments used were an old butcher-knife and a saw made from a piece of hoop-iron. The offensive members were cut off with the miserable knife, the bone severed with the improvised saw, and the stump seared with a hot iron, and then bound up with a poultice of bark,—which is always to be found in the villages and is carried on expeditions.

The savage who had to undergo the frightful operation was placed on the ground, and tightly held by another of his companions, while the victim held in his teeth a leaden bullet. Only a few slight groans were given, the poor man bearing up most manfully. Strange to say, all recovered from such savage surgical manipulations.

After the wounded had recovered, and the period of mourning for the dead had ended, a feast was given which continued uninterruptedly for fifteen days, in which horse-racing, foot-races and ball games were the principal amusements. The ball game among the Indians is very similar to a white boy's "shinny," and played with just such crooked sticks. The players are dressed with only a simple breechcloth and a pair of moccasins. Sides are chosen, and much in the shape of stakes is always put up on the result of the game.

The Comanches spoke the Spanish (or rather, the corrupted Mexican) with remarkable facility, and their frequent raids into New Mexico, with resultant successful plundering, had supplied them with many silver-mounted saddles, bridles, and spurs; and these were often of much intrinsic value. Consequently their ponies were gorgeously caparisoned, which was a surprise to the boys, until they learned from experience how the Indians got them, and were themselves possessed of some by the same means.

The arms of the Comanches for many years were confined to the primitive bow and arrows, but at thirty yards they could discharge them as rapidly, or even more rapidly in the hands of an expert warrior, than the repeating rifles of to-day. The boys' rifles were a new sensation to the old chief. Of course he had seen many of the trappers' guns, muzzle-loading and flint-lock, but those of the boys, especially Summerfield's and Burton's, were the then new Spencer breech-loading arm, and the warriors were surprised at their rapidity and accuracy in firing them. In a short time all the Indians of the Plains were well armed with the most improved weapons, by the munificence of the Government.

The village moved in the fall to the region of the foothills of the Rocky Mountains to gather wild gooseberries, cherries, and the nuts of the piñon. The operation of transporting the equipage and lodge goods of the savages was conducted entirely by the squaws. A long pole was strapped to each side of a pony, called a *travois* by the old French-Canadian trappers, with a platform fashioned on the parts dragging behind the animal, on which the tepees and very little children were carried. Many of the dogs, of which there are always hundreds in an Indian village, were made to do duty when moving. Small *travois* were constructed for them exactly like those for the larger animals; and everything not transported on these *travois* was carried by the women.

In packing the dogs, it is amusing to see the trouble that sometimes ensues, for many of the little brutes will not submit to the treatment of being made beasts of burden, and also worry those that are willing. Consequently, fights are of common occurrence, often including the squaws, who take sides with their respective dogs, and a general free-for-all scrabble is the result.

The warriors ride on the flanks of the moving band, leaving everything for the women to do, and always seem to take great delight in these fights between the dogs and their owners. Sometimes more than twenty thousand ponies, dogs, women, and children, together with the warriors, constituted the population of one of the Comanche villages in the past.

Arriving at their destination, after a temporary camp was selected by the chief the lodges were erected, which required the whole of the first day, and the next morning all the women started out to gather piñons and acorns.

The nut of the piñon tree is about half the size of a chestnut, and is used very extensively as an article of food both by the poorer classes of Mexicans and the Indians. It grows in a cone which contains twenty-five or thirty of the nuts, and is quite oily. The nuts are prepared for winter eating by covering over great piles of the cones with earth and then setting the heap on fire. This is allowed only to smoulder, in order to bake and soften the shells. When the cones are reduced nearly to charcoal, the nut and its kernel may easily be taken out.

Acorns are pounded into meal by a stone pestle, and are then boiled with corn mush. The squaws also gather immense quantities of wild currants, gooseberries, plums, and choke-cherries; but the choke-cherries of the mountains are entirely different from those found in the East. All of these fruits are dried for winter use, and, when the year is a prolific one for them, form a good portion of the savages' rations.

Before they started for the mountains, Carlos often said that he wished he had his dog Cyrus with him, if for only a single night; for, as he told the other boys, he would write a note, tie it to his neck, and tell him to take it home,—which he certainly would do, even though the distance were a hundred miles.

"It is not more than seventy in a straight line," said Pierre; "but there—we have n't got any Cyrus!"

"I wonder," said Summerfield, "whether your folks have ever attempted to find out where we are?"

"I know they have," said Carlos; "and they will keep on trying to find us until they do."

"Well, we 've got to wait our time," said Burton, "and if it were not for the worry and trouble I 'm giving my father and mother, and losing my chance at college, I 'd like to stay with the Indians a whole year. I like this wild life. Red Bear has treated us very nicely, and all the boys seem to be our friends. We might have fared much worse, if we had fallen in with any other chief."

This conversation was carried on while they were traveling to the new camp at the foot of the mountains. They had never given up the idea that soon they would be rescued by the Government, or that some trader would come down to the village and find out they were there.

They did not know, however, that several traders had been to the village while they were there, but the wily old chief had sent them out of the way on some sort of a mission, either herding the ponies at a great distance from the village, or hunting the buffalo with a party of warriors. The chief always knew when strangers were approaching his little kingdom, for the savages keep up a system of espionage through the medium of a well-trained corps of " runners," who give any information by signals of smoke or fire as already described.

Red Bear expected, when the proper time arrived, to receive a ransom from the Government, either in the form of money or goods, and for that reason was very good to his young captives.

The temporary camp in the mountains was located on the Rio Corralitos, in Old Mexico, and the slopes of the mountains were covered with the piñon, the stream abounded in fish, and wild berries grew in profusion.

During the stay of the savages in the (for them) charming region, there were no raids made upon the inoffensive Mexicans. The presence of the warriors was necessary

BRUIN IS CAUGHT ON A LEDGE.

to protect the women in their duties of gathering the winter supply of food; so the men idled away their time in smoking, gambling, and sleeping.

This leisure gave the boys, both red and white, lots of time to themselves, and they improved it by indulging in all sorts of amusements: fishing, swimming, hunting, shooting at a mark, playing ball, and everything else that the place and the time offered. They had many adventures while wandering through the somber mountains with their dogs, for as stated, the village was overrun with as motley a gathering of canines as it is possible to conceive of. There were none of them thoroughbreds, like Cyrus, Jupe and the others at the ranch on the Arkansas, for their pointed ears showed very plainly their close affinity to the wolves, with which they often affiliated.

The mountains were inhabited by various animals, especially the so-called California lion; and it was while living in the temporary camp of the Comanches that Summerfield, Burton, Pierre and Carlos made their first acquaintance with the ferocious beast, in which one of the largest and best of the Indian dogs lost his life.

The boys with half a dozen of their dusky companions were roaming through the hills one morning, and had gotten about five miles from the camp, when they suddenly came upon a lion, or cougar, that was sleeping in the underbrush, after partly devouring a deer which he had killed, portions of which were lying near the beast.

—14

The lion was evidently very sluggish, for even the noise the boys made did not awaken him as they walked by his retreat; but one of the dogs ferreted him out of his lair, and the now astonished brute attempted to escape by climbing a pine tree near by. Before he could effect it, however, one of the dogs caught him by the leg, and both lion and dog rolled over on the ground, biting and tearing each other terribly in the conflict. At last, by a supreme effort on the part of the lion, the poor dog's side was ripped wide open by the sharp claws of the lion's hind feet, just as one, of the Indian boys fired a sharp-pointed arrow into the brute, which made him let go his hold on the poor animal.

The dog was too far gone when the boys came up to him, and he lived only a few moments. He was one of the best of all in the camp, and was called " White Swan " by the tribe. The young savages were almost inconsolable over the loss of " White Swan," but swiftly revenged his death by pouring a shower of arrows into the lion, in which the white boys assisted, and the brute died in a few seconds after he was completely riddled by the swiftly fired savage weapons.

The young Indians soon skinned him, intending to take his hide back to camp to show their prowess in killing such a formidable beast.

On their way back, they came upon the fresh trail of a bear, and all determined to hunt him up and kill him too. They tracked him to a ledge of rocks, on a projecting shelf of which he was taking his morning siesta, probably having gorged himself upon some animal he had caught on his predatory tour, the tracks of which the boys had come across.

Bruin was perched pretty high up on the ledge, and above him it was almost perpendicular, so that the only way for him to get down from the shelf was by the same trail he had gone up, and that led directly to where the boys were standing ready to give him a bloody reception.

The bear woke up, and eyeing his enemies for a few seconds, gave a low growl, and looked above him to discover some means of escape that way; but he saw it was impossible, so stood at bay, snarling, snorting, and showing his teeth.

Fortunately for the boys, perhaps, the animal was only a common black bear, for if he had been a cinnamon or a grizzly, their chances of killing him without losing one or more of their own party, or at least getting badly wounded, would have been very slim; but the black bear is not a very ferocious animal, unless when a she one has her cubs with her.

The bear evidently understood his awkward position, and the dilemma he was in, for he cried like a baby as he looked down upon his enemies.

It was a comical sight to the white boys, and they could not restrain their laughter at the hopeless-looking expression of the bear's face, as he seemed to realize perfectly that he was " a gone goose."

Presently, the Indians could stand the inaction of both themselves and Bruin no longer, so they drew up their bows and poured a shower of arrows at him, nearly all of which, owing to the shortness of the range,—for the bear was not more than thirty feet from the group of boys that were firing at him,—took effect, but none of them happened to hit a vital part until fifty of the feathered missiles had been poured into him, when, by a lucky venture of Carlos', an arrow pierced the beast's heart, and he tumbled off the shelf right at the feet of the delighted boys.

He had a beautiful robe, for he was very fat, and the work of skinning him occupied but a few moments. Then the two hides, one that of the lion and the other that of the bear, were rolled up, and transported on a pole borne on the shoulders of two boys, who took "turns about" in carrying them until they arrived at camp.

The tribe remained at the camp for more than two months, until all the nuts, fruit and other things the women had come after were exhausted, and then preparations were at once made to return to their old permanent ground south of Hackberry creek in the Indian Territory. All was confusion again,—the same general fights between the dogs and the squaws taking place, that had characterized their start from the village; but the animals were more heavily weighted than before with the vast accumulation of food the women had gathered at the foot of the mountains.

The tribe were many days on the road, and coming

across several vast herds of buffalo, some time was occupied in killing them; and as the tribe had hundreds of extra ponies with them, they could easily transport thousands of pounds of the meat.

When the tribe reached Little Red river, they found the prairie adjoining that stream's high banks literally black with the coveted animals. At a point near where they pitched camp one afternoon, there was a high precipice, at least five hundred feet from its brink to the margin of the water. Here they succeeded in surrounding a large herd of buffalo, in which all the warriors and the young men assisted, and stampeding them, the huge animals rushed over the embankment and were precipitated on the rocks below, hundreds being killed by the awful fall. All hands then went to work skinning. The squaws cut the meat into strips, salted it with salt gathered from the saline springs which abound in that region, dried it in a sort of twist, with a streak of fat and lean together, and put it into bales for packing. It took them all the next day to properly prepare what they had killed in that one lucky venture of the precipice, and they started on their way the next morning rejoicing at their unusual good fortune.

When the tribe arrived at the old ground and the lodges were erected and the village looked as it did before their migration to the mountains, a great feast and dance was given, in honor of their good luck.

The lost trapper boys and their companions were now

entering upon their second year with the Comanches.
Winter was rapidly approaching, though the name of the
month alone betrayed it, for the weather was delightful.
The only change observable to the young Bostonians, who
were used to cold, snow and fogs in their harsh New England climate, was that the trees had donned their autumn
dress of russet, and many varieties of birds with which
they had become familiar during the summer, now no
longer were to be seen, having departed on their migration
southward. The grass on the prairies was brown, the
woods rustled at every breath of the wind as their leaves,
dry and crisp, fell in showers to the earth. The notes of
the cranes high in midair were no longer heard, the pleasant " Bob-White " of the quail taking their place, or the
sharp whirr of the prairie-grouse as they took to the shelter
of the timber, their usual winter quarters.

With a general dullness in the character of the village
incident to the close of the busy season, the boys began
to long for those things which civilization brings: the
festivities of the Christmas season, and the conventionalities of the New Year. So, for the first time since they
were captured by the Indians, did the time hang heavy
on their hands.

They had become sufficiently conversant with the language of the Comanches to understand what were the most
frequent topics upon which the savages talked. They
heard of the meeting of the Peace Commission, and noted
the mutterings of disappointment at the failure of the

Government to ratify the stipulations of the treaty made at Medicine Lodge. Also, they learned shortly after their return from the Rio Corralitos, that it was the intention of Red Bear to remove the village to the Wichita Mountains, so as to be farther from the region of country occupied by the whites, as a general war was to be inaugurated by all the tribes.

The boys were much disappointed when they heard the decision of the old chief, for they thought the chances of their getting away from their captors considerably lessened if they went so far to the south.

By the last of November the new village was firmly established at the foot of the range known as the Wichita Mountains, though it is a misnomer to call them such. They are, in fact, but an aggregation of isolated peaks standing on a level prairie, principally composed of granite in various shades of color, green predominating. They are much broken up on their sides, and from the base of nearly every one of them a cold spring of water gushes. The region is well timbered, and is the home of innumerable songsters; the mocking-bird, one of America's sweetest warblers, and the thrush prevailing.

It was a favorite winter residence of the tribes that were friendly with each other, as the climate was all that could be desired, mild in the extreme, and the skies of a deep blue, rivaling the sapphire.

The boys were pleased with the change of location: it was more picturesque than the region of the old village, but the enchantment was dispelled when they considered how much farther off were those whom they loved and longed to see again.

The tribe was kept posted by a corps of runners, who from day to day reported to Red Bear all that took place; and of course the boys, through their young Indian companions, were kept informed.

They heard of massacres having been committed by the Cheyennes upon the Smoky Hill river, and that a general war was imminent. They saw, too, many of the most noted warriors of the tribe depart from the village and not return. These they were told had gone to join the allied forces in the field; and they began to think whether their own lives were any longer safe in the village. Although no difference was apparent in the conduct of the savages toward them, they instinctively believed it would be better to make their escape, if possible; and the sooner they could effect it, the better.

CHAPTER XI.

TEN days had elapsed at the ranch on the Arkansas, since the departure of the Delahoyde boys and their young guests on their buffalo hunt far south of the river. Then their non-arrival home began to give the parents of Pierre and Carlos some uneasiness, but they did not worry a great deal, until the evening of the eleventh day, the last moment it was probable they would remain away, and still no signs of the absent ones.

The Mexican cook came up to the dugout and expressed his surprise at the delay of the return of his employers. He told Mr. Delahoyde they had ever been very prompt in their dealings with him; he had never known them to break an engagement, or remain beyond the appointed time.

Mr. Delahoyde told him that he and his wife were much worried, and that if they did not make their appearance that evening (it was then about four o'clock), he intended to go and search for some sign of them, and would like to have him go along.

The Mexican said he would gladly go, and it was agreed that they should start at daylight in the morning. Mr. Delahoyde suggested that they ride the two animals of the Bostonians, as his own ponies were far out on the prairie, and he could not get them up in time to start at the appointed hour unless he went after them that evening. For this he really had not the time, as he must fix things so as to leave his wife without too much to attend to during their absence, for he did not know how long they might be gone,— intending to follow their trail as far as possible.

Mr. Delahoyde immediately went to work and put his stock into the big corral, so that his wife would only have to throw a little hay in to them occasionally; and as the spring was inside of the inclosure, she would have no trouble in caring for them.

The next morning at daybreak the Mexican made his appearance at the dugout with two of the young men's horses saddled. As both he and Mr. Delahoyde had already breakfasted, they started down the river on the trail to the Fort Sill ford, taking their rifles with them and a supply of dried meat.

Arriving there about noon, they saw the evidences of the boys having camped at the spring, and here they halted for an hour to eat their lunch and give their animals an opportunity to graze.

By two o'clock they were in the saddle again, following the trail south to the Canadian, and reaching that stream about dark, discovered where the boys had rested and eaten a turkey, for the feathers of the bird were lying upon the ground near their little fire by which they had cooked it.

Mr. Delahoyde and the Mexican stayed on the Canadian that night, and started out again early the next morning, still following the trail of the boys southward.

The first sign they discovered that the boys had killed any of the great animals was beyond Hackberry creek. The remains of the tough old bull, which Pierre and Carlos had rejected, were right on the trail. It was nearly devoured by the wolves, but by the freshness of the bones they knew it had been lately killed, and as no buffalo-hunters had been in the country for many weeks, they were certain that the old bull had been killed by the boys.

Owing to the multiplicity of tracks of both ponies and buffalo, caused by the boys chasing the latter over a wide area, and the preponderance of the tracks of the split hoofs of the buffalo, it was impossible to trail the boys any farther, and the search had to be abandoned. That any of them had been injured in the chase, seemed not at all likely, for certainly all of them could not have been disabled; some of them would have returned to the ranch and reported the fact if any mishap had occurred: so that theory was not entertained for a moment.

Reluctantly Mr. Delahoyde returned to his home, almost heart-broken at the disappearance of his two bright boys. To his wife he said that he did not believe they had been killed; the worst he conjectured was they had fallen in with some stray band of Indians and been captured; but as the several tribes were at peace with the Government, he did not think they would be harmed; only held for ransom, which although a mere theory, gave some comfort to the mother of Pierre and Carlos.

The shadow of profound grief brooded over the once pleasant home on the Arkansas, and until Curtis, the Indian trader, returned from Fort Harker, nothing could be done in furtherance of the quest of the lost boys; for Mr. Delahoyde could not leave his good wife alone in the isolated dugout, to himself go to the fort and report to the commanding officer there the disappearance of the young Bostonians and his own sons.

Ten more days of gloom shrouded the home in the valley of the Arkansas, when one evening just at sundown the long-looked-for Curtis drove up to the ranch. He was immediately informed of the absence of his charge, and at once he and Mr. Delahoyde began to formulate plans to find out what had become of the missing youths.

Curtis said that although the Indians were apparently inclined to be friendly, there was a spirit of unrest among them. The constant encroachment of the whites upon their hunting-grounds, and the advent of the railroad, which now had penetrated many miles into the interior, bringing with it a horde of settlers greedy for the public land, he feared would cause trouble soon, and that a bloody war would be inaugurated.

He said that he did not think the boys were in any immediate danger, for of late years most of the tribes had changed their tactics in relation to their captives: they treated them fairly well, in hope of receiving a ransom for them from the Government.

It was agreed that Curtis should return immediately to Fort Harker and acquaint the officers stationed there of the circumstances concerning the absence of the boys, and get their opinion as to the best means to be employed to find out whether they were with any of the tribes.

Curtis started back to the fort early the next morning, on horseback, leaving his teams and goods with Mr. Delahoyde, saying he would return in about four days.

The period of his absence was a time of suspense and agony to both Mr. Delahoyde and the anxious wife. They both mourned over their ill-fortune, sometimes despairing of ever seeing their boys again, then brightening up as some new theory would be advanced by either one of them.

Promptly on the evening of the fourth day after his departure from the ranch, Curtis made his appearance. He reported that it was the opinion of the commanding officer at Fort Harker that the boys had fallen in with some band of Indians, and were now with them up in the mountains, as at this time of the year they generally migrated there to gather nuts and berries for their winter's supply, and would not return to their permanent villages until November. Nothing could be done in the way of sending out scouts to learn whether there were any white captives among them, as it was not known at what point in the mountains the savages had gone. He told Mr. and Mrs. Delahoyde that the officers at the post all agreed that their sons were in no immediate danger, for if they were held by the Indians they would not injure them, as there was a sort of peace existing between all the tribes and the Government; but that the Indians were dissatisfied with the appearance of so many whites on their hunting-grounds, and that the Government had appointed a Commission to treat with them, and find out, if possible, what the cause of their grievance was. Congress had appropriated a very large sum to meet the expenses of the Commission, and it was to convene in August on Medicine Lodge creek, in Barber county, Kansas. All the famous generals of the United States Army, and several Senators, composed the Commission, and it was to be fitted out and start from Fort Harker, on the Smoky Hill, which point the Union Pacific Railroad had now reached.

The principal chiefs of all the Plains tribes, the Cheyennes, Kiowas, Arapahoes and Comanches, had promised to be present at the council and have a talk with the representatives of the "Great Father" at Washington.

"The Council won't meet, then, for two months yet?" said Mr. Delahoyde.

"No," replied Curtis; "this is only the last of June, and I suppose the Commission will not get ready until the last of August. You know how slowly these Government bodies always move!

"The commanding officer at Fort Harker thinks that I would better go on down to the Cheyenne village in the Wichita Mountains, and find out from any old Indians who may have stayed there while the rest of the tribe are away, whether their friends the Comanches had any captives among them. You know that the Cheyennes and Comanches are never hostile with each other, and are always well acquainted with the doings of their different bands."

"I think that you are correct," said Mr. Delahoyde. "I suppose you are ready to leave here by to-morrow morning?"

"Yes, I have a load of goods for the Cheyennes, and will start at daylight."

The trader left the ranch early the next morning, taking the Mexican with him, who, having nothing to do, was anxious for a job, and gladly accepted the offer to drive the team.

Curtis was gone about ten days, when he returned to the ranch and reported that there were four boys who had run into the Comanche camp one night, and that they were now with the tribe in the mountains of Old Mexico.

They were all right, said Curtis; had been treated just as if they were of the tribe, and had been adopted by it.

This was good news to the lonely family at the ranch, and their worry over the possible death of their sons ceased, now they were assured of their safety.

The days dragged along very slowly until August came, when the Delahoydes heard that the Commission had left Fort Harker, escorted by cavalry, the famous regiment commanded by the intrepid General Custer.

Red Bear was too old to attend the council in person, so he sent his son to represent him, who was told by his father to say nothing of the presence of the white captives in their village, as the old man had become attached to the boys and did not want to part with them.

This may seem strange to the uninitiated in Indian character; but they are possessed of strong likes and dislikes—so it was not derogatory to their vagaries that he should become attached to his young captives, and did not want to give them up.

The meeting of the famous chiefs at Medicine Lodge creek was one of the most important that has ever occurred in the history of Indian treaties.

There were about six thousand members of the four tribes assembled there, and some of the greatest soldiers the United States has furnished. General Sherman, then General of the Army, Generals Harney, Terry, Marcy,

Auger, Gibbs, and others of lesser fame, together with Senator John B. Henderson, of Missouri, and other prominent civilians in the public service, composed the representatives of the Government. This body is known to history as "The Peace Commission," whose duty it was to learn from the Indians themselves the cause of their grievances, and make such a treaty with them as would forever put an end to the continuous hostilities which year after year devastated the frontier.

An agreement was entered into, after much parleying, which came near ending in a row; and there would have been another massacre if it had not been for the excellent disposition which had been made of the troops, which completely surrounded the Indians, who outnumbered the soldiers by many hundreds, and who foresaw nothing but a terrible slaughter of their warriors if they took the initiative.

The treaty was signed, as they always are, by each chief touching the pen, (some of them were mounted and riding furiously around,) while a clerk handed it to him, the ignorant savage having no more idea what he was subscribing to than if it had been a Greek manuscript.

Congress failed to make any appropriation to carry into effect the stipulations of the treaty, and after waiting patiently for nearly nine months for the Government to fulfill its pledges, the Indians became disgusted at the broken faith, allied themselves for one grand demonstration, and commenced a series of raids along the border, extending from the Nebraska line to the northern confines of Texas.

Then the Government sent General Sheridan to commence an active campaign against the allied tribes. He took the field in person, and inaugurated his memorable winter march, with such lieutenants as Generals Custer and Sully. In seven months the savages were completely vanquished, and a peace was brought about that has never been broken on the Central Plains.

The first battle occurred in September, 1868, on the Arrickaree Fork of the Republican river, just over the Nebraska line north of Kansas, when General Forsyth, of the commanding general's staff, with fifty-two picked men, all civilians, held at bay for over a week more than eight hundred of the savages, who were at last compelled to retreat. It was one of the most terribly unequal battles in all the history of our Indian wars.[1]

At the commencement of hostilities all the settlers, scattered at varying distances on the river and creeks, were compelled to abandon their claims and seek the protection of the military at the several posts. The Delahoydes left their beautifully timbered home and went to Fort Harker, which was then the largest military post near to them. The cattle, ponies, and the many pets of Carl and Pierre were also taken there, and excited considerable wonder

---

[1] For a detailed description of this fight, see "Tales of the Trail," Crane & Co., Topeka, Kansas.

among the children of the officers, and of course were kindly cared for by the boys and girls, under whose charge they were placed.

In October following the battle on the Arrickaree Fork of the Republican, General Sheridan changed his headquarters from Fort Hays, on the railroad, to Fort Dodge, on the Arkansas, where were to be concentrated the troops for active service in the field against the allied tribes, as he had determined to strike a blow at those savages in their winter quarters; something which had never before been attempted in all our wars with the Plains Indians.

The expedition intended to operate south of the Arkansas—one of the favorite haunts of the Indians—was comprised of the larger portion of the famous Seventh United States Cavalry,[1] General Custer's regiment, and some companies of the Third Infantry. It had early in September already crossed the Arkansas, under command of General Alfred Sully, whose reputation as an Indian fighter, during the celebrated Sioux campaign of 1864, placed him at the head of the list.

When General Sully's command reached the Cimarron it encountered the savages, who fought him all day, but at night, as is usual, suspended hostilities,—for they seldom attack after dark.

The next morning, as his command got strung out, a

---

[1] *Seventh Cavalry*, the famous regiment commanded by the lamented Custer, and which has fought more battles with the Indians than any other in the service. It was nearly annihilated by Sitting Bull, the great Sioux warrior, at the battle of the Little Big Horn (sometimes called the Rosebud), where Custer lost his life.

band of two or three hundreds warriors dashed at the rear of the column, and succeeded in cutting off a few led horses and two of the troopers who had lingered behind. The rear guard, commanded that day by Captain Louis McLane Hamilton,[1] of the cavalry, immediately wheeled his troops about and prepared to charge the savages, who were about to carry off the two captured troopers. The savages, who were within pistol-range, were gallantly charged, and obliged to give up one of their prisoners, but in abandoning him, cruelly shot him through the body and left him on the trail, supposed to be mortally wounded, while they succeeded in escaping with the other unfortunate trooper.[2]

As the command moved along, the Indians harassed it at every step, and at about three o'clock in the afternoon a general engagement took place with the allied Cheyennes, Arapahoes, and Kiowas, resulting in the retreat of the troops toward Fort Dodge, which they reached the next day, after almost continuous fighting, and having exhausted their ammunition. Luckily, the savages abandoned the conflict, satisfied with driving the troops away from the vicinity of their villages.

Effective measures were at once decided upon. It was determined to establish a temporary base of supplies at

---

[1] A grandson of Alexander Hamilton.

[2] The poor fellow was tortured to death, as was related by the Indians themselves after the war had ended. He was tied to a stake, strips of flesh cut from his body, arms and legs, burning brands thrust into the bleeding wounds, the nose, lips and ears cut off, and finally, when from loss of blood and terrible pain, he fell to the ground, the younger savages were allowed to rush upon him and dispatch him with their knives.

some point yet to be chosen, about a hundred miles south of Fort Dodge, from which place forage and rations for the troops operating against the savages could be drawn.

On the 12th of November all was ready for a grand movement, and an immense train of four hundred army wagons, loaded with forage for the cavalry horses and rations for the troops, started from Fort Dodge, escorted by a few companies of infantry, who were to guard it and become the garrison of the cantonment[1] to be selected. They crossed the Arkansas at Mulberry creek, twelve miles below the fort, and, camping there that night, the next morning began their march to the Indian Territory.

On the afternoon of the sixth day after leaving the Arkansas, the command arrived at the junction of the Beaver and Wolf rivers, those streams forming the North Fork of the Canadian, where it was determined to locate the base of operations, and to which was given the name of Camp Supply.

Two or three days after the arrival of the troops at Camp Supply, General Sheridan made his appearance, and immediately relieved General Sully from command of the forces, placing General Custer at their head, who was at once ordered to prepare for an aggressive campaign against the hostile savages.

As many of the best wagons and teams as were considered necessary for the impending expedition were selected

---

[1] *Cantonment:* Literally, a canton, or district where soldiers are quartered. In common military parlance now, temporary rude shelters, in the field or elsewhere.

from the immense train, and rations and forage to last thirty days were loaded into them. The Seventh Cavalry, Custer's own regiment, comprising eleven companies, aggregating about nine hundred men, now awaited orders for their search of the whereabouts of the Indian villages.

On the 22d of the month, General Sheridan issued orders for the command of General Custer to move out at daylight next morning. That evening a terrible storm of snow, sleet and hail commenced,—one of the worst ever known in that region; and when the morning broke, although the storm had abated, the ground was covered with snow to the depth of a foot, and snow was still falling.

It was scarcely daylight when the several troop commanders reported to General Custer that they were ready to move. "Boots and saddles"[1] was quickly sounded. Then, as every man had fixed his trappings, "To horse!" woke the silence of the somber camp, and after the usual commands, "Prepare to mount," and "Mount," were given, each trooper sprang into his seat, the "Advance" was blown by the orderly trumpeter, and with the band at the head of the column, just as it struck up "The Girl I Left Behind Me" the troops moved out in the snow and wind.

Not a man of the whole of the large command had ever before been in that part of the country, excepting the Osage Indian guides, Little Beaver and Hard Rope, and even they stated that they could not tell anything about

---

[1] "*Boots and saddles*," a bugle-call to prepare for the march, in the cavalry service.

which way to travel until the snow stopped falling and they were able to see the landmarks with which they were familiar. Thus, progress was very slow, handicapped as the command was by the condition of the atmosphere; nor could it camp that night where originally intended, on account of the inability of the guides to tell where they were.

They marched on through the storm until about two o'clock, when a place was selected on Wolf creek at which to remain until morning; although the snow continued to fall, with little prospect of its stopping. Fortunately, there was an abundance of timber on the stream, but it was very difficult to procure, on account of the depth of the snow. However, fires were soon kindled, and the warmth of their blaze had the effect of putting every one in good-humor, and when the supper was ready contentment pervaded the camp.

Morning came with a clear sky, but as the snow had continued to fall during most of the night, the earth was now covered to the depth of a foot and a half, and the march that day was a wearisome one; but when camp was reached at night, the same difficulties had to be contended with, excepting that the storm was no longer a disturbing element.

Out on the route early on the morning of the third day from Camp Supply, nothing of any particular importance occurred, and the command plodded wearily along, and encamped in the same valley that night.

The next morning, after ascending a high divide for some hours, the descent began, and the Indian guides said that the valley the command was to enter was that of the Canadian; and upon its bank camp was made that night.

In the morning the river was crossed with some difficulty, on account of the rapidity of the current and the great masses of floating ice with which it was burdened.

It was firmly believed that the villages of the hostile savages were located somewhere south of the Canadian, and every one was on the alert, particularly the Osage guides, to discover a trail leading from the river to them. At last it was found, about twelve miles up the stream, and preparations were made to follow it.

The wagon train was to be left in charge of a detail, and only such supplies as could be taken by the men strapped to their saddles were allowed. One hundred rounds of ammunition were allotted to each trooper, a little ground coffee and hard bread, together with a small amount of forage for his horse.

The route carried the anxious troopers through the snow, which was over a foot deep, and the ground very rough, which made it terribly bad for the horses to get along; and it was nine o'clock at night before the command halted for rest and to feed their tired animals.

It was at first proposed to continue the pursuit of the trail by the light of the moon, but Little Beaver, the chief of the Osages, strongly advised against it; he gave no valid reason for his objection, however, and the order was given. So at ten o'clock the men were all in their saddles, and silently the column stretched out,—not a word allowed to be spoken or a bugle-note to be sounded, for it was not known how near the savages might be.

The Osage scouts, famous trailers, led out, with whom General Custer rode, the cavalry following in the rear at a distance of a quarter of a mile. This was the disposition of the command, for the reason that the snow was crusty, and the tread of so many horses breaking through it would make too much noise, that might be heard a long way off.

At last one of the guides stopped, and when General Custer asked him what was the matter, he replied that he smelt fire. He was then told to proceed again, but to be very wary; and when he again halted and the General came up to him the second time, he said, "Me told you so!" and looking in the direction indicated by the Indian, the almost extinguished embers of a fire could be seen, just on the edge of the timber not a hundred yards away. That it had been built by an Indian was beyond the possibility of a doubt; and to make sure that the savages had been there, and how many of them there were, the General ordered the scouts to dismount, and, with their rifles ready for use at an instant's warning, to proceed cautiously to where the still-glowing coals could be seen, and investigate.

Anxious moments passed while the Indian scouts were gone on their mission. When they returned they reported that the fire had been deserted, but that from the great number of pony-tracks in the vicinity it must have been kindled by herders, and that it was their feeding-ground on which the fire had been made.

From these facts, which were not to be disputed, it was believed that the command were not more than a mile or two from the main village; so the utmost caution was now necessary, in order to surprise the savages in their lodges. The Indian scouts were then ordered to go on, and accompanied by the General they stole silently up a little divide. As they neared its crest, one of them went ahead (as was always their custom), and looked over into a little valley below.

After listening intently for a few moments, as he peered into the darkness, he turned to Custer and said in a whisper, " Heap Injuns down there! "

The General vainly gazed to where the scout had pointed, and then inquired of him why he thought there were Indians over there.

" Me hear dog bark! " was the reply.

That was very satisfactory to General Custer; because if the Osage really had heard the dogs bark, it was an assurance that a village was close at hand, for the savages never take their dogs with them on a raid, while their villages are infested with them.

Listening again, the General was himself rewarded by distinctly hearing the growling and snapping of dogs away off in the heavy timber, and very shortly after, the faint tinkling of a bell was wafted to his ears on the still, wintry air, which indicated that a herd of ponies was near. Then another unmistakable sound came—that of an infant (for of course Indian babies cry as do those of the white race). And now, doubly assured that an Indian village lay below him, he returned to the main body of the scouts and Osages, and by one of them was sent a message to the troops, ordering the most perfect silence on their part, and directing every officer to hasten and report to him.

When the officers had all noiselessly arrived at the point where their commander stood, he told them what he had seen and heard, that they might personally know the exact location of the village and the character of the ground their troopers would have to charge over in making the proposed attack. Sabres were then taken off, gently laid on the snow, and with the General his officers carefully crawled to the summit of the crest, to there obtain a view of the valley below.

In suppressed conversation, so as to prevent a sound reaching the unsuspecting savages, the General made his plans and assigned to each troop-commander just what he was to do. The idea was to completely surround the village, and at daybreak, or as soon as it should become light enough to see, to charge in upon the Indians from every side.

It was intensely cold as the morning approached, but fires were an impossibility, and for four terrible hours the shivering troops had to wait for the dawn which would enable them to see where to go. Stamping their feet to excite the blood, and thus put some warmth in them, was forbidden, and there was nothing to do but stand and suffer. During all those fearfully long hours, every man stood at his horse's head, bridle-reins in hand, anxious for light and to be away from such dismal surroundings.

The first streaks of the coming day at least began to light up the eastern horizon, and all were to prepare for the advance. Although the air was freezing, overcoats, haversacks, and all other things which might interfere with their quick movements, were ordered removed,—and especially were the men forbidden to fire a shot until the signal to attack was sounded.

The plan of operations for the command, as it was now formed, was for each squadron in its assigned place to get as close to the village as possible without being discovered, and at daylight the band to play at the instant the charge was to be made.

The command approached so near the lodges that Custer really feared he had been discovered, and that they had all been deserted some time before; but noticing smoke issuing from some of them, he was satisfied the village was still inhabited.

The General was in the lead, as ever, while immediately in the rear of his horse came the band, all mounted, each musician with his instrument glued to his lips, waiting for the signal. The leader had been told before, that when they struck up, the tune should be " Garry Owen," as an initial piece. At the moment when Custer was about to give the signal for the attack to begin, a single shot from a rifle rang out clearly on the crisp morning air, and suddenly turning to the band-leader, the General ordered him to strike up. At once the long-familiar tune to the troopers of the regiment sounded forth through the timbered valley, and the cheers of the men as they recognized the rollicking, fighting air, were reëchoed from the squadrons on the opposite side; and while the trumpets blew the charge, quickly the impatient soldiers dashed right into the sleeping village. It was like a thunderbolt from a cloudless sky. Caught napping, the savages came rushing out from their lodges as the gallant Seventh Cavalry struck them. The Indians soon rallied from their surprise, however, and in a few moments, from behind trees and from the banks of the creek, they began a vigorous defense of their homes and little ones.

It was the humane intention of General Custer to fight only those who were classed as the warriors of the tribe; but when the little boys, often not more than from seven to ten years old, expert in the use of the bow and arrow as well as of the more murderous revolver, began getting in their work on the soldiers, it became necessary as a measure of self-defense to get them out of the way as well as the older men. The gallant Colonel Benteen, than whom a better or braver soldier never drew saber, had to kill a mere lad of fifteen, who persistently, in spite of all the efforts of the Colonel to save the boy's life by taking him prisoner, fired shot after shot from his revolver at the Colonel's head, and who would not listen for a moment to peace overtures and be saved. He had fired several times at the Colonel, always missing him; but at last a bullet went through his horse's neck and another in a very uncomfortable proximity to his own head. He now made another effort to induce the plucky redskin to surrender, to which he paid no attention, but aimed his revolver for a fourth or fifth shot. Then, with deep regret for the necessity of his action, the Colonel dispatched him.

The center of the village was soon gained by the troopers, and a terrible hand-to-hand fight took place, as they found it impossible to dislodge the infuriated warriors from their places of refuge behind the trees and the bank of the creek, which they were utilizing as a sort of rifle-pit. So every man fought for himself, observing the same tactics as the savages, taking advantage of the shelter the trees afforded, where by their superior aim they effected the dislodgment of their enemies.

An incident occurred during the fight which is an exponent of the savage instincts of the Indian race. A squad of troopers came upon a squaw who was endeavoring to get away, leading a little white boy, a captive of the tribe, taken by the warriors during some recent raid on the settlements. When the woman saw that she was about to be surrounded and that escape was impossible, she drew from beneath her blanket a big knife and plunged it into the almost naked body of the hapless child. The men could not resist their own savage impulse on such an exposition of devilishness, and in an instant the fiendish act was punished by a volley of bullets fired into the body of the squaw, and she died instantly.

The warriors fought with a desperation worthy the cause for which they struggled—the defense of their homes and all that was dear to them. At one point, in a natural depression in the earth, seventeen of the savages had intrenched themselves, and every attempt to drive them from it failed, as only when a warrior raised his head to fire was it possible to hit one. At last they were all killed by some of the sharpshooters securing a place of cover and picking them off one by one.

Ten o'clock came, and still the fight continued. It was supposed, of course, that *some* of the warriors had escaped; but greatly to the surprise of the General, through his field-glass he saw on the divide more than a hundred mounted savages, all in full war-paint,[1] their lances at poise, and their gayly colored war-bonnets flashing in the sunlight. It did not seem possible that so many could have succeeded in getting out of the village at the first attack, surrounded as it was by the excellent disposition of the troopers, and the General was at a loss to account for their presence in the vicinity. What were his thoughts may be imagined, on being told by one of the

[1] Painted warriors. All North-American Indians bedaub their faces and bodies before going out to battle.

captured squaws that immediately below, on the same stream, were located a succession of villages of the hostile Indians,—Comanches, Kiowas, Arapahoes, and Cheyennes; that the one which he had just taken was but a portion of one of the Cheyenne villages; that the nearest was only two miles distant, and the farthest ten.

It was becoming serious, for the General felt certain that he would soon be attacked by greatly superior numbers, the moment the horde of savages below on the stream could make their preparations,—which they had probably been doing ever since they had heard the firing in the village he had just captured, the battle having virtually ended there.

On every side the savages could be seen mustering their forces, and from having surrounded a village, the troops were now themselves surrounded; the situation of affairs was completely changed. The command was hastily reformed and posted in readiness for the attack which was expected as soon as the chiefs and warriors could reach there from the lower villages.

A temporary hospital had been established in the center of the captured village, and the wounded cared for as well as they could be under the circumstances. Captain Hamilton was killed early in the fight, just as the command entered the place, and he fell by the side of Custer, with whom he was riding at the head of his squadron. Captain Barnitz, another squadron commander, was terribly wounded, and in a dying condition, having been shot through the body in the region of the heart. Of Major Elliott, the second officer in rank to Custer, nothing had been seen or heard since early in the morning, when he rode with his detachment of troopers into the village. He had nineteen men with him, including the sergeant-major of the regiment; and upon inquiry of all the other officers and many of the enlisted men, they declared that nothing had been seen of them since the first charge into the village. The conclusion was arrived at that he and his force had by some means been cut off from the main command. It was at last developed by one of the scouts, that immediately after the attack upon the village he had noticed a number of warriors escaping through a gap in our lines, and that Major Elliott had started in pursuit. Shortly after their departure he had heard sharp firing in the direction taken by him, but it soon ceased, and he had thought no more about it until the Major and his men were reported among the missing.

A small detachment was immediately sent in the direction indicated by the scout, to find out if possible what had become of Major Elliott and his brave command, but they returned without accomplishing their mission.

The large herd of ponies, numbering over a thousand, were then ordered killed by the General, as it was impossible to take them along, and to leave them for the Indians to again collect would be a very unwise thing. To deprive a savage of his means of transportation would

—16

be as severe a blow to him as could be inflicted. So an officer was detailed to take a detachment of troopers and shoot them. Enough were saved from the lot to carry the prisoners to Camp Supply, and the remainder were dispatched—a cruel necessity.

The last act of the tragedy ended, the command was re-formed, and dispositions were made to overcome any resistance to the advance of the column by throwing out skirmishers. It moved out with colors flying, the band playing, and the prisoners (all women) mounted on their ponies, strongly guarded, immediately in rear of the troops.

The command pushed on, and continued its march until long after dark, by which time it had arrived at the villages, which it was found had been deserted, their occupants having fled when the news of the attack on Black Kettle had reached them. There the General faced his forces about, and it was the intention to reach his train of supplies as soon as possible. Arriving at the battle-ground again, but not halting, the troops took the same trail they had followed in going to the village, continuing on until about two o'clock in the morning. Then it was considered prudent to bivouac until daylight, after sending a squadron ahead to reinforce the guard at the train.

As soon as day broke, the troopers were in the saddle again and marching toward the train, which they reached about ten o'clock, and which to their great joy they found safely encamped.

The mules were immediately hitched to the wagons, without waiting for breakfast, and early in the afternoon camp was reached in the timbered valley of the Washita. There the men and animals took their first " square meal," and the pickets having been posted, horses were unsaddled, the tents pitched, and every one made himself as comfortable as possible.

From there General Custer sent his official report of the engagement to General Sheridan, who was still at Camp Supply, waiting anxiously to hear from him.

In a few days, without any incident of importance occurring, the command arrived at Camp Supply; but the rest there was to be very short. In less than a week the command was in the saddle again, reinforced by the addition of a portion of the Nineteenth Kansas Cavalry, which had been raised at General Sheridan's request, and on the way south, over the same trail taken when the attack on Black Kettle's village was made. Upon reaching there, measures were at once taken to discover the remains of Major Elliott and his men, no doubt longer existing of their fate. General Sheridan, who accompanied this later expedition, thus in his report describes the result of the search for the bodies of the unfortunate men,—an epitome of that made to him by General Custer:

" After marching a distance of two miles in the direction in which Major Elliott and his little party were last seen, we suddenly came upon the stark, stiff, naked, and horribly mutilated bodies of our dead comrades. No words were needed to tell how desperate had been the struggle before they were finally overpowered. At a short distance from where the bodies lay could be seen the carcasses of some of the horses of the party, which had probably been killed early in the fight. Seeing the hopelessness of breaking through the line which surrounded them, and which undoubtedly numbered more than one hundred to one, Elliott dismounted his men, who tied their horses together, and prepared to sell their lives as dearly as possible. The bodies of Elliott and his little band, with but a single exception, were found lying within a circle not exceeding twenty yards in diameter. We found them exactly as they fell, except that their barbarous foes had stripped and mutilated the bodies in the most savage manner."

The punishment inflicted upon the Cheyennes by General Custer at the village of Black Kettle virtually ended the war. Since that time the savages of the Great Central Plains have been forced on reservations, and no serious disturbance with them has occurred.

CHAPTER XII.

BY THE first of November, all the various tribes—
the Comanches, Kiowas, Cheyennes, and Arapahoes—had established themselves in their winter
quarters on the Washita, their villages extending for more
than twenty miles on both banks of the stream, with that
of Black Kettle's near the head of the river.

In the Comanche village, where the boy-captives were,
there was a continual round of feasting, dancing and
amusements peculiar to the savages, for the season had
been very prolific in game and fruits, so they had an
abundance to eat; and when an Indian is sure of a meal
he is contented.

Runners brought the news that Creeping Panther[1] had
taken the war-path with thousands of his " Long Knives,"[2]

---

[1] General Custer was called by the Plains tribes "The Creeping Panther," because
of the manner in which he always succeeded in surprising them, like that sly animal
creeping upon its game.

[2] "*Long Knives*" has been the designation for the cavalry among the Indians, ever
since they first saw those troops with their sabers, in the early days of the century.

and soon ball-playing and other games gave place to the scalp-dances and other fêtes preceding an impending war. In a short time after it was ascertained that the Government had sent troops into the field against the tribes, nearly all the able-bodied men had left the Comanche village to join the allied warriors under the lead of the celebrated chiefs Satanta, Bull Bear, Kicking Bird, Satank, Yellow Bear, Little Raven, and a host of other famous savage braves, leaving only the very old men, the women and children in the village.

Summerfield, Burton, Carlos, and Pierre, who had now become proficient in the strange language of their captors, were ever on the alert to catch portions of the conversations which daily took place between Red Bear and his runners or spies; and they listened with eagerness to the report that a camp of the soldiers had been established at the confluence of the Wolf and Beaver rivers, which they found out was only about a hundred miles distant as the crow flies.

The vigilance which was for so many months exercised to prevent their possible escape, gradually relaxed, and now that only the very old men and squaws were left in the village, the opportunities for consultation among themselves were frequent. Heretofore they had been closely watched whenever they were found talking together, and made to separate. Only late at night, in the quiet of their lodge, when sleep had overpowered their captors, could they indulge in anything like an animated conversation.

One day, when it was their turn to watch the herd of ponies which grazed far down the prairie, and for some lucky reason none of the other Indian boys were with them, they formulated a plan to make their escape as soon as the moon, which was now rapidly waning, had disappeared.

In three days more, on pretense of going on a fishing excursion, they quietly selected four of the fastest ponies in the herd, knowing well from a long experience which they were, and secreted them in the timber late in the evening,— determined to that night make the attempt for freedom.

They had for several days previously quietly carried a supply of dried buffalo-meat and hidden it in the hollow of an old cottonwood tree, for rations on their anticipated journey, as they knew that they would not dare fire a shot on the way for the purpose of procuring food, although they intended to steal their rifles from the lodge of old Red Bear, where the wily chief had most religiously kept guard over them ever since they were taken. They knew, however, just where they were, and saw them every time they entered his lodge; and being on good terms with the chief, they believed themselves smart enough to get the rifles without his being any the wiser.

On the night when all their plans were consummated, Pierre and Carlos went into the old chief's tent while Summerfield stayed on the outside, according to the plan they had decided upon by which to get the four rifles. Carlos engaged the old fellow in conversation, and he became much interested. He liked to talk with the white boys sometimes, and to-night, as luck would have it, he was in a particularly good humor. So he did not notice Pierre gently remove the rifles and belts of cartridges from their place on the floor, and slip them under the edge of the skin which formed the wall of the lodge, where Summer-field was watching for them, and who, the moment he got his hands upon them, made off to the timber and hid them near where the ponies were tied.

Carlos and Pierre saw that their plans had matured, and still interested the old chief until they thought that sufficient time had elapsed for their confederate to accomplish his part of the work. Then they too got up, made their salutations to Red Bear, and took their departure as happy as can be imagined.

All went to their lodge at the usual time that night, and there they remained, wide awake, but perfectly quiet, until long after the village was wrapped in deep slumber. Then they silently rose from their bed of buffalo-robes, gathered a few things they might need, and passed out into the darkness. The dogs, of course, came around and smelled of them, but, satisfied that they belonged to the village, quietly walked away to their accustomed places, curled themselves up, and took no more notice of the boys, who wended their way to the timber.

The night was propitious for the escape of the young captives. There was no moon, but the stars shone brilliantly as the boys silently mounted their ponies, and guided by the North Star (no mistake this time) they rode out on the open prairie with light hearts and breasts filled with hope.

Pierre was the first to break the silence, after they had ridden for more than an hour without saying a word:

"I think we had best strike straight for the Canadian, and then follow it toward the west, as the Wolf and Beaver rivers[1] both run into the Canadian, so we can't miss them."

"It may be a little farther that way," said Carlos, "but as the old saying has it, ' The longest way round is the shortest way home.' "

The ponies the boys had chosen were fast walkers, and they made about four miles an hour over a very level prairie, after they got away from the breaks[2] of the Washita, which lasted for three miles or more. They did not dare lope their animals, as they did not propose to make a halt until daylight. Then they would hide themselves in some ravine, graze their ponies, and lie perfectly quiet until darkness came on again, when they would resume their journey. They knew that runners from the various hostile tribes were constantly on the go between the soldiers and the villages. These runners hanging around the flanks of the former, without themselves being seen, could watch every movement and report it to their war-chiefs,—for the Indians have a most perfect system

[1] *Wolf and Beaver rivers*, two streams south of the Arkansas, in the Indian Territory.

[2] The "*breaks*" of a stream are the hilly, rough region contiguous to its banks; sometimes stretching on one or both sides for a distance of many miles.

of espionage[1] and signals, as stated in a previous chapter. The boys did not fear one or two of the spies if they should run across only that number of them on their way, but frequently a party of warriors, detached from the main force, went out on their own hook on a horse-stealing foray, and it might not be very healthy to run into one of their camps. If they were¯ Comanches, perhaps it might not go so hard with them; but if Kiowas, Cheyennes, or Arapahoes, they would stand no chance for their lives, as now the savages killed and scalped every white person who came in their way, irrespective of sex or age.

When daylight showed its first faint streaks in the east, the boys sought a well-sheltered, rocky ravine, and getting down into its deep bottom, picketed their ponies on the grass, which is generally good in those places. After eating their breakfast of the dried buffalo-meat, and having for their drink only water, which they found in a spring or little rivulet running through the diminutive cañon where they had stopped, they laid down and went to sleep, taking turns in watching.

They had to guess at the time for each one's turn at guard, for both Summerfield's and Burton's watches had been taken from them and broken up, the first day after their capture, by the old chief Red Bear.

They slept very soundly, each one taking his turn, as he was called when apparently two hours had elapsed, and so the time passed until darkness spread its welcome

---

[1] *Espionage*, a system of spying.

mantle over the earth. Then they saddled up, and again taking their direction from the North Star, continued on that course until daylight made its appearance, when they once more sought a sheltered ravine, and camped in its friendly depth all that day.

Just before they laid down to rest in the early dawn, they began to figure upon how many miles they had made during the one night and part of a night they had been traveling.

"Let 's see," said Summerfield; "it was about ten o'clock when we started from the village, and daylight comes by seven. That would make nine hours that we were on the way before we stopped yesterday morning, so we must have made thirty miles, at least, the first night."

"All of that," said Carlos; "and we did better last night, for we got an earlier start by four hours; don't you think so, Pierre?"

"Yes," replied Pierre; "we must be more than seventy miles from the village, and close to Hackberry creek."

"I wonder where we 'll cross it?" said Burton. "Would n't it be funny if we should strike it at the same place where we camped and ate the turkey Pierre shot?"

"Perhaps we may," said Pierre. "Were we traveling in daylight, I could tell something about where we are going to strike it, but we won't know anything until we are right on top of it."

"But even if it is as dark as a pocket, we can tell

whether we have ever been at that particular point or not," said Carlos.

"Well, I think that we are not very far from Hackberry now," Summerfield said; "for I fancied that I could see a dark line ahead of us just as we came down into this ravine, and I think it was timber."

"If you were right," said Pierre; "we can't be more than two or three miles away from it, for you could n't see farther, it was still so dark when we came down in here. I 'll wait until day fairly comes, and then I 'll venture on top of the ridge and take a look for the timber. There are lots of rocks out on the ridge, I noticed as we came here, and I can skulk behind them."

"Do you think it 's safe to take any chances?" asked Burton. "Some devil of a savage may be prowling around; and confound them, they have such a faculty of seeing farther than any white man I ever knew!"

"I 'll risk it," replied Pierre. "I want to get our bearings anyhow, and I can't do it at night. It 's my first turn to stand guard, and while you fellows sleep I 'll go up on the ridge and take a peep around."

After they had all eaten their meager breakfast, all excepting Pierre laid down on their saddle-blankets to rest. He waited until it grew lighter; then, taking his rifle, he sauntered to the top of the ravine, where the ground was covered by great granite boulders, many of them as high as a man's head. He wandered around cautiously among them, hiding behind their smooth surfaces, and at last got a good glimpse of the prairie away below him to the north. There, sure enough, he plainly saw the line of timber which Summerfield declared he had noticed, about three miles off, and he made up his mind that it must be that which fringed Hackberry creek.

While carefully peeping around the angular corners of the boulders, he thought he saw something resembling a bunch of feathers, which seemed to move very slightly, as if by a breeze; but as there was no wind at all, not the slightest breath of zephyr blowing, he thought at first it must be a bird. On thinking a moment longer, however, he decided that it was impossible that a bird with such gaudily colored plumage, like that of the mallard duck, could be in the region at the present time, in the midst of winter.

Pierre watched the object which had so riveted his attention for a few moments, when to his surprise he saw that there stood a savage dressed in his war-bonnet,[1] with his bow and quiver full of arrows, behind one of the huge masses of granite, and that he was watching him with all the cunning of his race. He further noticed that the Indian was fingering his bow, evidently with the intention of shooting him,—believing, perhaps, that Pierre had not yet discovered him.

In an instant, without any compunctions, Pierre sud-

[1] "*Bonnet*" was the name originally given to a head-dress for men, before the introduction of hats. It is a cap without a visor. An Indian war-bonnet was probably so called from the Scotch bonnet, but it in nowise resembles it, excepting that it has no visor. It is simply a band, into which feathers, generally of the eagle, are stuck, and sometimes extending away down the back of the wearer.

denly drew his rifle to his shoulder, and, taking deliberate aim, pulled the trigger, and with a convulsive shudder the savage dropped dead in his tracks.

The report of Pierre's rifle brought the rest of the boys to the top of the ridge in a moment, with their rifles ready for instant use,—for they knew that Pierre would not have discharged his weapon without an urgent reason.

Upon arriving at where Pierre now stood, over the dead savage, they were astonished, and Carlos excitedly asked whether there were any more skulking among the rocks.

" This is the only one I 've seen," replied Pierre; " but there may be more, and you fellows would better take a turn around and see. Be awfully careful, and don't let them, if there are others, get the drop on you. I don't believe you 'll find any more, however, or they would have made their appearance when this one fell."

All the boys, leaving the dead Indian where he laid, made the rounds of the boulders, and not finding any signs that others had been there, returned to examine the one Pierre had shot.

" He 's a Cheyenne," said Carlos, picking up his quiver and scrutinizing the arrows.

" That 's so," echoed the others, who had made themselves familiar with the different weapons of the several tribes; for one who is used to them can easily determine to what band they belong. Moccasins, too, are a distinguishing feature, as the savages of each tribe have a different style.

"I would like to have his war-bonnet," said Summerfield, as he took it off the head of the dead warrior; "that is, if I am ever going to get back to Boston."

"Take it, if you want it," said Pierre, "and this handsome quiver and arrows, too. You can easily pack them on your pony. As for the dead savage himself, we 'll just let him stay where he is. The wolves will soon have a feast off his bones. We could n't bury him if we wanted to—the ground is too hard; besides, we have n't got anything to dig with."

"I can't find the tracks of any more," said Pierre, who had been scrutinizing the ground. "I suspect the fellow had been trailing us, and expected to make an easy capture of our ponies. Those Cheyennes can't let the chance of stealing a horse go by."

"Well, he 'll never steal another," said Carlos; "he 's dead as a poisoned wolf!"

"Boys," said Pierre, "I guess that we can chance making the timber on the Hackberry. I 'm satisfied there are no more Indians around here, and we can hide just as well there. What do you all say?"

"We 'll do just what you and Carl think best," said Summerfield, which was also agreed to by Burton.

So they waited until their ponies had filled themselves, then saddled up, mounted, and, keeping under the shadow of the divide, followed it down to the creek and entered the timber.

When they reached the water, which was about three

miles from the ravine where Pierre had killed the Cheyenne, they found themselves at the precise spot where they had camped the afternoon before their capture. Of course there were no signs of their ever having been there, so far as any remains of their camp were concerned; but all recognized an immense cottonwood, and a curious tree which grew up into a single trunk, then divided into two limbs, one of which was an elm and the other an ash. They had noticed this freak of nature when they camped there, and it alone was sufficient to determine the question, for such anomalies are very rare. Originally there had been two distinct little twigs, one of them an ash, the other an elm. So closely did they come together that eventually they became a single trunk, and at the point of separation (the " crotch") one fork was an ash, the other an elm.[1]

Where they camped, they discovered that only very recently a large body of cavalry had bivouacked[2] at that point, and imagined that some of General Custer's command in following the trail of the Indians had remained there over-night, for the hoof-prints of the horses showed that they had been shod; besides, there were the remains of scattered grain on the ground, which would not have been the case if only a band of savages had halted there.

The boys kept themselves hidden in the deepest timber

----

[1] This curious tree was in existence a dozen years ago. The author of this volume saw it when camping there, on the trail that Custer took to the Canadian.

[2] Bivouac, a military term meaning where troops are without tents or shelter, in a state of watchfulness, ready for a sudden attack.

all day, and just as night began to fall they mounted their ponies again and started on their lonely journey. They hoped to make many miles by daylight, but had not proceeded a great way when the wind suddenly sprang up from the northwest, and the snow began to fall in great flakes, indicating one of those fearful storms which characterize the Plains in the early winter.

"It's going to be a terrible night," said Pierre; "we're bound to have a tough time of it if this wind keeps up."

"Well, we'll have to stand it," said Summerfield, "until we reach the Canadian,—as you say there is no timber between here and there,—but I wish that we were back in our warm skin lodge, until the storm blows over."

"Pierre," said Carlos, (as at dawn they arrived at the Canadian, almost frozen,) "don't you remember that old buffalo cabin somewhere along about here?"

"Yes, now I come to think of it. It was just about three miles from Spring creek. I don't suppose it's there now, though. It's more than a year that we've been away, and if the Indians could destroy it they would."

"If we could only find it," said Burton, "what luck it would be! We could make a fire and keep warm anyhow."

"Keep a good lookout for it," said Pierre; "if it is in existence we must be pretty close to it. We passed Spring creek some time ago."

In half an hour, peering in the darkness and through the almost blinding snow, now falling thick and fast, Bur-

—17

ton, whose eyes were always good, said, " Pierre, what is that dark-looking object looming up over there like a mountain ? "

Pierre and Carlos both strained their eyes in trying to penetrate the inky blackness, and in a moment Pierre said, " Good! That's the old buffalo shanty! Let's get to it as quickly as we can. It's right on the trail, and can't be more than a hundred yards ahead."

Presently they arrived at the rude structure, which had been built of rough stones, with a fairly good dirt roof on it. It contained one room, and diagonally across one corner was a huge fireplace built of cobblestones from the bed of the Canadian. The door (it had no windows) was made of saplings, chinked with prairie-grass, and it hung on wooden hinges, having a sort of latch of the same material. It had been built by the buffalo-hunters some three years before, and connected with it was a small stone corral and shelter for a dozen horses. Near it, too, was a fine spring. It was common property; every buffalo-hunter occupied it in storms, and, strange to say, it had been left intact by the savages on their raids; probably because constructed of stone and they could not burn it.

The boys were almost wild with delight as they rode up to the crude cabin and found that it would protect them from the awful storm, which by the time they had reached the shelter raged more furiously than ever, so that their ponies could hardly face it. They, too, were almost stiff with cold. At once they jumped off their ani-

mals and rushed into the welcome hovel, which they found
had not a flake of snow in it, the roof completely whole,
and the room fairly comfortable; at least, the change from
the outside was so great that the temperature was hot by
comparison.

Fumbling around, Pierre found some dry pieces of
wood, and taking out his flint and steel, which he had
somehow managed to get hold of before he stole away
from the Comanche village, soon had a cheerful blaze
roaring up the fireplace.

Warming themselves for a few moments, so as to thaw
out, they then went to take care of their ponies, which
stood on the lee side of the cabin. They took them into
the corral, and found the shed in good condition, under
which the true little animals hurriedly betook themselves.
The saddles, blankets and bridles were then taken into
the cabin, and the blankets spread out before the fire to
dry, for they were soaking; and in a short time the boys
were quite comfortable.

While they were drying themselves and sparingly par-
taking of their dried buffalo-meat, which now was almost
exhausted, they talked over the situation in which they
found themselves.

"Well, the poor ponies will have to stand it to-night,"
said Pierre; "but in the morning, as soon as it gets light
enough for us to see, we 'll have to get them some cottonwood limbs[1] to feed on."

[1] In places where timber grows, in all cases where the white man finds himself
snow-bound and it is impossible for his horses to get at the grass, he cuts down cotton-

"It will be mighty hard work to cut them with nothing but our knives," said Carlos; "yet it 's got to be done, for the ponies are our only dependence. If we lose them, we 're gone up."

"The wood is getting short, fellows," remarked Burton. "We had best get outside and hustle some, for we can't stay in here to-night without fire and only four horse-blankets for covering."

"Then, out it is," said Carlos, jumping up and going to the door, the rest of the boys following him. The wind was howling at a terrific rate, and the snow was blown into their faces with the force of a hurricane; it stung even their hardened cheeks, as the great flakes struck them like nettles, while the fitful blasts nearly carried them off their feet, as they stood for a moment trying to catch their breath in the freezing wind.

Pierre saw a white pile near the door as he stepped outside, and putting his hands on it, to his delight discovered it to be a heap of wood, now covered with about a foot of snow. The wood had evidently been left there by the last hunters who had occupied the place.

"That 's a streak of luck I did n't look for," said he, as he told the boys what he had found, and they almost yelled with delight as they brushed the snow off the wood and commenced to carry it into the cabin.

wood trees, the bark of which the animals are fond of and which sustains life as well as does the grass, for a time. Where the mulberry can be found, it is preferred to the cottonwood; but the former is limited to a relatively narrow belt on the border of the Great Plains, while the cottonwood abounds along the margins of most of the streams all over the West.

There was more than enough taken in in a few minutes (and even then the pile was not exhausted) to last them until broad daylight. They piled the fresh fuel on the glowing embers, and instantly the red flames shot up the throat of the huge chimney like the blast of an iron furnace, for the wind gave it a terrific draft.

It required about two hours for the blankets to dry, and then spreading them out on the earth floor, the boys found them only wide enough to allow two to lie down at a time; so they determined to watch by twos and sleep the same way.

Summerfield and Pierre, declaring themselves by seniority to be entitled to watch first, insisted that Carlos and Burton should lie down at once, and when they had slept three hours, as nearly as Pierre and Summerfield could guess, they were to be called and take their turn.

The room, which was only about ten feet square, was thoroughly warmed, and although there were no windows, the immense fireplace, which was almost the width of the entire room, gave perfect ventilation, and the boys did not suffer in the least from vitiated air.

Carlos and Burton, Pierre and Summerfield both insisting, reluctantly threw themselves on the blankets, thinking that it was unjust for the older boys to stand guard first. While the latter seated themselves on their saddles (the other two were used by the sleepers for pillows) they commenced to talk quietly, so as not to disturb their worn-out companions.

Summerfield, of course, had to fill his pipe. He was more like an Indian than the others in that particular. But he was now confined to the savage's tobacco, the bark of the red willow. The genuine article he had not even seen for more than six months, when he happened to get a little from old Red Bear one day when he was in a specially good humor, and gave Summerfield about two pipefuls of the precious stuff.

After the two had sat quietly for a few moments while Summerfield was struggling with his pipe to keep it lighted,—for his tobacco had become very wet in his pocket,—the wolves set up a most dismal howling, apparently but a short distance from the cabin.

" They 're after our ponies," said Pierre; " but they can't get at them,—the stone wall is too high; and as I told you a great while ago, the wolf is a mighty poor climber. They will have to satisfy their appetites with yelping. It 's a mighty lucky thing for us that there is a corral here, or we should certainly have lost our ponies to-night if we had been obliged to picket them out. The wolves are terribly bold now during such a storm. I suppose there are at least twenty of them outside, judging from the howling they keep up. They would probably like to get at us too, but they smell the fire, and dare not come any nearer than the corral. They 'll all be gone by daylight."

" Let 's eat a bite," said Summerfield; and he went to the *parflesche* packet which held their dried buffalo-meat, and as he took out a portion, said to Pierre: " I guess we won't have anything to eat to-morrow night, if we don't kill something to-morrow; there is only meat enough left for breakfast and dinner!"

"Well, then we 'll have to shoot something," said Pierre. "I hoped that we would have enough to last until we got to the forks of the Beaver and the Wolf, but this storm has played hob with all our calculations, and it may continue all day to-morrow. We can't start out while it snows, and after it stops we must wait until some of it is melted so we can see the trail, and find some grass for the ponies."

When they thought their three hours were up, they woke Carlos and Burton, who promptly obeyed the summons, and took their places near the fire on the saddles, while Pierre and Summerfield threw themselves down on the warm blankets to rest for their three hours.

Carlos and Burton talked about all sorts of things, and forgot all about going to sleep again until daylight came streaming down the throat of the great chimney. Then they went to the door and looked out. It was still snowing hard, but the wind did not blow so furiously as during the night. The earth was now covered to the depth of nearly two feet, and Carlos told Burton he had never seen so much snow on the ground before,—that it was the worst storm he had ever known of since he was born.

Of course the daylight was a dull ashen gray, and as they could not tell by any possible means what time it was, thought best to wake Pierre and Summerfield, and all go and attend to the ponies, which must be nearly starved by now.

Pierre and Summerfield got up the moment they were called, and without thinking of their breakfast, after washing at the spring and taking a good drink of the water, started out to get some cottonwood limbs for their animals.

Before they had left the cabin, Carlos in prowling around came upon an axe, which, though not very sharp, was a prize to them just then, for without it they had nothing but their hunting-knives with which to cut down the small trees necessary to the salvation of their ponies.

Going to the corral, Burton and Carlos took the animals down to the spring, while Pierre and Summerfield went out into the timber, and selecting some of the smallest of the cottonwood saplings, commenced to work at them vigorously with the axe, taking " turns about " until they had felled what they thought would be enough to last the ponies until the next morning, at least. When Burton and Carlos had finished watering the ponies, they went to where Pierre and Summerfield were chopping, and carried the trees to the corral, getting them all there by the time sufficient had been cut down.

The boys returned to the cabin well satisfied with their success in getting forage for their favorite animals, ate their own breakfast, and found that only enough of the meat was left, as Summerfield had suggested, to last for one more meal.

"We've got to get something to eat," said Pierre. "Suppose that Summerfield and I go out and try to find something, while you and Carlos," addressing himself to Burton, "stay here and keep up the fire and watch things, as it won't do to leave the ponies and our things alone."

"All right," said Burton; "Carl and I will bring in enough of that wood to last us while you and Summerfield are gone."

"Get your rifle, Summerfield," said Pierre; "we must start right away, for we don't want to be out in this storm any longer than we can help. All we can hope to get will be a deer, as nothing else will be here in the timber, and we can't venture out on the prairie to hunt for an antelope."

Summerfield filled that everlasting pipe, and both he and Pierre started out for the river, wading through the snow up to their knees, knowing that if they kept alongside the stream there was no danger of their getting lost. It was terribly cold, but the wind had moderated so that it did not bother them much, as they walked as briskly as they could, hoping to find something in a short time, and not be obliged to wander many miles without seeing any animal good to eat.

They had proceeded about half a mile from the cabin, when Pierre, who was a little in advance, stopped short, and put his hand on Summerfield's shoulder, at which the latter, too, halted. Pierre pointed with his hand to a large box-elder tree, about two feet in diameter, and

showed him a deer, whose head was completely masked
by the trunk of the tree, but whose left side was boldly
beyond it. Raising his rifle, and taking careful aim, he
pulled the trigger, and the doe (for such it proved to be)
dropped dead without a struggle.

They both went up to their lucky quarry, and while
Pierre cut the animal's throat to let it bleed, Summerfield commenced to take off its hide, at which in another
moment Pierre assisted him. Then, throwing the skin
away, for they had no use for it there, they eviscerated
the doe, and tying its legs together, hung it on a pole they
found near, and so transported it to the cabin by resting
one end of the pole on a shoulder of each.

Burton and Carlos had heard the report of the rifle,
and when Pierre and Summerfield approached the cabin
they were standing outside eagerly watching for them,
and when they saw the doe on their shoulders they took off
their hats and waved them, congratulatory of their success.

When Pierre and Summerfield entered the cabin they
found that the boys during their absence had not only
brought enough wood in to last until morning, but that
they had built an unusually hot fire for their especial
benefit, knowing they would be very cold after their hunt.

While they were all cutting up the doe, which weighed
over seventy-five pounds, Carlos said: " Well, we 've got
enough meat now to last five days without another morsel,

and the beauty of it is that we shan't lose any, for it will keep in this weather without drying."

"Yes, said Pierre; "but if the weather clears off, I hope we shall be in the fort on the Beaver before five days have passed. We ought to be able to start out to-morrow night if it clears any time to-day—though I did not see any signs of it when we were out."

The meat was cut up into convenient strips for carrying at the backs of their saddles and apportioned equally to each one, but was hung outside of the cabin on a tree, for it was too warm inside.

By the time the meat was taken care of, the boys, although they could not tell what the hour was, felt by the cravings of their stomachs that it must be time to eat again. So each one cut off choice portions of the deer, and, hunting some fine branches of the willow, trimmed them into skewers upon which they broiled their portions before the glowing embers, the fire having purposely been allowed to go down, as the room was warm, to make just the right kind of coals to cook it.

The fireplace was large enough to permit them all to broil their meat at once, and there was a general sputtering as they sat down on the earth floor and each one put his stick with the meat upon it before the coals, and patiently watched it until it was done to a turn.

"How I wish that we had some salt!" said Summerfield, as he tore off a little piece of the meat with his hunting-knife and put it into his mouth.

"I brought some along," broke in Carlos; "I forgot all about it;" and he reached down into the inside pocket of his coat and pulled out a buckskin package, which he opened, and displayed about two ounces of the precious stuff.

All grasped some of it with avidity, and then their meat tasted much better, with the addition of the necessary condiment, they all declared.

"Which would you rather have—salt, or tobacco?" asked Pierre of Summerfield.

"Tobacco, of course," replied he. "A man can get along without salt, but if he loves to smoke, he must have tobacco."

They all laughed at him, and even Burton, who was an inveterate smoker, said, "Well, I'll take salt in mine every time."

"I should like to get a taste of the real stuff once more," said Summerfield as he vigorously puffed his pipe, "and I shall be glad if we ever get where there is a sutler's store, so I can beg, borrow or buy some."

"I guess that we would better cook all the meat," suggested Pierre; "for we may not be able or dare to make a fire after we leave here."

So they watered the ponies, and finding that there was not enough cottonwood to last them during the day, Pierre said, "We'll have to get them some more roughness,— then we'll cook the meat."

"Roughness!" said Summerfield; "what's that?"

"That's a Western term for anything that a horse or cattle will eat, excepting grain,—grass, hay, or cottonwood limbs."

Summerfield and Burton laughed, and the latter said, "I should think that they had *roughness* enough where they are!"

Cutting cottonwood limbs and packing them to the corral occupied all the rest of the forenoon, and after eating their dinner the boys went diligently to work and broiled the rest of the doe, which required pretty much all the remainder of the day.

That night the storm abated somewhat, but it was still very cold, and the snow did not melt at all; so for two days more they were compelled to remain in the old stone cabin, eating, cutting cottonwood for the ponies, and sleeping.

On the afternoon of the fourth day since they had occupied the cabin, the sun came out, the air from the south was very warm, and the snow began to melt rapidly.

By night the trail was plainly discernible, and they made preparations to leave as soon as it grew dark. The ponies were saddled, and were in fine condition after their long rest, notwithstanding they had eaten only the bark of the cottonwood trees. The remains of the cooked deer-meat were divided equally, tied behind their saddles, and they rode out into the night feeling very hopeful that in two more nights, at least, they would reach the forks of the Beaver and Wolf.

They traveled all night, and just at the break of day

camped in a sheltered little bend of the river, under a
high bluff which formed the boundary of the stream on
the south side. They had hardly gotten the saddles off
their ponies, when their ears were greeted by a strange
sound.

"Hark!" said Summerfield; "what's that?"

They all listened, and Pierre spoke up: "It sounds
like a bugle!"

"So it does!" all reëchoed as they stood still to catch
the strange sound.

"Let me go on top of the bluff," said Summerfield,
"and perhaps I may find out something. Soldiers are
certainly somewhere in the vicinity!"

Summerfield started quite lively for the top of the
bluff, and after having been gone only a few moments,
came rushing down, waving his hat, and almost out of
breath, said: "It's the fort! I can see the flag waving
in the breeze, and it's not more than two miles away!"

"Hurrah!" shouted Pierre. "Saddle up again.
"Don't let's wait for breakfast or anything else, but get
there as soon as we can!"

So, with feelings excited at the thought of the ending
of their eventful journey, they hurriedly saddled and
rode up on the bluff, to take a look at "Old Glory," and
the haven of all their hopes.

CHAPTER XIII.

THE second of December, 1868, broke over the cantonment at the junction of the Wolf and Beaver rivers with cloudless skies and a temperature delightful in its mildness. It was a charming day, characteristic of the midwinter weather on the Central Plains after such a terrible storm as had just ended, and during which General Custer made his memorable march and attack on the village of the Cheyennes on the Washita; through which, also, the lost boys persistently plodded in making their escape from the camp of Red Bear, the chief of the Comanches. The snow still covered the prairie in spots, but was rapidly disappearing under the influence of the warm south breeze.

Flags were flying everywhere over the rude buildings of the primitive fort, in honor of the great victory General Custer and his gallant troopers had effected, who were now taking a well-deserved rest after a campaign almost unparalleled in its hardships. The prisoners taken in the fight, numbering fifty-three, were encamped on the margin of the creek, guarded by a detachment of infantry, anxiously waiting for the morrow, when they were to be transported by wagon-train to Fort Dodge, on the Arkansas, where they were to remain until their final disposition was determined upon by the authorities in Washington.

General Sheridan and his brilliant personal staff were still at Camp Supply, and that morning, in company with several other officers belonging to the garrison, were indulging in a buffalo-hunt, as the whole region for miles in every direction was covered with the shaggy animals. As it was not at all probable that the immense herd would remain in the vicinity for more than another day, advantage was taken of their presence for a few hours' exciting sport.

With the party of hunters was the renowned chief of scouts, W. F. Cody, afterward known all over the world as " Buffalo Bill," and probably the most successful all-around shot in the world at that time.

When they had reached a point about three miles from the fort, there suddenly appeared coming over the bluffs bordering Wolf creek, a party of four individuals, who from their dress seemed to be Indians. The General immediately dispatched Cody and two other of his couriers

GENERAL CUSTER'S WELCOME TO THE CAPTIVES.

to ride toward them and find out who they were, as leading men of the various tribes were daily coming in to surrender themselves and followers.

When Cody and his scouts arrived within hailing distance of the strange-looking group, he stopped, still believing them to be Indians, and putting up both of his hands with the palms outward, the sign of friendship, called out to them to halt.

The boys (for they were our old friends) immediately responded by gestures similar to those which the chief of scouts had made, and then rode boldly toward him. As they came up, they were instantly recognized as white, notwithstanding their bronzed faces and savage garb.

"Who are you?" inquired Cody as they drew up on their ponies within three feet of him.

" We are the Delahoyde boys, and two other young men, Summerfield and Burton; have just escaped from the Comanches, where we have been prisoners for more than a year and a half," answered Pierre, who acted as spokesman for the rest.

"Don't you know my dad,—Delahoyde, the old trapper?" interrupted Carlos.

"Why, certainly!" said Cody; "every one in the whole country knows him. So you are his boys, and these other young men are the ones whom General Sheridan has been having so much correspondence about with their parents in Boston."

—18

" Where is our dad ? " anxiously inquired Pierre of the scout. " Do you know ? "

" Yes," quickly responded Cody, noticing the look of filial solicitude on the countenances of the two boys, as Pierre asked the question. " Your father, and mother, too, are all right. Your father is at Fort Harker, employed in the quartermaster's department. They have grieved very much over your disappearance from the ranch, but your father has always said that you would turn up sooner or later, and get away all right from the savages.

" You would better all go with me now to General Sheridan; he 's over there," pointing with his quirt[1] to where a group of officers were standing watching the meeting of the scouts and the strangers.

Then they rode up to where the General was waiting for them, and upon arriving, Cody said: " General, these two youngest boys are Delahoyde's sons, and the others— what are their names ?—those parties whose fathers have written to you so continuously about them."

" Oh, Summerfield and Burton," interrupted the General, as he cordially shook hands with the four young fellows, and congratulated them upon their escape from the Indians.

" It 's a mighty fortunate occurrence for you," continued he, " that you effected your escape before the battle of the Washita, for all the captives held by every tribe,

---

[1] *Quirt*, a riding-whip with a short wooden or stiff leather handle and a braided rawhide lash: used in the western United States and in Spanish-American countries.

with one or two exceptions, were brutally murdered the moment the news of the defeat of Black Kettle reached their villages, as I have been told by my scouts.

"You would better go on to the fort now;" and turning to one of his couriers, he ordered him to conduct the young men there. "We shall soon be through our hunt, and will see you later, as I want to have a long talk with you. To-morrow I will send you to Fort Harker with the train which is going to take the Indian prisoners there, and from there you young Bostonians," addressing himself to Summerfield and Burton, "can go to Fort Hays and take the cars for home. How are your ponies—in good condition?"

"Excellent," replied Pierre; "they are good for any trip."

Turning to Summerfield again, the General said: "You will find lots of letters at the sutler's store[1] for you. They have been accumulating for months. I've had considerable correspondence with your parents, and will send a telegram to them by a courier who leaves this evening for Fort Harker, that you are safe and well. You would better send one too. I suppose that you are out of funds, so I will pay for it. Your parents will immediately forward money for you to get home with; but if you want to start before you receive an answer, I will furnish what funds you may need."

---

[1] "*Sutler's store,*" a store at military posts, or in the field, for the accommodation of the troops. The proprietor is called a sutler.

Summerfield and Burton both thanked the General for his kind offers, and then all followed the scout to the fort, where they arrived in about fifteen minutes.

On the way, Pierre asked the scout what had become of Dick Curtis, the Indian trader; and at the same time Summerfield inquired after his faithful valet, Romeo, the Mexican.

"Poor fellows!" replied the scout, "they were both killed by the Cheyennes. We found their bodies on the trail to Fort Sill. Curtis must have been surprised by the savages, for his head was resting on his saddle, in a little ravine where he had incautiously gone to sleep; his breast filled with arrows, his scalp missing, and his body horribly mutilated. We did not find the Mexican until the next day, about fifteen miles from where Curtis was killed. I suppose they captured him alive, and getting tired of taking him to their camp, just murdered him to save themselves the trouble of bothering with him any further."

All the boys felt grieved over the news of Curtis's death, for he was an excellent man, and had been a lifelong friend of the Delahoydes; and Romeo had become quite a favorite with the young Bostonians, because of his faithfulness in their service.

Upon arriving at the fort, all the boys were introduced to General Custer, who was standing at the entrance to his tent watching their approach. After shaking hands very cordially, he ordered their ponies taken care of by an

orderly. Then, inviting the boys inside his tent, he began
to question them quite at length concerning the Comanches; their strength, the locality of their village, the number of the warriors they could muster, and everything else
by which he could profit.

After the bright young fellows had imparted all the
information the General desired, he ordered an excellent
dinner prepared for them by his own cook, and when in
about half an hour they sat down to it, and tasted coffee,
hard-tack and butter, their feelings of gratification at once
more eating like Christians may better be imagined than
described.

After dinner was over, the Bostonians spent an hour in
writing letters, as at the end of that time the courier would
be ready to start with the mail for Fort Harker. They
also sent the telegram suggested by the General, when
they first met him on the open prairie.

Upon invitation, that evening the boys had the honor
of taking supper with General Sheridan and his staff.
When the meal was disposed of, all gathered in front of
the tent, where a brisk fire was burning, and they passed
a delightful evening in roasting buffalo shinbones and in
conversation. The conversation was kept up until after
ten o'clock, the young adventurers having to do most of
the entertaining, by answering the host of questions put
to them relating to the incidents of their eventful lives
while prisoners among the Comanches.

Summerfield told the group of officers assembled that

all the trouble and sufferings they had experienced were caused by his great desire to obtain a buffalo-head to take back to his home in Boston; but that the result was zero, so far as a head was concerned, and he had brought only hardship upon his companions.

The General said, laughingly: "There is an old adage, 'All things come to him who waits.' We got some magnificent heads to-day on our hunt, and you shall each have one, which proves the truthfulness of the saying, for you have certainly waited with commendable patience for your desire." Then, turning to one of his orderlies standing near, he said to him: "Give my compliments to Mr. Cody, the chief of scouts, and ask him to send a couple of the best heads down to the Indian camp to be prepared, so that they will keep until they reach Boston. Then," addressing himself to Summerfield, "you can there have a regular taxidermist finish them for you."

Summerfield and Burton were profuse in their thanks to the General for his kindness, and after the orderly had departed on his mission, all retired,—the boys in a tent assigned to them by General Custer near his own, where with plenty of buffalo-robes they slept very soundly and peacefully for the first time in two weeks.

The next morning, contrary to all expectations, opened with a fearful blizzard of blinding snow and furious wind from the north; but after a good breakfast, the train of eight hundred wagons, with the Indian prisoners stowed in as many of them as were necessary, with an escort of one squadron of cavalry, two hundred and forty dismounted troopers and one company of infantry, started for Fort Harker via Fort Dodge. Accompanying the train were one hundred and twenty-seven worn-out horses of Custer's command, which it was the intention should be taken to the fort to recuperate. The commanding officer of the escort, however, expressed his doubts to General Sheridan whether he would be able to get them there, on account of the terrible storm, and there was no dependence for what they were to subsist upon but such grass as they might find under the snow. The General replied, not by any means to allow them to be caught alive by the wolves, but to exercise his own judgment as to their disposition in case he could not get them along.

The buffalo-heads and the equipage belonging to the boys were placed in one of the ambulances, but they themselves preferred to ride their ponies instead of using an ambulance,—particularly as the commanding officer was compelled to stick to his horse at the head of the column, where, with a compass on his saddle-bow, he led the way on the now obliterated trail down the river, the terrible wind and the blinding snow making it impossible to see ten feet ahead!

The poor horses were trailing slowly behind, and it required the utmost efforts of the infantry in the rear to prevent the wolves, which hung in packs on their tracks, from getting at them.

By dint of almost herculean heroism on the part of the

soldiers, twelve miles were made by three o'clock, when, with frosted feet and hands, they camped in the friendly timber of the Beaver.

Tents were put up, and large fires kindled, by means of which all were soon rendered relatively comfortable. The played-out cavalry horses were so harassed by the wolves, which kept increasing in numbers as night came on, and as there was no forage for them, it was deemed advisable to kill them to prevent their falling alive into the rapacious jaws of the persistent brutes which were snarling and snapping among themselves by the hundreds, almost inside the very camp. So the poor animals were taken a few rods from the trail and mercifully shot, in order to save them from the more cruel fate of falling by the wayside to be torn to pieces by the rapacious monsters which were sure to get them eventually.

After the slaughter was ended, such a growling, fighting, snapping and snarling while the famished brutes pounced upon their now easily acquired quarry, has rarely been heard; and before morning the bones of the luckless animals which had done such good service, were picked as clean as it is possible for a wolf to accomplish it.

During the night the storm abated, the snow ceased falling, but the wind continued to blow furiously, and it was bitter cold. After the command had gotten fairly strung out on the trail, it was discovered on counting the Indian prisoners, that two or three of the youngest, mere babies in fact, were missing, and upon inquiry through

the interpreter, it was learned that the squaws had purposely abandoned them in the snow at the camp! An
ambulance was immediatcly sent back for them; they
were gathered up without any apparent injury having
happened to them, and returned to the train.

Before the train started on again, the commanding
officer, through the interpreter, informed the savages
that if that occurred again he would hang five of them to
the first tree he came to on Bluff creek, which they would
reach by noon the next day. The threat had its effect; no
more babies were left in camp, but the best of care taken of
them all the way to Fort Dodge, where the train arrived
on the afternoon of the fourth day from Camp Supply,
crossing the Arkansas, which was filled with floating ice,
right at the Fort.

The next day the command left for Fort Harker, where
they arrived after about two days' travel.

The meeting between the Delahoyde boys and their
parents was very affecting; nor was their joy at seeing the
Bostonians again less sincere. That whole evening was
passed in relating the sad experiences through which they
had all passed, and reading the mass of letters found at the
sutler's by Summerfield and Burton.

The next morning an ambulance was to start for Fort
Hays, on the Kansas Pacific Railroad, in which, after an
affectionate farewell, and protestations of undying friendship, the Bostonians rode, they promising to write the moment they arrived home, the Delahoydes watching the
vehicle until it passed out of view over the divide.

A fortnight had scarcely elapsed since the departure of Summerfield and Burton from Fort Harker, before long letters were received from both the boys and their parents, full of praise for the bravery of Pierre and Carlos, with the assurance that each vacation, until they were graduated, both sons would spend with their companions in so much pleasure and hardships, on the beautiful Arkansas, a stream so fraught with sad and delightful memories.

In a few days after the receipt of the letters, a large box came by express, filled with a choice selection of books, and a magnificent repeating-rifle for Carlos and Pierre, with an abundance of cartridges.

The war having ended after Custer's punishment of the savages, the rest of the tribes were placed on reservations provided for them by the Government, and peace once more spread its wings over the land. The Delahoydes moved back to their ranch on the Arkansas, where a neat stone house was erected to take the place of the old dugout destroyed by the savages.

The next season Summerfield and Burton, true to their promise, came and spent their vacation of three months at the place, where they fished and hunted as of old, but now they could go anywhere without fear of running into a Comanche camp!

In less than three years the Bostonians had completed their studies at Harvard, and were graduated with honors; but so attached had they both become to the wild and exciting life of the frontier, that they lost all taste for the conventionalities of Eastern civilization, and their fathers, being wealthy, purchased for their boys a couple of sections of land, not many miles from the ranch of the Delahoydes, stocked it with fine cattle, and both places are considered to-day as among the finest and best equipped frontier homes in the whole Western country.

Every fall, Pierre, Carlos, Summerfield and Burton took an outing of five or six weeks, going to the localities which years before were so fraught with thrilling adventures for them, camping on the identical ground; and while smoking their pipes, renewed, in reminiscence, the strange story of their young lives.

At first, for a few years, the buffalo, antelope and wild turkey still lingered in their old haunts; but as immigration poured in, they too became a mere picture on memory's walls, and only the ubiquitous wolf, the cowardly little coyote and the cranes were left to form a living picture of the long-ago. The Polled Angus, Herefords, and the broad-backed Shorthorns on the ranches usurped the place of the great shaggy ruminants, the once monarchs of the Plains, and that which was originally a wild but picturesque region was transmuted by civilization into the most charming pastoral landscape on the continent.

The "old folks" of both families visit their sons very often, and the only regret ever expressed is that there are no girls, so there might be a closer relationship than now exists, of only a deep friendship.

www.ingramcontent.com/pod-product-compliance
Lightning Source LLC
Chambersburg PA
CBHW020936120726

47905CB00008B/2544